A Good Day
to Pie

FORTHCOMING BOOK BY CAROL CULVER

Never Say Pie

A Good Day to Pie

A Pie Shop Mystery

Carol Culver

MIDNIGHT INK
WOODBURY, MINNESOTA

FIRST EDITION
First Printing, 2011

Book design by Donna Burch
Cover design by Ellen Lawson
Cover illustration © Tom Foty/The Schuna Group Inc.
Edited by Rosemary Wallner

Midnight Ink, an imprint of Llewellyn Worldwide Ltd.

Library of Congress Cataloging-in-Publication Data

Culver, Carol, 1936–
  A good day to pie : a pie shop mystery / Carol Culver. — 1st ed.
      p. cm.
  ISBN 978-0-7387-2378-5
  1. Bakeries—Fiction. 2. Pies—Fiction. 3.
Murder—Investigation—Fiction. 4. California—Fiction. I. Title.
  PS3603.U628G66 2011
  813'.6—dc22

                                                                    2011009336

Midnight Ink
Llewellyn Worldwide Ltd.
2143 Wooddale Drive
Woodbury, MN 55125-2989
www.midnightinkbooks.com

Printed in the United States of America

ACKNOWLEDGMENTS

With thanks to my wonderful agent Jessica Faust for her encouragement, support, and her great ideas.

ONE

"I swear your grandmother has a better social life than you do." From the overstuffed chair in the corner of the small commercial kitchen, my friend Kate Blaine gave me a look that was somewhere between pity and concern.

I winced, because I suspected "social life" was a code term for "sex life." And I suspected it was true.

"Everyone has a better social life than I do," I said lightly. "I'm up at dawn, chopping, slicing, rolling, mixing, you name it. By the end of the day I can barely make it home to collapse in front of the TV to watch the Food Network." I pointed one floury finger at the flat above the store. "Good thing I don't have to commute."

To illustrate just how busy I was, I proceeded to measure and mix the ingredients for a basic pie crust.

Kate got up, poured herself a cup of coffee from the pot on the vintage black and white porcelain stove, and peered over my shoulder. "Wouldn't that be easier with a food processor?"

"This is a small pie shop, not a factory," I said, shaping the dough into two flat circles with the palm of my hand. "Grannie did it all by hand and so do I. It's the only way to make a good crust. One at a time. At least for now. Later, when I've got dozens of orders to fill and a line around the block, I'll automate, but for now I'm mixing the old-fashioned way. Grannie's way."

Kate eyed the empty butter wrapper with suspicion. "I thought your grandmother used lard."

"Well, yes, but Martha Stewart and I use butter. Tastes better. But I'm not a complete Luddite. See, I bought a new high-tech rolling pin." I held out my new pin with the chrome caps and the pink silicone surface. "Go ahead, try it. Totally nonstick. Ergonomic. Comfortable to hold, don't you think?"

Kate rolled the pin over the dough and it stuck to the silicone mat even though the manufacturer promised it wouldn't.

I sprinkled some extra flour on the dough. "Roll from the middle, then turn one quarter," I said. "Act quickly while it's still cool. That's the secret. Once you let the dough get warm, it gets sticky."

She sighed and handed it over to me. "Some people have the touch, some don't. I'll do the eating, you do the baking. What happened to your grandmother's old wooden rolling pin?"

I pointed to the stoneware utensil crock on the counter that held her scarred and battered rolling pin along with a whisk, a ladle, and an oven thermometer.

Above the stove I'd hung a framed photograph of Grannie wearing a blue ribbon the year she won first prize at the county fair for her Fuji Apple Southern Pecan Caramel Pie. She seemed to be looking right at me as I rolled smoothly just as she'd taught me when I was barely tall enough to reach the counter. "I thought

I'd like having her here with me in the kitchen," I said to Kate, "but when I roll out the crust, I can hear her saying, 'The chunks of butter are too big. It's too thick. No, too thin. Try it again.' So let's put her in the window. She won't mind and maybe she'll attract customers."

We were standing in the window, me in my baggy T-shirt and faded jeans covered with a large white apron with The Upper Crust stenciled in red across the bib, and Kate in her designer jeans under the "Grand Opening" sign trying to decide where to put the picture. The low clouds and patchy fog that are common along the California coast in summer hadn't burned off yet. By noon it would be another beautiful cloudless day in paradise. A woman with a hybrid labradoodle wearing an all-season stretch dog coat walked by and I almost lost my balance.

"Oh my God, that's Mona Grimes," I said. "Grannie's best customer. Where has she been all this time?" Since I opened the shop three weeks ago, the business had been painfully slow. I'd sold a grand total of seventeen pies since I reopened the pie shop. And two of them were to Kate.

I jumped down from the window ledge, pasted a welcoming smile on my face, and opened the front door just in time to see Mona walk right on past and down the street. Not even a backward glance from her or her dog. Slowly I closed the door and stood with my back to it, blinking back tears of frustration.

"Probably on her way somewhere," Kate said.

"Somewhere? Where is there to go in this town?" Crystal Cove prided itself on its small-town ambience. The little town I once found claustrophobic—the one I escaped from some fifteen years ago—was the one I'd recently returned to. Sometimes I missed the perks of big-city living and a job with a regular paycheck. "The destinations around here include the bank, the park, the library, and the occasional neighborhood block party."

"That's not fair," Kate said. "We have a small farmer's market that you haven't even visited, we have great beaches you say you don't have time for, and we have an old-fashioned downtown that you ignore."

"Okay, okay, I'll get to the market."

"Don't just go to the market, rent a booth and sell your pies there."

"But Grannie never …"

"I know she didn't, but that doesn't mean you can't."

"And who minds the shop while I'm at my booth?"

"I will or you can hire a high school girl. You don't have to be everywhere."

"So you think I should expand. Today the farmer's market, tomorrow you'll have me setting up franchises."

"I want you to be where the customers are."

"They're not here in droves yet, but I'm hopeful." She was right. It was time for me to think outside the box. But I always had an excuse. "At the moment I can't close up to go anywhere during the day or I might lose customers." I knew what she was thinking. What customers? "So first things first. I'm going to sell some pies. Now. Today. Why shouldn't I? Fortunately it's not like I'm selling turnips. It's pie. Who doesn't like pie?"

"Hanna, nobody doesn't like pie. It's the world's most unpretentious food. It reminds people of their grandmother, or *your* grandmother."

"Then why haven't I been named Crystal Cove Entrepreneur of the Year? What am I doing wrong besides staying inside the shop?"

"Nothing. You're making delicious pies. Their loss."

Fortunately, the oven timer went off before I lost my cool and started to blubber uncontrollably about my slow business. I rushed back to the kitchen to take a strawberry rhubarb pie out of the oven.

Kate followed me and collapsed in her chair. I couldn't blame her. With three small kids to chase around at home, she came to the bakery to relax and sample my pie and keep my spirits from flagging. Not an easy job these days. She closed her eyes and let the steamy air and the scent of fresh-baked pie oozing its tart-sweet juice wash over her.

"I'm in heaven," she murmured. "Pie heaven."

"While you're there, would you ask God to send me some more customers?"

"God says be patient. If you bake it and take it where they are, they will buy your pie. She also says to tell you to hang in there. And you should hire me as your official taster and PR person. But you're the expert. Didn't you do marketing when you worked in San Francisco?"

"Yes, but that was then. I want to be in the production side of things now—we'll see how it works," I said vaguely.

"Okay, we'll be partners," Kate said. I could tell she was excited about it. Being a stay-at-home mom wasn't enough for her. She was smart and ambitious, and we did work well together. But I couldn't be anybody's partner. Not now. Not ever again. I'd learned my lesson the hard way.

I tried to explain. "I don't do partners. Too many complications. I work better alone, like Grannie."

Kate shrugged. "Whatever. I'll work for you then."

I nodded, not surprised she didn't ask me why I shied away from a partnership with my best friend. Even though she might want to know. That's why she's my best friend. She'd never pressed me about what happened to me in the city, why I'd been so eager to come back and take over the pie shop if I was such a raving success where I was. Why she didn't hear from me for a long period. And I hoped she wouldn't ask. There were some painful memories I'd wanted to bury, and that's where they would stay: buried.

Determined to lighten the mood, I took the battered old rolling pin and waved it in her direction. "I pronounce you my royal taster and Public Relations Official and future franchise director. You get a ten percent cut of every pie you help me sell."

"I'll take my commission in pies."

"You got it."

Kate closed her eyes and sank farther into the overstuffed chair Grannie had left behind. She wore a blissful smile on her flushed face. The prospect of a slice of warm strawberry rhubarb pie with a double crust hot out of the oven will do that to you.

As if in answer to Kate's prayer, the bell over the door to the shop rang and I dropped the rolling pin, dusted my hands off on my apron, and ran out to the shop. A fit-looking gray-haired woman in a sweat suit and running shoes stood in front of the refrigerated glass display case and stared at the Luscious Lemon Meringue Pie and the Velvety Key Lime Pie topped with swirls of whipped cream. Finally, was this someone who appreciated a tart-sweet citrus pie as much as I did?

"Hi. Welcome to the Upper Crust. What can I do for you?"

"Is Louise here?"

"No, actually she retired a few months ago. I'm Hanna, her granddaughter, uh, taking her place. Not that anyone could replace her, of course, but I'm trying. Did you have a favorite pie that you don't see here because..."

"What's that one there?"

"That's Extreme Chocoholic Chunk Pie. It's very rich. Most people can only eat one tiny slice, so it goes a long way. One pie will feed twelve to eighteen people. There's a crunchy chocolate cookie crust and when you bite into the filling you're hit with the blend of exotic spices like cinnamon and nutmeg and mace and a touch of rum, then the intense flavor of the chocolate wraps around your tongue..."

I was convincing myself but losing her. I could tell by the way she wrinkled her nose.

"Your grandmother made her chocolate pie with a pudding mix and a graham cracker crust. It was delicious."

"She had the magic touch," I agreed. "But after all those years of getting up early to bake pies, she's earned the right to sleep in and play Bridge all day instead of slaving over a hot oven." Her life was sounding better and better to me, and I was looking ahead at thirty years of this. I didn't mind baking the pies; thinking up new, innovative recipes was a challenge I welcomed. It was selling them that was so hard.

"Tell her Zelda said hello."

"You should stop by and see her. She's up the hill at Heavenly Acres."

"That place with the miniature golf course and the huge swimming pool?" she asked incredulously.

I knew what she was thinking. How did Grannie make enough from pies to afford to move to the five-star retirement home? She didn't. Her ex-husband died last year and left her a bundle of money.

I didn't say that, I just nodded. "In the meantime, I have a strawberry rhubarb pie still warm from the oven with your name on it."

I could see her waver.

"You used Louise's recipe?"

"The crust is different. Mine is all butter."

"You should ask her how she made hers. She'd never tell me. She always said she used a touch of magic."

"I know. She told me the same thing. Why don't you take a pie with you, and if you don't like it I'll refund your money." I could hear Grannie's voice in my ear. *Refund your money? Are you out of your mind? That's no way to run a business.* But I was desperate for a sale.

"Fine," she said.

I took a cardboard box from the shelf and slid the fresh strawberry rhubarb pie inside. She paid me and I thanked her.

"You brought me luck," I told Kate, trying to act like it was no big deal. "I sold a pie."

She jumped up and gave me a high five. "I was just thinking. Maybe in some cases, a whole pie is too much of a commitment. What if you offer a piece of pie and a cup of coffee, an introductory special?"

"Grannie never wanted to turn the place into a café. Making coffee and tea didn't appeal to her, and then what if they wanted their pie à la mode? She'd have to get a big freezer and ice cream."

"May I remind you it's yours now. Give it a try, why not?"

"Well, maybe. I've got that little patio table of hers upstairs and some matching chairs."

"I'll watch the store, you go get them."

"Watch the store? For what? The hordes of customers?" I snorted. "Come up and help me."

Shortly afterward, we had Grannie's little glass-topped table with the wrought-iron legs and its matching chairs set up opposite the pie case. Ever hopeful, I pressed my face against the glass door and gazed outside, but all I saw through the fog was the one-story wooden-frame police station across the street with the small cropped lawn and bushes framing the windows. On the door was an enlarged badge with a logo of blue waves and green mountains and the name of our town—Crystal Cove—in bright yellow, a symbol of the three hundred days of sunshine we get per year. After the morning fog burns off, that is. But not an officer in sight. No crimes. No activity. No surprise. But where were the men who used to come in, kid around with Grannie about the lack of felonious activity in town, and take out a pie for the staff?

In a burst of optimism, I measured some Sumatra coffee into my own 12-cup brew maker I'd installed on the counter of the pie shop kitchen, thinking *If I brew it, they will come.*

A middle-aged man came in wearing a classic cotton golf hat, shirt, and Bermuda shorts. He said he was new in town. He'd heard about my pies. I wanted to ask who, where, and when and how, but I didn't. But I did talk him into a lemon meringue since a lot of men don't like things too sweet. I was off to a ripping start. Two sales already in one morning. But Kate still wasn't satisfied. She wanted the shop to be full of happy pie eaters. She went out in front and looked up and down the street. So did I. I could tell she was restless. So was I, but I had nowhere to go. She looked at her watch. Said she had to pick up the kids or her dry cleaning. Or maybe both.

"Okay," I said. "But come back for lunch if you can. I'll make a savory pie. A Wild Rice Quiche. You'll love it."

"I know I will, but how will that help your business?"

"You'll sit at the table next to the window, and when people walk by they'll think you're a customer and they'll say, 'Hey, wonder what that woman is eating,' and they'll come in and see."

"When they do, I'll lick my lips and rave about your pies. And they'll say, 'I'll have what she's having.'" She paused and put her hands on her hips. "Wait a minute. I'm just a stooge. You're using me, aren't you?"

I nodded. "What are friends for?"

After she left, I went inside and set Grannie's picture on an easel I found in the storeroom. Then I walked back outside and looked in the window to get the perspective of a casual prospective customer. I was proud of the gigantic pie I'd painted on the window with the white blobs of paint indicating wisps of steam billowing from the browned crust.

The picture of Grannie told people she was still there in spirit. At least I hoped that's what it told them. I was trying to update the shop without sacrificing the cozy ambience people expected. I thought I was getting close—not too fussy, not too cute, but not too spare either. The kind of place I'd want to hang out in if I was a customer.

I went back to the kitchen and was about to roll out the crust I'd made, when I thought about Grannie and her recipes. How her pie crusts were so flaky, so mouth watering, so irresistible. On a whim, I reached into the back of the cupboard for a can of vegetable shortening and made a flaky crust just like she used to do. Fifteen minutes later, I took it out of the oven to cool while I made the filling, sniffing it to see if it had that delicious crusty smell I remembered so well when it filled the bakery and the apartment upstairs with warmth, comfort, love, and Grannie's special magic.

Grannie now had her meals at Heavenly Acres, wine included, and all my old friends had either left town or gotten married to their high school sweethearts. Which left me the odd girl out. Not that I cared. I hadn't come back to the Cove to find love. Finding the perfect man was almost as hard as making the perfect crust. Isn't that what drove Grannie all these years, looking for perfection? According to her old customers, she'd found it and I hadn't. I'd given up on finding the man, but not the crust. As I told Kate, I had no time to socialize, not when I was trying to prove to myself, Grannie, and the world I could start a new business that was once a thriving old business. And now I had to expand as well.

I followed the recipe for Wild Rice Quiche, beating the eggs with a wire whisk. I'm sure Kate would have said I should use an electric mixer, but there's something satisfying about doing things by hand and seeing real tangible, edible results when you're finished. Especially after shuffling papers in an office for a few years.

After topping my quiche with a mixture of aged Parmesan and Harvarti cheeses, I slid it into the oven and had just poured myself a cup of coffee when the bell rang again. I jumped up from the stool at the counter and faced two women with kids in strollers who looked vaguely familiar. The women, not the kids.

"Hanna Denton, is that really you?"

Damn, these were girls from my high school class I hadn't seen for years. Part of the popular crowd that didn't include me. Tammy and Lindsey had married their high school boyfriends. I hadn't. I didn't know what I'd say to them, unless it involved pie. I could only hope they were hungry. Too late to brush the flour out of my hair and change into a clean apron and some skinny jeans so I wouldn't look like such a slob.

"We heard you were back in town," Lindsey said, tossing her long blond hair over one shoulder.

Tammy, looking not a bit older than the day we'd graduated with her feathered bangs and chin-length brown hair, paused and sniffed the air. "Smells good in here."

"How are you?" I said, wishing I'd taken the time to put on some eyeliner and brushing some color on my cheekbones. I'd been up for hours and I was sure I looked as tired as I felt.

"We should get together," Tammy said. She was scanning the pies in the case. My hopes were rising like a cheese soufflé. Then she said, "Do you have any cupcakes?"

"Uh, no, just pies. Lemon Meringue, Key Lime, Strawberry Rhubarb…"

"We heard somebody in town is making cupcakes. Thought it must be you."

"Not me." Cupcakes. Why didn't I think of that? That's all I needed was some competition in the bakery department. "How about a cup of coffee?"

They exchanged glances.

"On the house, of course."

"Hanna, you can't give away coffee," Lindsey said, opening her purse. "We can afford it. This is my treat."

I went to get the coffee. Maybe someone would walk by and see a veritable crowd in here. I could only hope. Because no one wants to hang out in an empty pie shop no matter how inviting the interior or how mouth-watering the pies. So much better to be where the action is.

We sat around the tiny table. Half listening to them gossip about old classmates, their divorces, and their own kids who were both blissfully asleep in their strollers, I fantasized about getting more tables for more customers eating pie and drinking coffee and the sound of money in the vintage cash register. Maybe I'd put tables out on the sidewalk. It would be more than a bakery. It would be like a European café. I'd serve tarts and quiche. Or was that too pretentious for little Crystal Cove?

"….won't believe who's the Chief of Police," Tammy was saying.

"No, who?" I asked. Whoever he was, he wasn't a customer, and he should be.

"Sam Genovese. You remember Sam?"

I almost spilled my coffee. Of course I remembered him. How could I forget? What was he doing here?

"Thought we'd never see him again, didn't you?" She gave me a funny look. She couldn't possibly know I had a history with Sam, could she?

"Never," I agreed. The town bad boy was now the Chief of Police? I stared out the window at the police station as the sun broke through the clouds and shone on the center of law and order. If he worked there, why hadn't I seen him or anyone from the station come into the shop? Because he was avoiding me or my pies, obviously. When Grannie was here, the cops were her best customers.

"Almost as unbelievable as you back here making pies," Tammy said. "Just like your grandmother."

"Not exactly. She taught me everything she knew, but I have some new recipes. You'll have to try one."

"Not me, I'm on a diet." Lindsey sucked in her cheeks and gazed at the walls I'd painted persimmon and the mirror on the wall that I thought made the shop look bigger. "Looks different," she said. I wasn't sure whether she meant it looked better or not.

"Oh, there he is now." Tammy stood and stared out the window. Across the street, a tall man in street clothes got into a squad car and drove away. I forced myself to stay seated, though I wanted to run outside for a better look. From where I sat, it could have been Sam. It could have been anybody.

"If that's him, why isn't he wearing a uniform?" Tammy asked. Which made it unnecessary for me to ask that same question.

"Duh. He's the chief. And he's a detective. They don't wear uniforms. Don't you watch 'The Closer'?" her friend asked.

Instead of answering, Tammy turned to me. "What do you think? Would you have recognized him?"

I shook my head and changed the subject. I didn't come back to Crystal Cove to rekindle an impossible teen crush. And I wasn't running away from anything. At least that was my story and I was sticking to it. I was here to carry on a family tradition, which is what I told my grandmother. Also to make a big change in my life. I didn't want to talk about Sam for fear of dragging up old memories, both mine and Tammy's and Lindsey's. Enough speculation about Sam. "If there's a pie you'd like to special order, I'd be glad to make it for you. Parties, holidays? They make great birthday gifts for that special person. And I deliver."

Lindsey stood and pushed her stroller to the door where she paused and looked thoughtful. "Actually, I'm having a sex toy party next week and I wanted to serve something, something, you know, sexy. Any ideas?"

"What about 'I'm too sexy for my crust' Italian Bittersweet Chocolate Silk Pie?"

"Ooooh, that sounds good."

"I thought you were on a diet," Tammy said to her friend.

Lindsey frowned. No one likes to be reminded they can't eat pie. "I have to serve something at my Pleasure Party, don't I?" she said.

"For how many?" I asked.

"Fifteen or twenty. All women, of course. My husband's out of town so I'm doing a 'Girls Night Out' thing."

"I suggest having a blueberry pie to go with it. Did you know blueberries are a powerful antioxidant and they fight wrinkles, not that you need to worry about wrinkles, but still..."

"Okay, one of each. And Hanna, if you want to stay for the passion products..." She didn't seem at all embarrassed that she hadn't invited me. Maybe she thought since I'm probably a swinging single I didn't need any sex toys. "I would have invited you but I wasn't sure you were around."

"Oh, I'm around," I said, "but I can't really come to the party. I never mix business with pleasure." I might have sounded a little stiff, but a pleasure party with girls was the last thing I'd want to do no matter how desperate I was for company. Lindsey gave me instructions, when to arrive as well as her address. Fortunately, she didn't insist on my staying for the "fun." As soon as she mentioned her address, I thought "big time." Because her street was definitely in the best part of town.

After they left, I went back to the kitchen and took a look at the quiche in the oven. It was puffed, set, and golden brown around the edges. Just perfect.

When Kate came back, the temperature outside was climbing into the mid-seventies. Crystal Cove prided itself on its eternal spring weather. If I'd had my sidewalk café set up, we could have sat out there. I cut two pieces of quiche and poured two glasses of white wine Grannie never would have served, and we sat at the table in the window.

"What would you think of my expanding out on the sidewalk?" I asked with a wave of my hand toward the street.

"Now you're thinking," she said with a smile. "Great idea. I picture little tables with umbrellas." That's the thing about Kate, she's so upbeat. She keeps me thinking positive when sometimes in the middle of the night I'm afraid I've made a mistake coming back here.

"By the way," I said. "Guess who dropped in? Our old friends Tammy and Lindsey."

"Good. They'll tell people and you'll have more business. Tammy goes to water aerobics with the old crowd and Lindsey knows everyone in town. And they're both way up on the food chain, if you'll pardon the expression."

"And why didn't you tell me Sam was back in town?" I asked. "I could have been prepared."

"Must have forgotten," she mumbled, her mouth full.

"Do you like my crust?" I asked, turning my attention to the quiche.

"Mmmmm, hmmmm," she said.

"I used Grannie's recipe this time." I chewed thoughtfully. "It's good but it's not great. I've got to ask her what her secret is."

"If she tells you, it won't be a secret. Don't worry about it. This is delicious. She never did savory pies, did she?"

"I don't think so, but I wanted to try something new. Maybe that's my problem. People around here don't like change."

"Then we'll have to educate them. As your PR person I'll get busy. I'm going to write a profile of you for the *Crystal Cove Gazette* and take a photo of you and your pies."

"That would be great." I managed to sound enthusiastic, but I was tired, worried about the future, and worried about running into the Chief of Police. Sooner or later it was inevitable, considering he worked across the street. We'd probably have an awkward conversation that would go something like this:

"So, what brings you back to little Crystal Cove?" I'd ask. Or I might insert "boring, monotonous, dull, but scenic Crystal Cove."

"The job. And you?"

"Same."

"Good to see you."

"You too."

I'd force a smile. He wouldn't. He never smiled. Unless he'd changed drastically.

"So … how are you?" I'd ask, because I really wanted to know, damn his blue eyes.

"Fine. How about you?"

"Great. Couldn't be better." I'd say it so sincerely he couldn't doubt I was feeling and, I hoped, looking fabulous.

And that would be it. We'd get our awkward meeting over with and then get on with our lives, such as they were. The past would stay in the past. I had no intention of bringing it up, and he probably wouldn't either.

Fortunately, Kate had no idea my mind was wandering. She retained the enthusiasm of the cheerleader she once was and the ability to focus, which I seemed to have lost. I still have a hard time believing Kate and I ever became best friends. I was the geek, she was the popular girl, but we were on the newspaper staff and went out and did interviews with teachers, students, and townspeople together. We shared many laughs and we still do.

"You're doing terrific," she said, wiping the crumbs from her mouth. "Your savory pie was divine. But no one knows about it. That's why you need me to spread the word." She pulled out a small digital camera from her purse and had me pose with a pie in my hands.

"Wait, I didn't even comb my hair."

"You look fine," she assured me. "Very natural. Besides, it's the pies we want to feature, not you."

She gave me a thumbs up, promised to get me the publicity I needed, and drove away in her SUV filled with the kids' car seats. If I'd stayed around fifteen years ago, would that be me? A happy and contented small-town housewife with two kids and a husband who adored me? No point in dwelling on what might have been. I'd had some interesting experiences and some not so interesting, which made me determined to appreciate my new independent life here.

The phone rang and I reached into my apron pocket.

"Hanna," my grandmother said. "You've got to come over here right away."

I frowned. "Why, what is it?"

"There's been a . . . an incident. The police are here and they're asking questions."

"What do you mean an incident? What kind of questions?"

There was no answer. She was gone. Disconnected. Grannie is not the type to cry wolf, so I hung a "Closed" sign on the door of the shop and immediately drove up to Heavenly Acres in Grannie's '71 two-tone Buick Estate Wagon while I pondered what kind of an incident it could be in this quiet, geranium-and-forget-me-not town that would require the presence of the police? A stolen iPod? A lost diamond ring? Someone skinny-dipping in the infinity pool? Or overindulging at Happy Hour? Whatever it was, she needed me and I was going to be there for her.

TWO

I DROVE UP THE hill past the iron gate with the Heavenly Acres sign on it, and into the parking lot marked "Visitors." As I got out of the car, I took a moment to admire the sweeping view of the sparkling azure cove the town was named for. The tasteful one-story buildings were built around a patio fringed with palm trees. Once again I realized how lucky Grannie was to have the money to afford the monthly fees at this upscale facility where the staff-to-resident ratio was three to one, there was water aerobics in the afternoon, first-run movies every evening, Yoga and Pilates on Wednesdays, but best of all there were nonstop Bridge games in the card room.

A tiny fear niggled at me. Not about the incident that prompted her call, but selfishly I worried about where I'd be at her age. No ex-husband to foot the bills for me. I'd be lucky to find someone who'd marry me so he could share Grannie's flat and have pie twice a day.

I found Grannie pacing back and forth in the formal reception hall along with other residents who were milling around, staff in uniforms, and administrators in what I call smart, casual outfits appropriate for a Friday afternoon at an active adult community such as Heavenly Acres. Grannie herself looked fit and chic for her age, wearing a linen pants ensemble, giving me hope that I'd inherited her genes if not her fortune. When she came into the money from Hubby Number Two, she offered me her shop with living quarters upstairs, then picked up the phone and ordered herself a new wardrobe from Talbots. Next she applied for a spot at Heavenly Acres and signed up for all the activities that didn't interfere with Bridge. It was as if she'd never been simply "the Pie Lady." She was now "the Bridge Lady."

Right now she was slightly pale and so shaky she looked like "the Scared Lady." But why?

"What's going on?" I asked.

She blinked rapidly and looked over her shoulder. Then she pointed toward the South Wing. "My room."

Her room was actually a small apartment with a gleaming miniscule kitchen she never used, not even to boil water, because she said after years of making her living baking, she was happy to let someone else do it. Like me. Beyond the kitchen was a large bedroom with a luxury bath, and a small living room filled with brand-new furniture straight out of the Pottery Barn catalog with sliding doors to a patio. She'd furnished her patio with redwood chairs, a table with an umbrella, and an actual lemon tree heavy with ripe fruit.

"Sit down," I said. "You look like you need a drink."

She sat on the Italian-designed white sofa, buried her head in her hands, and braced her elbows on her knees. I went to the sideboard and poured her a glass of Scotch, added a little water the way she always did it, and handed it to her.

She reached for it and gave me a wan smile. "They think I did it," she said.

Puzzled, I leaned against her mahogany dish cabinet and entertainment center and studied her face. "Did what?"

"Killed Mary Brandt. The woman who died on Wednesday."

"But that's ridiculous. I don't know who Mary Brandt is, but people of a certain advanced age do die from time to time. Why would anyone think someone killed her, and for heaven's sake, why would they suspect you? Surely it was natural causes."

"If you knew her, you'd know people like her don't die of natural causes. She's the type that gets murdered."

Murdered? At Heavenly Acres? Good grief, had Grannie gone completely off the deep end?

"What do you mean? What type gets murdered?"

"The type that cheats at Bridge. Everyone knew it."

Grannie lived by a few rules, Never eat at a place called Mom's. Never sleep with a man who has more problems than you, and never, ever cheat at cards or love.

"She wanted to win that badly?"

"She wanted to go to the tournament. We were tied for points. She couldn't beat me fair and square so she had to use other means. Right after she ate a piece of *my* Cranberry Walnut Cream Pie. The one you made for me."

"So what did her supposed cheating have to do with her dying?"

"It wasn't supposed, Hanna. It was real. She's dead, gone, and deceased. Here's what happened. I'd put up with her hand signals, her sighs, her looks, her twiddling with her glasses long enough. On Wednesday right after lunch I got mad. We'd just started playing when I let her have it. I told her what everyone knows. 'You're not fooling anyone,' I said. 'We all know you're sending signals to your partner.' That's Donna Linton, by the way, who's turning bright red when I say that because she knows, of course, she knows. 'Well, you're not getting away with it this time,' I say. She says something I don't understand. Then she turns white as the tablecloth, drops her cards, and slumps over."

"That's hardly murder."

"Easy for you to say. I knew she was taking something. She had her meds there on the table in her itty-bitty antique pillbox like usual. She's always bragging about her special pharmacy where they mix the drugs on site to order. Expensive, but worth the cost, so she orders them by mail instead of patronizing our own local drug store. I know she's got problems like hypertension and deep vein thrombosis, because she talks about her health all the time like it's so fascinating and we really want to know. And who doesn't take something for something? I should have kept my mouth shut."

There was a knock on the door. "Mrs. Denton? Crystal Cove Police Department."

I grabbed my grandmother's arm. "For God's sake, Grannie," I hissed. "Don't confess to anything. You didn't kill the woman. She obviously died from accidental causes. Period. End of story."

Grannie nodded. I smiled at her, then turned and opened the door with a flourish to show Grannie just how confident I was.

Sam Genovese, my old high school flame, stood at the door in classic dark slacks and an Oxford blue button-down shirt. Sam, a button-down professional? It was not the way I'd pictured him. It was too much for my mind to process. His dark hair, once shoulder length, was now cut short. So it was true. As a thirty-something adult he was outrageously more gorgeous than as a rebellious teen. And he was the absolute last person in the world I'd ever expect to be on the side of the law standing on the other side of the door tonight. Even when I'd heard he'd come back to run our little police station.

I should have guessed he'd be on the scene after hearing about him from my supposed old high school "friends." I stood there staring at him, trying to reconcile the tall, muscular guy looking positively mainstream with the tattooed teenage rule-breaker I once knew. And trying to remember what I was going to say at this meeting. There was no need. He looked right past me at my grandmother.

"Ms. Denton? How are you? I'm Sam Genovese. Crystal Cove PD. I'd like to ask you a few questions about Mary Brandt if you don't mind."

Then he turned to me. "Hello Hanna," he said, his voice deeper than I remembered, but just as casual as if we'd met yesterday on the street. It was a cinch his heart was not pounding like mine. And that he'd not practiced what he'd say to me when we met. But then he was as super cool as ever and it wasn't his grandmother being questioned by the law. "If you'll excuse us."

"Of course." What else could I say? "Hello, Sam, how are you?" I said as smoothly as I could. "You're interviewing everyone, right?"

I said that more to reassure Grannie than to hear something I already knew. "I mean Mary's death was an accident, wasn't it?" I wanted him to know he wasn't getting rid of me so easily. This was my grandmother he was talking to.

"Initially Mary Brandt's death appeared to be an accident, but in the meantime we've had the report from the coroner as well as some additional information from her family. Which means in a case like this we're treating it as a homicide. This was no accident."

"No accident? A homicide?" I repeated like a parrot. So Grannie wasn't paranoid after all.

He nodded rather curtly I thought.

"In a case like this?" I asked, still reeling from the shock. *Like what?* I wanted to know. But he didn't answer. I didn't know where Sam had been all these years. If he was working as a cop in some big city, maybe he was accustomed to finding murder victims every other Friday night. He ought to know how rare murder was, especially in peaceful Crystal Cove. Especially at a retirement home.

"Where the family insists on an investigation and the evidence points to murder."

I gulped, but when I recovered from hearing the M word, I shot Grannie a confident smile I hoped pumped her up, then I left and stood just outside with my ear pressed to the door. I shouldn't have been surprised, but it was amazing to hear my grandmother switch from frightened suspect to her Lady of the Manor mode. All signs of the nervous, worried, supposedly accused murderer were gone. After offering him a drink which he declined, she asked him how he liked Crystal Cove, as if he was a newcomer. He told her he was actually a native.

She said, "Oh, of course, how silly of me. How could I forget. You're the Genovese boy. You'll have to forgive an old lady, my memory isn't what it used to be." Then I swear, she giggled. She probably hoped he'd tell her she was far from being "an old lady." Around here anyway. But he didn't, so after a pause she continued.

"It's lovely having you back in town. I hope you're here for good," she said. "Crystal Cove is such a wonderful place to settle down and bring up children ..." I couldn't hear what she said next, but knowing her I assumed it was something like, "So, do you have any?" I knew exactly what was coming next. *Not married? Really? Either is Hanna. She's back in town too.*

Just as Sam told her to sit down because he had a few questions for her, two of Grannie's friends walked by. I jumped back as if I wasn't listening at the door, and greeted them as if I was just innocently hanging out in the hall.

"Isn't it awful?" Helen said to me in a stage whisper. "Of course you never want your opponent to win a hand, especially when you're playing for a chance to move on to the Big Time. But Louise only said what everyone knew. Mary cheated at cards. She got other people to cover for her. We all knew it. But nobody had the guts to tell her until Louise did. That's what I told the officer. She was just being our mouthpiece. That's Louise."

I swallowed hard. Maybe she shouldn't have volunteered to be their mouthpiece. Reluctant to leave the vicinity, I hooked my arms with theirs and the three of us walked down the hall to the well-appointed TV lounge, which was empty since everyone was out watching the police cars. I turned off the TV and closed the door.

We sat down in front of the faux fireplace faced with antique marble with a faux fire burning cheerfully. I took a deep breath and spoke as calmly as possible. "What did she say, actually?"

"Louise was right," Grace said. "Right after we had our coffee and pie on Wednesday, and by the way your pie was absolutely delicious, and so unusual. Who would have thought of combining cranberries with walnuts in a cream pie? Anyway, Mary started in. She bids six of Spades, she leads with the Ace, and bingo, she starts pulling her ear, twisting her ring, and staring at her partner. It was so obvious, and it's not the first time. So finally Louise couldn't take it anymore. She's the only one who had the nerve to call her on it. That doesn't mean she did it."

I leaned forward. "Did what? Who did what?"

"Killed Mary," Helen said. "I don't care what they say, nobody killed Mary. All Louise said was 'Cheating is a crime, you know. In the old days it was punishable by death.'"

Uh oh. No wonder Sam was questioning Grannie.

"It's not her fault Mary got caught," Grace said. "And got what was coming to her. What happened was she had a stroke right there at the table and keeled over. She was guilty as hell and she knew it. That's what I told the officer too when he asked me if anyone had a motive for wishing Mary was dead. Did you see him? I thought he was new in town, but it turns out he grew up here. Very handsome fellow, don't you think? If I was a few years younger…" She tilted her head to one side and stared off into space for a moment while she tapped her red fingernails on the coffee table.

My head was spinning. A picture was forming in my mind, but there were still a few pieces missing from this puzzle. "So Mary had a stroke on Wednesday," I said. "Then died the same day."

"That's right. The ambulance came and took her away and later we heard she'd passed away at the hospital," Helen added. "They flew the flag at half-mast and we had a moment of silence at the dinner table, just like we always do."

I admired the matter-of-fact way the women accepted death, and I hoped some day I'd be able to do the same.

"So why are the police here?" I asked. "If it was an accident." I knew what the official explanation was, but I wanted to know what they thought. "That's unusual, isn't it?"

Helen and Grace exchanged looks. Then Helen shrugged.

"It's her crazy family. She told us and everybody who would listen to her someone was out to get her, so when she croaked, her daughter decided she was telling the truth." Helen sighed. "So here comes the police and the big investigation. Kind of exciting in a way."

Grace chimed in. "I've got to say, Mary would have loved it. She always wanted to be the center of attention. Dead or alive."

"Not that Mary didn't have enemies," Helen said. "Let's face it, she was not a lovable person. Some might even say she was conniving and controlling. But murder? At Heavenly Acres? It's ridiculous. It was her conditions that killed her. Any booby knows that. We're all just lucky to be alive. Do you know what the life expectancy was in Queen Victoria's time?"

I shook my head.

"I don't either," she said, "but I think it's about forty. We're living longer, but at our age we've all got something to complain about. What I always say is if you can't stand the heat, get out of the kitchen. Know what I mean? If you can't take the stress of Bridge, if you haven't got the chops anymore, have the decency to quit and stick to Go Fish. But now that she's dead, she's out of the tournament. Your grandmother Louise will move up and represent Heavenly Acres in Sacramento. We'll rent a van and we'll all be there to root for her."

Grace clapped her multi-jeweled hands together and smiled at me.

I leaned back in my chair and contemplated what I'd learned from the two of them. Sam must know by now that Grannie not only called Mary out on her cheating, perhaps causing her stroke, but she'd directly benefited from her death by moving up in the Bridge tournament. That didn't seem to bother these "girls" in the least. Were they as ruthless and cutthroat as they seemed? Or were they just realistic? When you face the fact that death is just around the corner for all of us, maybe you accept it more easily. Again a knock on the door and this time I wasn't surprised to find Officer Sam standing there.

"I'm asking all the residents to gather in the dining room." He looked at me as if he knew I'd try to escape. "This means you too, Hanna. If you would."

"But I don't live here," I explained as calmly as I could. Did I really need to explain that I wasn't over fifty-five and eligible for admission to a seniors-only facility? I was just about to tell him I had a shop to run when he said, "Be there," in a tone that brooked no disobedience.

THREE

In the lounge with the blue and gold striped wallpaper and the folding chairs filled with residents, I hung out in the rear doorway and tried to make myself invisible. And I wondered what in the hell I was doing there as I canvassed the place. There was Grannie flanked by her two Bridge buddies. I wished I'd had a chance to ask her what else Sam had said to her, but there was no time. I just hoped she gave the right answers and he'd look elsewhere for his murderer. Across the room was a dapper old gentleman elegantly dressed in a cravat and a smoking jacket whose gaze was fixed on Grannie. For a moment I thought he winked at her. Was this the murderer? Or the boyfriend she'd only hinted at?

I shifted my gaze when Sam introduced himself.

"As your new police chief," he said, "I hope you will feel free to come to me with any problem you have, legal, criminal, or otherwise. My door is always open."

He paused and looked around the room as if he thought someone might jump up and spring a problem on him on the spot. They didn't. Then he continued. "I was born and bred right here in Crystal Cove and I love this town as much as you do." He mentioned the hills and the sandy beaches and the beautiful weather and pledged to uphold the law and keep the streets safe for all citizens. I almost gagged. He sounded like he was running for mayor. Maybe he was. Maybe police chief was just a stepping stone. Safe streets? Come on. This was no New York City. It wasn't even Sacramento.

Was this some kind of role Sam was playing? Or had he really changed that much? What happened to the fast-talking, wild-eyed guy who put the cow on the roof of the high school the day of graduation? Where was the champion wrestler who could drink anyone under the table? Who left town under a cloud of suspicion? I swear he looked straight at me when he said his door was always open, as if daring me to walk in and confess to something. Anything.

You hear about zombies eating human brains. I never believed in them before, but I was beginning to wonder. If it wasn't a zombie, maybe it was aliens that stole his original bad-boy brain and exchanged it for one from an ultimate law-and-order guy.

"I want to apologize for interrupting the Friday afternoon Bingo game," Sam continued, "but I am opening a murder investigation into the death of Mary Brandt."

The whole room gave a collective gasp.

Sam ploughed on. "I hope you will all bear with me as I have a short meeting with each and every resident right here at Heavenly Acres to get to the bottom of this crime on these premises. Not to alarm anyone, but the majority of murders take place in the home or workplace. I can't leave any stone unturned or any party uninvestigated. I hope you understand my only goal is to keep you safe from harm."

A cacophony of murmurs spread through the crowd.

Again he seemed determined to ignore them. "So as not to cause anyone to disrupt their daily activities," he continued, "the management has graciously allowed me to use the housekeeper's office for my interviews. A schedule will be posted outside the door. See me if you have a scheduling conflict."

I looked around. The excitement in the dining room was palpable. I had to think they weren't too shocked to welcome this unexpected turn of events. I would have thought they'd be worried and frightened, thinking there was a murderer right here where they lived. Maybe they were. Or maybe they didn't understand the implication of what he'd said. Instead they were on the edge of their chairs, alive, alert, and stimulated. All eyes were glued to Sam, the picture of a tough, good-looking TV detective, all hearing aids turned up to full volume as they appeared to relish the idea of a criminal investigation, not on television, not in Miami or Chicago, but right here before their very eyes.

Maybe they were also riveted by Sam's unexpected presence on their turf, because most of the women were staring at him as if the star of *Die Hard 2* had suddenly appeared to solve a crime right in their serene, secure, pricey retirement home. The new Chief of Police paused again and then cut to the chase.

"In preparation for your interviews, I would like you all to search your memories for any information concerning the deceased Mrs. Brandt. If you have any theories, or can think of any small detail, an overheard conversation perhaps or any suspicious activities that might help us solve the murder of one of your residents, I would like to hear it. I'm counting on your help in this matter. And your discretion."

Murmurs swept through the room once again. *Murder? Suspicious activities?*

Sam went on. "Naturally, whatever you choose to tell me will be held in complete confidence."

Hands shot up.

"You mean we're supposed to rat on our friends?" a man in tennis shorts and a Lacoste T-shirt asked, his eyes wide behind his bifocals.

"'Rat' is not a word I would have chosen," Sam said calmly. "I'm sure you are just as anxious as the police department is in solving this mystery and keeping you safe from wrongdoers in our midst. I'm asking you for whatever information you have, that's all. My job in this town is to protect the innocent. To do that, I must prosecute the guilty to the full extent of the law. Whoever killed Mary Brandt may still be in our community. He or she may be someone you know. I don't want to frighten any of you in this room, but my goal, which should also be yours, is to find Mary Brandt's killer as soon as possible. Then we can all go back to enjoying the perks of living in this small, beautiful, law-abiding town we call home."

"What if my interview is the same time as flower arranging?" a woman wearing a pale gray cashmere sweater set and pearls asked. I had to give her credit. She'd doubtless heard the words "murder" and "kill" in conjunction with the people in this room and yet she was worried about missing flower arranging. First things first. I wondered if this was a typical reaction.

"I'll be happy to change the schedule to accommodate your prior commitments," Sam said.

"What if I heard something suspicious but I don't know if it means anything?" a man in a San Francisco Giants visor cap asked.

"I welcome hearing anything that you can think of. Anything at all. No information is too small or trivial. I will be able to judge if it's relevant or not. Please don't hold anything back no matter how insignificant it may seem."

After a few more questions of this nature, I could imagine Sam rolling his eyes, wishing he didn't have to deal with these elder citizens, but to his credit he seemed ready to stay there until everyone was satisfied. He actually looked genuinely interested in what they had to say. Maybe they had a class at the Academy in Listening and Respecting the Public No Matter How Dumb Their Questions Are.

A woman in tailored slacks and a printed scarf arranged artfully over a sweater asked, "How can we get in touch with you if we have something to tell you that can't wait until our interview?"

Sam gave her and everyone his cell phone number and said he was looking forward to hearing from them, anytime, night or day. Solving this crime was his number one priority. Lacking a piece of paper, I wrote the number down on my arm with a pen I borrowed. I intended to call him ASAP to tell him to lay off my grandmother.

He closed the meeting by apologizing once again for disrupting their lives at the residence, but there was a murder to be solved. He was sure he could count on every one of them to be discreet and helpful. Then he wished everyone a good evening, left the room, and pealed away in his patrol car.

The place was jumping. The noise level was in the high decibel range. Everyone was milling around. I edged my way through the crowd to find Grannie.

"I've got to get back to the shop," I said. "I hate to close up in the afternoon like this."

"You don't want your customers to go away disappointed," she said. "But thanks for coming." I could tell her mind was elsewhere.

"What's wrong?" I asked, noticing how pale she was. "You're not afraid of Sam, are you?"

"The question is—Is he afraid of me?"

I managed a little chuckle. Then I quickly sobered up. "What do you mean?"

"He asked me to come to the police station tomorrow morning. He wants to ask me some questions."

"That's nothing to worry about. He's asking everyone questions. That's why he's coming over here to set up shop."

"But my interview isn't here. Mine's at the station. I'm the only one. You know why? He's got a lie detector there." She gave a little shudder. "He suspects me of murdering Mary."

I tried to chuckle again at this laughable idea, but instead I choked. I caught my breath and said, "If he's got a lie detector, you'll pass with flying colors and that will be the end of it. Of course, you'll tell him everything you know. He'll give you a medal for bravery and full disclosure and you'll be out of there in no time, free as a bird."

We walked out to the parking lot together. I don't know if she was reassured because she didn't say anything for a long moment. When we got to the classic wagon she'd driven for years, she ran her manicured hand absently over the hood. She insisted she didn't miss driving. Heavenly Acres had a van to take the residents anywhere they wanted to go and that was just fine with her. But I thought I saw a gleam of nostalgia in her eyes as she stroked the surface of the vehicle she'd loved.

Suddenly she frowned as if she'd just remembered what we were talking about. "Weren't you listening?" she asked, her gaze fixed on mine. "Didn't you hear him telling us to rat on each other? Everything I've ever said about Mary, and believe me I've been critical of her, to her face and behind her face, will come out in the wash. Not just what I've said about her Bridge playing but other things. I'll be in chains before you know it."

"Chains?"

"Whatever they put you in, I'll be there. I may have even said I'd like to kill her."

"Given how unpopular she was, you can't be the only one."

She stared at me for a long moment. "So all I have to do is find out who else wanted her dead. Is that what you're saying?"

"Not at all," I assured her, afraid she'd be off on a witch hunt. "If he's as smart as we expect from a Chief of Police, he'll soon find out you didn't do it and he'll discover the real perpetrator," I said softly with a glance over my shoulder. "You're a competitor, but you'd never go that far to win." I stifled the urge to add, *Would you?*

She didn't say anything and the look on her face didn't assuage my fears that there was something she wasn't telling me.

"There is no need to feel guilty," I said firmly. "Or take responsibility for solving this crime. Sure, you upset Mary, but you didn't kill her."

Or did she? Did she cause the stroke that killed Mary? What did kill Mary? How did he or she do it without anyone noticing until she slumped over at the Bridge table?

"I can't help it," she said. "You should have heard what Sam said to me."

I wanted to say, I *did* hear what he said to you, but I couldn't admit to eavesdropping.

"All you have to do is tell the truth tomorrow," I said. "Nothing to worry about."

"The truth is I wanted Mary out of the way because I didn't want any competition at the state tournament. Is that what you want me to say?"

"Not in those words. Because while he'll probably learn you were rivals, that doesn't mean you've been anything except a serious competitor. All you've ever done is to play with your whole heart, just like you used to bake pies. You always put your full self into what you're doing. That's no crime."

"I'm glad someone is so sure," she said.

I got in the car and she leaned down to face me from outside the open window. "One of my friends will bring me down tomorrow and I'll come by the shop after my interview."

"You'll do fine," I said, reaching out to squeeze her hand. But I wasn't sure about that. I wished it was just an interview, but if he was hooking her up to a polygraph, then it was more than an interview. I'd heard a lie detector machine was a psychological tool for exacting confessions the way torture was in the olden days. And it gave me the chills.

I drove away, and when I looked in the rearview mirror she was still standing in the parking lot staring straight ahead and looking thoughtful. Was she thinking about her "interview," or who else wanted Mary dead, or her chances at winning the Bridge tournament, or, much better, the man who was giving her the eye at the meeting just now?

As I crushed graham crackers in the blender for a pie crust the next morning, I wondered how far my grandmother *would* go to win at Bridge. Had she verbally attacked her rival hoping to provoke a reaction that would throw Mrs. Brandt off her game? That wasn't a crime. If she was cheating, it was time someone called her on it. Did Grannie really want her out of the way? If she did, she probably wasn't the only one. I couldn't help worrying about her. My wonderful, warm, caring grandmother was not a murderer. In a few hours she would take a lie detector test, she'd pass with flying colors, and Sam would turn his attention elsewhere and we could all relax. All of us except the real killer, who would fade into the woodwork now that Mary was gone. It might be one of those unsolved mysteries, or Sam would find the murderer after a brilliant investigation and we could all sleep better once the arrest was made.

I pictured a time in the near future when the seniors and other residents of Crystal Cove would drop in to my shop for coffee and pie regularly. And while in the shop, I'd overhear comments about the Chief of Police. I had to admit I was curious about his life. What had happened to him between when he dropped out of high school and now? Even if Sam never came into my shop, and I only ran into him by chance, I might find out from my customers what he was really up to. Had he done a complete turnaround? Or was this an act? Or a secret undercover assignment?

It seemed obvious that Mary couldn't be the first resident in her age group to be struck down and die in a hospital. There must be a protocol for such events that included an investigation if the family requested or the coroner had reason to think this was murder. What was in the coroner's report? The method of her murder? And who did the family believe was out to get Mary? Or did they just dismiss her as an old lady with paranoia?

While I was simmering the mixture on the stove for a chocolate marshmallow pie, I thought about how much I owed my grandmother, not just for giving me the chance at a new life, but for filling in for years and giving me a home when my parents were living out of the country.

She was finally getting a chance to enjoy life and by heaven, I wasn't going to let any overzealous small-town Chief of Police try to pin a murder on her. No matter how eager he was to solve the first murder in years and make a name for himself in this bucolic seaside paradise. Which is probably why he'd come to this town anyway, where there was no crime, or practically none. How else would he justify his being in a town where nothing happens except to make a quick arrest of some helpless senior citizen who wished her Bridge nemesis was out of the picture?

I tried not to think about getting old and dying of natural or unnatural causes, whether it was at Heavenly Acres or the Poor House. Instead, I concentrated on my pie. After I'd put it together and it was cooling in the fridge, I wrote "Special Today Only—S'Mores Pie" on a blackboard and leaned it against a tree outside on the sidewalk. Then I hung an "Open" sign on my front door, ever hopeful that today would be the day I would ring up a lot of sales. It was eight thirty in the morning, and I'd been up for three hours. Baker's hours.

I walked out in front of the shop several times looking for Grannie. I noticed a classic Mercedes parked in front of the station. Maybe that was her friend's car. Maybe she was in there right now hooked up to the lie detector. I couldn't concentrate on anything until I heard she'd come through the test okay. Finally, she showed up with her friend. She was beautifully dressed as usual, in a tailored flowered shirt, a navy blazer, a matching skirt, and comfortable walking shoes.

"How did it go?" I asked anxiously. I didn't like the way she looked. When I put my arm around her shoulders, she felt small and vulnerable. Damn that Sam. What had he done to her?

"It was terrible," she said collapsing into a chair.

I immediately poured her a cup of coffee and cut her a piece of S'Mores Pie. I sat down across from her. "What do you mean? What did he ask you?"

"Everything," she said. "Have you ever had a lie detector test?"

I shook my head.

"Well, first they ask you things like 'Did you ever lie to get out of trouble?' I said yes, because you know, everyone has. Then a bunch of other questions that seem easy, but they're there to trick you."

"So you knew what to say," I said slightly relieved.

"The important thing is to believe what you say," she said.

"Well then," I said. "If you did, I'm sure the machine will back you up."

"Then why did he tell me not to leave town?"

I bit my lip. That wasn't good news. "I … I don't know. Maybe, I don't know, to corroborate others' stories or just more questions. The police always say that. Sam's seen too many movies. Don't worry. It's nothing personal, I'm sure." But I wasn't sure at all.

"There's only one thing I can do to clear my name," she said. "And that's to find the real murderer."

"But that's Sam's job," I protested. I pictured her setting up a rival investigation to his. I imagined her poking into the private lives of her fellow residents, which wouldn't win her any points in life or in Bridge.

"You'd think so," she said. "But after today, I can't count on that. And neither should you. He's out to get me, Hanna. And I have to stop him."

I opened my mouth to protest, but she wasn't in any mood to listen to me, so I closed it. If Sam was really out to get her, I couldn't let that happen. How could she, a senior citizen under suspicion, stop him? I'm the one who had to take action.

"There's my ride," she said, glancing out the window as the Mercedes pulled up. I tried to see who the driver was, wondering, was it Grannie's new boyfriend?

"What about your pie and coffee?"

"I couldn't eat a thing. Not with so much on my mind. Besides..." She looked at her watch. "I have a Yoga class at eleven. Believe me I need some deep breathing and relaxation exercises after what I've been through."

Before I could stop her she lifted her chin, stood up straight, and walked out of the shop. Not for the first time, I was in awe of her gumption. She'd been through a lot in her life—building a business, raising me, dealing with an ex-husband—but this was the first time anyone had accused her of murder. I shouldn't be surprised that she wasn't taking this lying down. The old car had barely pulled away with her in it when Sam came to the shop.

"Officer Genovese," I said, trying to stay calm and imitate Grannie's gracious hostess voice and formal manner even though I was seething with anger. I tried but I just couldn't do it. My manners crumpled like a collapsed soufflé. "How dare you accuse my grand-mother of murder!" I demanded.

"Wait a minute," he said. "I gave her a lie detector test. That's all."

"The implication is that you suspect her. Do you or don't you?"

"I suspect everyone who had dealings with Mary Brandt. Your grandmother is one of those people."

"How many are getting tested?"

"That's confidential."

I exhaled loudly. I decided it was time to switch gears. Who was it who said you can catch more flies with honey?

"How about a cup of coffee on this cool morning along with a slice of tropical key lime pie?" I was proud of myself for turning on what I hoped was the charm. I was going for something be-tween polite and effusive.

A hint of a knowing smile touched his lips as if he knew what I was going through. The Sam I used to know would have had a sarcastic reply. He would have made fun of my turning into my grandmother. The Sam who stood in my shop said, "Sure, why not?" so casually I did a double take. I expected him to turn me down flat.

I went to the kitchen, cut a slice of key lime pie, one of my per-sonal favorites that reminded me of a vacation in the Florida sun where I'd gone on a rare trip with my usually absent parents.

After I set the pie on the table, I stood in front of the coun-ter, crossed my arms over my chest, and watched him eat. I'd be damned if I'd break the silence.

"Very good," he said after a few bites. He set his fork down. "I'd like to ask you a few questions."

"Of course." I tried to act normal but my stomach was in knots. I should be glad he hadn't hooked me up to his lie detector. It was only because I didn't fit his description of someone who'd had dealings with Mary Brandt. "I'm not busy at the moment. I wish I was busy, but unfortunately business is a little slow these days. As you know, it's a very quiet town. Or it was."

"Is that why you left?" he asked. "Or should I ask why you came back?"

"That *is* why I left. I thought life was too slow, too boring and quiet for me here. I wanted to get out and live an exciting life in a big city where things happened and no one knew me. No one knew I was raised by my grandmother, that I lived above a pie shop and spent my free time working in the shop after school or doing my homework."

"I understand that," he said. "I felt the same way. I had to get out. Somewhere where no one knew I was kicked out of high school or that my parents were deadbeats. At least you had support. You weren't on your own from early on."

"No, but I wanted to be. I didn't want to be Louise Denton's granddaughter, the serious nerdy girl who studied all the time to get on the honor roll. I wanted to be the popular cheerleader kind of girl or a goth. But I was neither." I smiled ruefully at the thought of it.

"You were never nerdy," he said with a long sideways look at me that made my toes curl. Even now, more than fifteen years later, it all came back to me as if it was yesterday. Every word he'd ever said to me, and there weren't very many, were engraved in my subconscious. I thought I'd forgotten, I wished I'd forgotten, but I hadn't.

"I was. You just don't remember."

"I remember you," he said. "I remember prom night."

I swallowed hard. I would have thought he'd have forgotten. Of course I hadn't, being the girl who wanted to be hip but never was.

"I never thanked you," I said.

"For what?"

"For what you did," I said.

"For telling the truth?"

"Yes. It couldn't have been easy." I knew that and I always wished I'd had the chance to speak to him.

He shrugged. I hoped we could drop the subject. It was painful reliving that embarrassing scene after the prom when my date ran out on me. It was downright humiliating even now. I didn't want to know why Sam did what he did or why he left town so fast. I didn't want him to know how often I'd thought about it. How often I'd thought about him. Instead I answered his other question. Sort of.

"Why did I come back? Why not? As you know, Crystal Cove is as close to paradise as you can get. You said it yourself, we have the hills and the ocean, the sandy beaches and the safe streets." I emphasized the word *safe*. "What's not to like? Besides, my grandmother wanted to retire. I'd done the big-city thing, lived in an apartment, had an office job, went to singles' bars at night until all that got old. I was ready for a change. I also really like baking pies. It's a job and it's challenging, but there's no desk, no time clock, and no boss, so it seems more like … I don't know … a hobby or a habit. Anyway, here I am."

I stood there brushing my hands against my apron while he looked around the shop until he finally focused on me and looked at me, really looked as if he could see the girl behind the woman

44

behind the apron. He was waiting for me to go on, as if he wanted to know more. But I wasn't about to tell him or anybody what stupid thing I'd done. I just wanted to put it behind me and keep it buried in the past.

"There isn't much more to know," I added, hoping to put a cap on this discussion. He didn't say anything. He just looked at me as if maybe I was still hiding something.

"What about you?" I asked, eager to change the subject. "Why show up in Crystal Cove after all these years?" He probably wouldn't tell me, but I just had to ask, especially since we were both pretending he didn't suspect my grandmother of murder. "Isn't it boring for a law man to be back in the small town where nothing ever happens except for old people dying?" I waited for him to tell me she didn't just die, she was murdered. But he didn't. I waited for him to explain his assignment was some kind of punishment for letting a mobster get away or speeding on the freeway in his sports car. Knowing Sam, he'd have an explanation. But he didn't do that either.

"It's not boring," he insisted. "Not at all. I went to the Police Academy in San Francisco, worked on the streets for a few years. Then this job came up so I took it."

"What was it like being a street cop?" I asked.

"Fine, until things go wrong. Until your partner gets killed on your day off." He stared off into space with a look on his face I'd never seen before. His lips were pressed together, and his jaw looked like it was locked in place.

"That's awful," I murmured. "How did it happen?"

He didn't say anything for a long moment. I was afraid I'd gone too far. Afraid he'd say it was none of my business.

"A domestic disturbance. He was out with a rookie because I wasn't there. I should have been."

"Where were you?"

"I took the day off to take a kid to school. I'm a big brother."

"I thought …"

"You thought I was an only child. I am. Big Brothers is a program I got involved with in the city. You mentor a kid, someone who needs a little help. I got assigned to this boy …" He broke off. "You don't need to hear all this."

I shrugged as if it didn't matter whether I did or not. But it did matter. I wanted to know what happened in those years I lost track of him. I wanted to tell him I cared, but I was afraid to. I didn't move. I just stood there waiting, hoping …

"The kid reminded me of me. Bad home situation. Full of himself. Acting out at school. You know I did. So it was parent day at his school. I went. Not that he asked me to, he wouldn't do that. In fact he told me he didn't want me to come. I went anyway. And that was the day Eric got shot by the guy who was beating up on his wife. The domestic disturbance I missed."

"You might not have made a difference," I said. "Or you would have been shot, too."

"Or I would have been shot instead of my buddy who had a wife and two kids. But I wasn't." He said it so matter-of-factly I almost thought he'd put it behind him, but there was something about the way his eyes were narrowed that made me realize it was still a big part of him.

"What happened to the boy, the one you were mentoring?"

"Michael? His uncle came and took him to Nevada. I went to see him, but he'd already gone."

"Still, you made a difference."

"Did I? I don't know."

"Well…" I waited a long moment, then I went to the kitchen and came back with a strawberry pie just out of the oven.

"Would you take this as a welcome-back present for the guys at the station? I don't see enough of your uh… staff… force, I mean." What did you call a group of policemen anyway?

"That's because they're all on a fitness regime," he explained. He sounded better. Back to the present. I wasn't sure if I'd opened a can of worms by asking all those questions.

"It's a badly needed program of exercise and diet," he explained. "Which is partly why I got this job. To shape up the officers. To re-model the whole department. When I got here six months ago, the staff was about five hundred pounds overweight, collectively."

"Does this fitness program of yours have anything to do with the police avoiding my shop?"

"It could."

"Okay, I see you've got a job to do. Shape up the department. I agree that pie should be eaten in moderation, but some pies are re-ally good for you. Take this strawberry rhubarb here. It's all natu-ral and all delicious. You have fruit—the strawberries and rhubarb, which is actually a vegetable with high-quality fiber, and dairy in the buttery crust into which I added some whole grain. I call it the ultimate food."

He didn't say anything; he just looked at me as if he was try-ing to reconcile the former local nerdy hippie-wannabe girl who once died her hair black and purple with the homey, flour-covered baker in front of him. No makeup, brown hair pulled back in a rubber band, and my body covered with an apron. So I'd changed. Well, so had he.

"I'll cut you a piece right now," I said, setting it down on the table.

"I don't usually eat dessert," he said. "And besides, I just finished a piece."

"Well, this isn't dessert, it's a food group," I said and without waiting for his answer, I took the pie and hurried into the kitchen for a knife and two clean plates. I cut two pieces of warm strawberry rhubarb pie oozing ruby-red juice, and then I poured two cups of coffee. I was counting on the fact that hardly anyone can resist a piece of warm pie when it's put in front of them, no matter how much will power they have. I put everything on a tray and came back into the shop.

But instead of digging in, he was standing at the window looking across the street at the police station.

"What's up?" I asked. "Another emergency?"

He shook his head. "You know at one time I hated that place, the police station. I thought they were out to get me. Old Officer Jarvis would drag me in and ask me questions like where was I when ... something happened. Whatever it was, he was sure I was behind it. Or he'd ask why did I skip school the month of whenever. Not that I didn't deserve it. I broke enough rules and got into enough trouble in my time."

"I'm not a psychologist," I said, "but does your return to Crystal Cove have something to do with what happened in the city or your showing the town and yourself that you've redeemed yourself? You've not only done a complete turnaround, you're going to bury your past, solve a murder, and keep us all safe from harm while you're at it."

"Not bad," he said with a pointed glance at me, "for an amateur. But if I were you I'd stick to pie baking and leave the pop psychology to someone else."

Of course he'd say that. Especially if I'd come anywhere close to guessing the truth.

He turned and regarded the plates and the forks and the cups of coffee along with the old-fashioned sugar bowl and matching creamer with some suspicion. But he sat down again and so did I. I wanted so badly to acknowledge the elephant in the room, the subject we were both avoiding, and say, "How did it go with my grandmother? How did she do?" but I continued to keep it to myself.

I held my breath until I saw him take one bite and then another of the pie. When he finished, he set his fork down and finally spoke. He got down to the real reason he was here. He wanted to talk about pie, but not this one.

"The cranberry pie you made for your grandmother on Wednesday…" Sam said.

"Yes?"

"Whose idea was it?" Sam asked.

"Mine," I said. "I'm the one who offered to make the pie for my grandmother's Bridge group."

"Were you the one who decided on the type of pie?" he asked.

I hesitated. Did I dare lie? Was there any point to it? Did he already know the answer? "She asked me for Cranberry Walnut."

"I don't suppose you knew that a drug called warfarin interacts with certain foods like cranberries, spinach, cabbage, coriander…" he said.

"Of course not," I said hotly. "How could I? I'm not a pharmacist. And I had no idea what anyone was taking. If they were taking anything. Although considering the facility, I would think some, maybe most of the residents are taking something."

"Someone knew Mrs. Brandt was taking warfarin to prevent blood clots and served her cranberries, which interacted with her medicine," Sam said sternly.

"Was she? Did it?" I asked.

"Her relatives say she was on several meds but not sure which ones she took that day. Whatever she was taking interacted with the pie she was eating and had a deadly effect," he said.

"Just an unfortunate accident, then," I said hopefully.

"No, Hanna. This was no accident."

"You don't really think my grandmother had anything to do with her ... death, do you?"

"Do you?" he asked.

"Of course not," I said squaring my shoulders and looking him in the eye. "She wouldn't hurt a flea."

"She said it was your idea to bake a cranberry pie."

"I ..." I knew what was going on. I've seen enough TV dramas to know how they divide and conquer. Put the suspects in separate interview rooms and ask the same questions and try to catch the suspects in lies or evasions. "I'm not sure. Maybe it was. I had a bag of cranberries in my freezer and I like to combine them with walnuts. So does Grannie. We think alike when it comes to pie." I paused. "Actually, I believe someone requested something with cranberries in it, and as a businesswoman I'm always happy to honor requests. Besides being a businesswoman, I'm really just an ordinary citizen. If you ask me, this was just an unfortunate accident."

"I'm not asking you. This is a homicide due to an overdose of a common medication."

"Maybe Mary ODed on purpose. She knew she'd been caught cheating and rather than deal with the shame of it, she killed herself."

His jaw dropped and he looked at me as if I'd lost my mind.

"Or not," I said quickly.

"Let's look at the facts," he said, "instead of wandering off in crazy-land. Mrs. Brandt was a wealthy woman. She was also an outspoken woman at the facility where your grandmother lives. I understand she'd made a few enemies. More than a few. Which is why I'll be interviewing everyone who was there the day of the demise as well as Mrs. Brandt's family, who are very anxious to get to the bottom of this."

And divvy up her property, I thought.

"As are we all," I said. "In regard to lie detector tests, I understand they're not at all reliable." I'd actually done some investigating on the Internet last night and stored up a few facts. "Did you know that the man who started the CIA's polygraph program thought that plants could read human thoughts?"

"No, I didn't."

"Also the alleged anthrax killer passed a polygraph test."

"Thank you, Hanna. It looks like you've been doing some research."

"Anything I can do to help," I said sweetly.

"What you mean is anything you can do to help your grandmother."

51

"I confess to that. She's an honest, sincere, kind, wonderful woman and you're right. I'd do anything to help her."

"Would you lie to the police?"

"I don't need to."

"You didn't answer my question."

I didn't intend to either. I wasn't under oath.

There was a long silence. Finally he spoke. "I understand the funeral will be this weekend with a memorial service at the retirement home and the interment following up at a later date after the autopsy."

"Autopsy? Is that normal procedure?"

"The family has ordered an independent autopsy."

"But why? I don't get why everyone including you assumes she was murdered. A paranoid old woman tells her family someone is trying to kill her, then she has a stroke during a particularly tense Bridge game and dies at the hospital. Yes, she ate a pie with cranberries in it, and she was taking certain drugs whatever they were, but isn't it possible they didn't cause her death? I can't imagine how big a dose it would take to kill a person. Or how many pieces of pie. And you insist this is a murder."

"That's right," he said. "Whether Mary was killed by an overdose of a drug or the interaction between her drugs and the pie she ate, it was not an accident. It was homicide. I understand how upsetting it is for everyone in this town to think there's a killer around, but we have to face the facts. That's what they're paying me for." He paused and gave me a steady look. "If you have anything else to tell me, I'd be glad to hear it. My door is always open."

"Yes I know. I heard your speech."

"Then you have my number."

I looked at my arm and nodded.

"That's all for now," he said. "I'll see you at the service. If not before." He put some money under his empty pie plate and walked out.

I stood there in the doorway thinking of everything he'd told me and wondered if he regretted saying so much about his past. It certainly showed me a side of Sam I'd never seen, and it left me with mixed feelings.

I considered all the things I might have said in defense of my grandmother, but didn't. Like why would Grannie murder Mary? Sam would be all over that. Motives, that's what Sam would be looking for. I could just see him thinking as he grilled Grannie: Did she have a motive? Was she ambitious?

Unfortunately for this murder investigation, Grannie was ambitious. Sam would probably figure that out eventually if he hadn't already. He'd hear from someone, perhaps Grannie herself, how much she wanted to win at Bridge and go on to the tournament. He'd learn that Mary was her chief competitor in earning master points. I didn't think for one minute I'd convinced Sam of my or Grannie's innocence. And all because I made and she'd served a cranberry pie.

I could picture myself confessing I'd tampered with Mary's meds and made the pie. If I had to, I would to save my grandmother, and she would do the same for me. Next thing you knew we'd be sharing a small cell in the county jail after being convicted by a jury of our Crystal Cove peers of murdering Mary with pie and an overdose of pills. We'd have visitors for sure. There would be an exercise facility outside so we'd keep in shape. Grannie would spend all her money on a hot-shot lawyer who worked tirelessly year after year to find the real killer and set us free. Maybe we could even help out in the prison bakery while doing our time.

I shook my head to erase these disturbing images. Instead, I forced myself to think about the memorial service and the gathering afterward for pie and coffee. Lots of pie. Many kinds of pie.

As I carried the plates to the kitchen, I took some satisfaction in seeing Sam had eaten every crumb and even paid for the privilege with a wad of bills he'd left under his plate. But I'd never forgive him for frightening my grandmother. I swore I'd get even with him for that. Sure, it was his job. Sure, he'd made something of himself since he left town. Yes, he was back in town to keep us all safe from harm, and to do something for his own damaged psyche after his partner was killed, but still…

That afternoon I was determined to find out more about the Brandt family. Since Sam was convinced Mary was murdered, the only way to save my grandmother was to find the real killer. She knew it and I knew it. Wasn't it possible one of the family members wanted to see Mary bite the dust so he or she could inherit her money? I figured she must have had money. The Brandt family sure did. They were well known around town. But maybe not wealthy enough. Who does have enough money? It didn't take a genius to see their motive would be greed.

Everyone who reads mysteries knows the two chief motives for murder are love and money, followed by ambition, greed, revenge, jealousy, and insanity. If anyone loved Mary I hadn't heard about it. If anyone was going to profit from her death it would have to be her family. I looked up Brandt in the slim Crystal Cove phone book and found a Hartley Brandt listed on Vista Lane in the hillside section of Crystal Cove, the side of our town with the winding streets and the lush vegetation carefully tended by gardeners, and the views of the cove from the McMansions perched on the steep acreage. Was Hartley Mary's husband or her son? I could have called first, but I wanted to catch Mary's relatives unawares in the guise of a condolence call. I knew it sounded naïve and crazy, but I hoped to stand outside and overhear them arguing over Mary's fortune, accusing each other of doing her in or talking about who they suspected of killing and threatening her.

I hung a "Closed" sign on my door with a little cardboard clock indicating I'd be back in an hour. I could only hope someone cared and that they'd come back later. I'd dressed the part of the entrepreneur/baker in a navy blue T-shirt I had made with "The Upper Crust—It's All About the Pie" printed in orange letters. Over that I had layered a natural linen blazer paired with khaki capri pants. Casual, as in Crystal Cove Casual, but personal too. I put a warm apple pie with double crust oozing a cinnamon/brown sugar juice into my wicker basket. Nobody doesn't like apple pie, I told myself.

Failing stumbling on a revealing shout-out or conversation, I hoped to be invited in and somehow learn something. Anything. If I was so lucky to hear something incriminatory, I'd discreetly tell the new police chief, as he suggested last night at Heavenly Acres, and generously let him take credit for what I'd done and make the arrest on his own. I didn't want any credit, I just wanted to clear my grandmother's name and see her win the Bridge tournament. Was that too much to ask?

The house was your typical beige stucco Southern California McMansion with a red tile roof surrounded by a rolling lawn and oak trees. There was an iron gate with one of those push-button devices where you have to have a code at the entrance to the driveway, so I parked on the street and walked up the path to the front door, the basket with the pie over my arm, dodging the leaves of a huge ficus plant that almost blocked the entrance. The ocean breeze blew through the leafy trees and the air smelled like old money.

I paused at the massive red door with the brass knocker just in case they were in there bickering over their inheritance or plotting to cut someone out like I'd imagined, but there wasn't a sound. The driveway, however, was lined with expensive cars, including a Lexus, a Mercedes, and another I didn't recognize. I refused to be awed or jealous. Grannie's old Buick wagon suited me fine. It was one of a kind. And I liked living above the shop in the cozy apartment filled with her furniture.

When I rang the doorbell, I was rewarded for my gutsy unplanned arrival when a gorgeous guy not much older than me opened the door. He stood there barefoot, in shorts and a T-shirt. He had a towel over one shoulder and water was dripping from his forehead.

He stared at me for a long moment, then gave me a big smile.

"Hanna? Hanna Denton?"

"Blake? Blake Wilson?" The Blake Wilson who was a high school football star, class president, and general hottie who now looked like a male model? He recognized me, a high school nobody? "What are you doing here?" I asked.

Even after fifteen years I remembered why all the girls were crazy about him. "I could ask you the same thing."

"I came about . . . about Mary Brandt."

"You knew my grandmother?"

"Not really. I came to pay my respects. I was sorry to hear about her . . . passing away."

"You and everybody else. It's been a regular parade. First the police, then the neighbors, now you."

"The police were here?" Sam hadn't mentioned questioning the Brandts, but why would he confide in me?

"Sam Genovese. You remember Sam from high school. What a shock to see him again."

"I know," I said. "Well, all I wanted to do was to pay my respects. I'm so sorry to hear about her … uh … passing away."

His smile faded and he rearranged his movie star good looks to appear appropriately saddened. "Thanks. It's a shock, even though she was old, you don't expect it. Now I feel bad I haven't been to see her in a few years. But I'm in New York, so far away."

"You got here fast." *As if you knew she was going to die* I thought. *As if someone in your family warned you, perhaps even sent you a plane ticket.* But that wasn't fair. All he had to do was get his own plane ticket when he learned his grandmother was dead.

"I left as soon as I heard. My mom was pretty hysterical on the phone, kept talking about losing her mother so suddenly, no time to even say goodbye. And how they were going to sue the retirement home. My dad's yelling in the background. I can't believe they called the police. Police, murder in Crystal Cove?" He shook his head. "Unbelievable."

Startled, I asked, "Sue Heavenly Acres?"

"For you know, negligence. You don't put your grandmother in a retirement home and expect to find her murdered."

I shook my head sympathetically as if I too would sue them if Grannie'd been murdered. After all, they're supposed to be taking care of our treasured antecedents and not let them be murdered on the premises. That wasn't too much to ask. Blake definitely said the M word. I looked over my shoulder, wishing I hadn't come here, wondering how long a condolence visit is supposed to last, and wishing I had a graceful way to ask who they thought had murdered his grandmother.

"Come on in," he said. "I heard you were back in town. That you took over the pie shop."

"That's right." Who did he hear from? Not Sam. But what did Sam hear from Blake, that's what I wanted to know. "I really can't stay. I just wanted to say how sorry I am and drop off a pie." I opened my wicker basket and took out the apple pie. Nothing fancy—just the right touch for an occasion like this, I thought. "And I wonder if you could use some pies for the … after the memorial service?"

"That would be great. The ceremony is at two on Wednesday at the retirement home with a what do you call it, not a party but a wake afterward. There will be a big crowd. Grandmother had so many friends. Although obviously someone had reason not to like her. The whole Heavenly Acres will be there, of course. I heard my mom say grandmother loved pie—in fact, wasn't she eating a piece when …" He broke off, his brow furrowed as if trying to remember the details. Or too overcome with emotion to speak.

I hoped he wouldn't remember the details of his grandmother's demise, but I didn't want to be around if he did since I had such a strong connection with pie and so did my grandmother. I shook his hand and murmured once again something about extending my sympathy to his family.

"I was just going to have a drink," he said. "Join me? Come on out on the deck. We have to get caught up."

Join me? Caught up? It was not as if we were old friends. Picture the high school popularity guy with the girl nobody knew. He must be desperate for company, rattling around in this big house by himself, if he wanted to have a drink with me and get "caught up."

I meant to say thanks but no thanks and explain about how I had a pie shop to maintain, but if Sam thought it was important to contact the Brandts, then I had to too. I set my basket down and found myself following him through the spacious high-ceilinged house toward a large deck with a spectacular view of trees and ocean in the distance. It was a glimpse of the kind of Crystal Cove life on the other side of the mythical tracks I had never experienced, but that he obviously took for granted.

He stopped at a wet bar, filled two glasses with something icy and sparkling, and we walked outside in the brilliant sunshine. He handed me my drink and we stood at the railing of the deck. I stole a glance in his direction. If you had told me fifteen years ago or even fifteen minutes ago I'd be having a drink with Blake Wilson at his family's house, I'd have said you were crazy.

"I always wondered what happened to you," he said.

"Me?" I almost dropped my glass.

"Yeah, you. The girl who worked in the pie shop after school. That was you, wasn't it?"

"Yes, but I don't remember…"

"You don't remember me, but I used to walk by and see you in there, waiting on people." He grinned at me as if we shared a secret of some kind. "You wore an apron over your short shorts and you even looked hot in it."

I felt a hot flush creep up my face. Talk about hot. Blake Wilson had noticed me? I couldn't believe what I was hearing. Blame it on the sun or the gin, but I giggled in spite of myself.

"So did you like it?" he asked.

"Working there? It was okay. It was just something I had to do. But now it's different. It's my shop. I'm in charge. No boss. I like that."

"Sounds good to me. I wish I didn't have a boss. Or sales quotas. Or a huge rent. I envy your life."

"Really?" What a difference it made to talk to someone who didn't suspect you or your grandmother of malfeasance, who though from a privileged background, still envied me my simple life and who thought I had looked hot as an apron-wearing insecure teenager. If only I'd known.

"Do you ever get to New York?" he asked. "I mean for research or to buy supplies or just for fun?"

"Not usually," I said. Make that never.

"I could show you the town," he said. "If you do."

"I'll think about it," I said. Me and Blake Wilson doing the town in New York? How improbable was that? I was feeling dizzy. Maybe it was the frosty drink that may or may not have been laced with gin or maybe it was the unexpected compliments.

"Do you still play football?" I said. "I remember your touchdown against Santa Nella your senior year." Victorious, he was carried off the field by his teammates at the end of the game.

"You do?" He seemed genuinely surprised. "That was a long time ago. No more football for me after I broke a toe kicking a field goal in college. But I'm in a soccer league on Long Island.

Come out for a weekend and you can cheer me on, win one for our team."

I nodded, but the image of me standing on a soccer field in Long Island cheering for our high school hero was like a scene from a movie I was watching from the back row. I set my glass down and said I had to get back to work. Back to reality was more like it.

At the door he gave me my pie basket and took my hand. He held it for a long moment before he laced his fingers with mine and said, "Let's get together again before I leave."

I said okay, but I really didn't think it was going to happen.

"I'll tell my mom you came by," he added. I really wished he wouldn't. "Just send her the bill for the pies. I'm sure she'll be cool with it."

As it turned out, he didn't need to tell her, because I recognized his mother, Linda Wilson, a young-looking blond woman, who pulled up in a sporty Porsche convertible with his father just as I was leaving. She leaned forward and glared at me as if she knew exactly who I was and didn't appreciate my coming to her house, no matter the reason. I waved and sped out of there thinking she hates me. But why? Because she thinks either I or my grandmother killed her mother? Or because she's afraid I'll find out she killed her mother for the inheritance?

How? A large overdose of warfarin or her heart drugs or whatever? For her money, of course. Just as I suspected. I knew nothing about drugs or overdoses, and for all I knew Blake's mother already had more money than anyone in the family—she was driving an expensive car, after all. Maybe his grandmother had nothing and was being supported by her children who preferred she spend her golden years at Heavenly Acres instead of in their guest room. In which case I had nothing to go on. All my theories were out the window. Blake's parents had always hosted the yearly benefit to raise money for the hospital, the school, and the restoration of the old City Hall. If you wanted to raise money for a good cause in this town, you asked the Wilsons for help.

At least I'd come away with an order for the memorial service pies. Even though I hadn't learned much. Had Sam learned any more than I had? I did find out that Blake actually remembered me from the old days. I was too old to get carried away by this jolt of flattery, but I guess I was not as mature as I'd hoped because I was feeling a definite glow all the way home. Chalk it up to a shot of gin and tonic on a sunny deck with a blond quintessential California guy, that's really all it was.

I did find out his family was suing the retirement home and that they were sure Mary had been murdered. I also learned Blake was even better looking than he used to be, he wasn't married if the lack of a ring was any indication, and he seemed like a genuinely nice guy. I'd never really known him in high school and he hadn't known me. But he had noticed me, the lowly freshman who spent Saturdays with her grandmother in the pie shop while other kids hung out at the beach. The town was divided then by the rich kids who lived up in the hills and the rest of us who lived near town on the flats. It probably still was. The haves and the have-nots and never the twain should meet.

I wished I could stay out of the Mary Brandt mess and go back to worrying about which pie to make next. But I had to keep at it. I had to find out who murdered Mary. I couldn't trust Sam to do it. Despite his visit to the Brandt house, he thought he already knew who did it. He'd only invited one person that I knew of to take a polygraph test. Or were there others? I had to find out.

FOUR

AT THE SHOP THE day before the memorial service, Kate and I were busy making pies for the occasion. Kate had left the kids with her mother-in-law so she could help me make a dozen pies, and we'd been at it since dawn. I had no explicit orders as to how many and what kind, so we were winging it with two Deep-dish Caramel Apple Pies with glazed crust, a Bourbon Pecan Pie that smelled sinfully delicious, and we still had another pie in the oven.

"I'm looking up Funeral Pie," Kate said as she leafed through my grandmother's cookbook. "Here it is. Raisins. Vinegar. 'Quick and easy. Made with no seasonal ingredients. Served at Amish funerals.' Ugh. I'm glad we're not Amish."

"If we were, we'd be wearing long hair and long skirts."

"The better to cover our sturdy unshaved Amish legs," she said.

Just as I measured the dry coconut for a creamy coconut custard pie, I remembered Grannie always grated fresh coconut. I hoped no one would notice the difference because I wasn't going to the store at this time, and what were the chances our little grocery would have fresh coconuts on hand? Kate closed the cook-book and asked, "What does Blake look like?"

"He looks like he never left town. He's still tan. His hair is sun-bleached. He wears shorts. But he lives in New York. Maybe he spends his weekends on the beach in the Hamptons with the rich and high and mighty. Oh, wait, he plays soccer on Long Island too. The best part is, he doesn't blame me or Grannie for his grand-mother's death. Or if he does, he was too polite to say so. Unlike some other people do," I muttered. "What a difference in people from our small-town high school," I said. As if she didn't know. As if I'd just realized what everyone else already knew and I was act-ing like I'd stumbled on a great secret.

"I had the biggest crush on Blake a million years ago during football season," Kate confessed. "Didn't you?"

"Not really," I said. It was true. He was so out of my league I didn't bother thinking about him. Until now.

"Did he ask about me by any chance?" Kate asked.

"No, but he's in mourning," I said. "I'm sure he wanted to but probably heard you were married, so ..."

"Dang," she said. "I missed my chance. And now he'll be rich *and* good looking."

I had to agree with the good-looking part. I purposely did not tell her we'd shared a drink and some memories on his deck the other day. It meant nothing, and knowing Kate she'd get all excited and have me married to him before he left town. That's how eager she was to find Mr. Right for me. Besides, I felt guilty about spend-ing all that time with him and not asking more questions about his grandmother. I didn't tell her Sam had been there before me either.

"How do you mean rich and good looking?" I asked Kate.

"I heard today Mary left millions."

"To her grandson?"

"To her family, to the town, to some of her pet charities, and to some other people," she explained.

"Not to my grandmother, I can tell you. No love lost there."

"Are you sure? Wasn't it just because they were playing against each other? I bet they made up after the games. You know how competitive they all are. But it's just a game, after all," Kate said.

"Tell that to the police. Sam made no secret of his suspecting Grannie or me of murder by cranberry pie."

"You're too sensitive, Hanna. You must have misunderstood. Sam's just trying to do his job. Give the guy a chance. We're lucky to have him in town. You know just the other day you complained about the lack of eligible men in town—now there are two, your old pal the new chief and Blake."

"I wasn't complaining, I was just stating a fact. I have no time for men. Besides, Blake will be off as soon as the funeral and memorial service are over and he's collected his millions in inheritance, and I'm guessing the new chief is only here until the department has been shaped up. Physically, I mean. And Sam thinks I'm holding out on him. He wants me to confess that I killed Mary or I know who did."

"That seems unreasonable," she said mildly. Knowing how she hated to criticize Sam, it was quite an admission on her part. "You said he actually ate your pie. Did he look like he liked it?"

"I guess so. Hard to tell. He doesn't show much emotion. He's a different person from the off-the-wall guy we went to high school with. I guess he's been through some stuff while he worked the beat in the city."

"What kind of stuff?" she asked.

I wished I hadn't said that. I was sure Sam wouldn't want his past bandied about. He probably was wishing he hadn't told me either. "Oh you know what police go through. Anyway now he's all law and order."

"What do you expect? He's the Chief of Police, for heaven's sake. Cut him some slack," she said, leafing through the three-by-five recipes in Grannie's tin box. "Oh, here's one for a sugar-free cherry pie. Some of those oldsters at the memorial service may be diabetic. What do you think?"

"Sounds good. If you watch the store I'll head out to the farm stand for some cherries."

"I'll go," she said. "What I was trying to tell you, Hanna, is that *if* you were interested in either guy, which you're obviously not or you'd get the flour out of your hair and wear a frilly little French apron over a short skirt and high heels when you're on duty instead of clogs and that heavy-duty cotton number, you'd have absolutely no competition."

"You mean since every other girl in our age bracket either left town or got married?"

"You came back. You've seen the world but you know the value of small-town life. You're a treasure. You're a link to the past, carrying on the pie tradition. You cook, you bake, you're old fashioned, but you're thoroughly up to date, you're cute, and you're unattached."

"And likely to remain unattached. If only the two men up for consideration one, didn't suspect me of having a hand in murder or, two, live three thousand miles away, I might do something with my hair and consider getting one of those sexy little aprons, but under the circumstances..." I might have told her that Blake invited me to watch him play soccer and do the town in New York, but she would have gone giddy and bought me a plane ticket on the spot.

"You're being ridiculous. No one has accused you of anything except trying to revive the fine art of pie baking. Think about it. An old woman dies during a Bridge game. If this wasn't Crystal Cove, if we didn't have a new chief, if, if, if... This whole thing will blow over in a week, you'll see. Sam will arrest the night watchman or a vagrant passing through town and you'll be off the hook. Everyone will breathe a sigh of relief. Then we'll go back to being the same old quiet, boring town we always were."

"I wish," I said. I could have told her how small the odds were that a stranger had poisoned Mary, but I didn't. I didn't tell her about Grannie being singled out for a polygraph test and told she couldn't leave town either. It was all too awful. When I'd cracked this case, we'd all have a good laugh about it. But not yet.

I opened the oven door to check on my buttermilk custard pie that smelled of just a hint of nutmeg and grated lemon, and a blast of hot air hit me in the face. After I inserted a knife in the pie and decided it needed a few more minutes for the custard to firm up, I closed the door and faced my friend in the very kitchen where Grannie started her business thirty years ago.

"Boring?" I asked when her words sunk in. "Wait a minute. After touting the sunsets, the quiet streets, and the old friends. After I give up my exciting city life to move here, I finally get the truth. It's *boring*! Which is why everyone's so excited about the murder of a prominent citizen and Bridge player. I bet if I confessed right now, I'd get the key to the city and a story in the local gazette for rescuing everyone from tedium as they hauled me away. If you're bored here, what does that mean for my future?"

She didn't answer. There was no answer. My future was up to me. My future started with Mary Brandt's memorial service.

———

The sun had broken through the morning overcast and was shining brilliantly on the crowd that was so big they held the memorial service outside in the Heavenly Acres rose garden, fortunately in full bloom. Sam was in plain clothes, of course. Did he even have a uniform and if so, on what occasions did he wear it? Today he was wearing dark denim designer jeans, a black blazer, shirt and tie. Oh, and sunglasses too.

He might have thought he was blending in with the crowd so he could do some sleuthing, but I and most of the residents probably noticed him right away. He'd stood out from the crowd in high school with his unruly hair and his wild antics and though no longer the wild child he once was, he was still hard to ignore. My heart gave a lurch when I saw him, as if this was still high school and I was a hormone-charged teenager. Only now that I knew more about him I felt a pang of sympathy for what he'd gone through, or I would have if he wasn't after my grandmother. I gave myself a stern warning to focus on the older residents and Mary's family members.

Still stung by Kate's remarks about how I'd let myself go, I was wearing a little black dress I used to wear in the city for weddings, the opera, and even job interviews, but this was the dress's and my first memorial service. With it I wore a pair of strappy black high-heeled sandals. The complete opposite of the usual professional attire I wore while baking. I felt good about myself and my pies and glad to see Grannie was looking smart though a little pale in a black lace dress surrounded by her group of friends, also dressed appropriately in black.

I was relieved there was no body in a casket, even though I knew the reason was the corpse was at the medical examiner's. Even a dead body couldn't put a damper on a beautiful summer day in Crystal Cove. The cool breeze off the ocean rustled the fronds of the palm trees that framed the patio. And the fragrance of dewy hybrid roses filled the air. It made a person glad to be alive. Glad to be back in a small Central California town even though there was a murderer somewhere nearby—perhaps biding his or her time? Plotting the next crime? Scoping out his or her next victim?

Maybe my suspicions were not that unusual. Not at the memorial service of a murder victim. Why else was Sam here if not to look around and see who was acting strange? On the other hand, I felt strangely upbeat. Maybe attending a service made one especially glad to be alive. Surely I wasn't the only one counting my blessings. I was alive and so far I was free to come and go. So far, Sam hadn't told me to stay in town. Although I would have been glad to, since my town was a beautiful, white-washed seaside town. Maybe that's why Grannie was able to bounce back from her polygraph test so fast. I hovered at the edge of the crowd behind a towering Bailey palm tree so I could watch the mourners file by and search their faces for signs of tears of revenge, duty, jealousy... whatever.

"Looks like the whole town is here," I muttered to Kate when she walked in with her husband, Jack, both looking properly serious.

She craned her neck and gave my dress a once-over then favored me with an approving nod. "Probably heard about the pies," she murmured. "Wouldn't want to miss anything."

I didn't want to miss anything either, which is why I was hiding behind my sunglasses, watching everyone who came in. The last people to arrive were the family. Blake was the only one who saw me and gave me a dazzling smile. His white teeth flashed in his handsome suntanned face. The others brushed by me and took their seats in the front row.

The service was brief, no mention of foul play, only glowing memories of Mary's life told by a minister, and nice words from the director of the retirement home about how Mary was such an active member of the community there at Heavenly Acres and how much she'd be missed.

"We will miss her at the Friday night Sing-Alongs, Bible Study, and, of course, the Bridge table," he said. As if he'd ever sat across from her at Bridge. If he had, he'd miss her hand signals and her other cheating ways I'd heard about. I held my breath when he uttered those last words, but the skies didn't fall, the earth didn't shake. I looked around hoping to see someone blanche or gag or give me a sign of their guilt. There were a few red eyes and at least one woman was sobbing. I heard the woman next to me say it was Donna, Mary's Bridge partner and best friend. I must ask her, would she look for a new partner or quit the game completely?

Then it was time for the reception. Chairs were cleared and tables set up. Pie wasn't the only thing on the menu. Her family had ordered the kitchen to prepare small appetizers, and staff members in uniforms were pouring California wines.

I went to the residential kitchen to check on the pie supply. I was happy to see a good selection out on the tables along with a coffee urn. With some kitchen staff women doing the cutting and serving, I almost felt like a guest at my own party.

I came outside again and was just starting to relax and enjoy the sun, the view, and the compliments.

"This is delicious."

"Wonderful pie, did you have the pecan?"

"Try the apple. It's the best."

I was feeling pretty good until I heard someone else say, "But not as good as her grandmother's."

Suddenly a scream split the air. It was Grannie on the other side of the rose bushes. I knew it.

I spun around. I gasped. There on the stone patio lay the same suave gray-haired man I'd seen the other night, the one who appeared to be interested in Grannie. He was flat on his back, a broken pie plate next to him in shards and an unmistakable stain of coconut custard on his cold lips. My grandmother was standing next to him, her hand covering her mouth, her eyes as round as the coffee cup in her trembling hand.

No, it couldn't be. Was this another suspicious death involving one of my pies? It took every ounce of restraint I had to keep from rushing over to wipe the telltale crumbs off the man's mouth and pick up the broken pieces of plate from the tiled deck. I looked across the crowd at Sam, and he met my gaze for only a second and shook his head slightly. Was he sending me a message to "Stay out of this" or was he thinking "There she goes again," or did the warning look on his face have nothing to do with me?

Whatever he thought, it only took seconds for our new Chief of Police to take charge. He motioned Grannie to step back. Then he cordoned off the part of the patio where the man lay and immediately began giving him CPR while the rest of us hovered on the periphery, watching anxiously. If only the victim had not eaten any pie before keeling over. Or if he had, I prayed this was not another murder where my pie was incriminated. In the distance I heard sirens. No doubt the ambulance knew exactly where to come, given the frequency of medical emergencies at Heavenly Acres. And the most recent catastrophe involving Mary Brandt and a piece of my pie.

When the paramedics arrived, they cleared the patio immediately and the mourners scattered, some to the lounge inside, others to the parking lot. I headed for the kitchen, where I had a good view of my pies and of the medics carrying the man out on a stretcher. When the ambulance left, I ventured out again and so did most of the other guests. The atmosphere was definitely subdued. People spoke in hushed tones and looked somber, but then this was a memorial service, after all. A reminder that death was always just around the corner.

When I found Grannie, she was looking even more pale than before and staring off in the direction of the ambulance. I said, "Did you know that man?"

She nodded and she blinked back a tear. "Bob Barnett. One of my good friends." She glanced over her shoulder and lowered her voice. "Actually, we were dating." Her cheeks reddened. "I can't help worrying about him. I should go to the hospital to see if he's okay. Can you give me a ride?"

"Sure. If you can wait while I check on the pie situation."

Dating, she'd said. What did that mean? Sitting together at the Friday night movie? Star-gazing from the rooftop garden? Dancing? Dining? Sex? I didn't really want to hear any details.

"Is it a secret?" I asked. "Your dating, I mean."

"This place is a hotbed of gossip," she said in a semi-whisper. "Don't get me wrong, I love it here, but you can't keep a secret if you tried. Especially after Mary..."

I nodded. "I can imagine."

She pulled me aside. "Bob and Mary were well, you know."

"No, I don't know."

Grannie cupped her hand around her mouth and fixed me with her wide-eyed gaze. "He was seeing her for a while. Before me. Until she drove him crazy. She was very possessive. Like a stalker. So he..."

"Yes?" I leaned in toward her. "What did he do?" *Did he kill her? If he did, you must tell Sam. If only to save your own skin. This is no time to protect a friend.*

"Louise." Grannie's chum Helen came up behind us and put her arm around Grannie. "How are you holding up?"

"Fine. I love a good service, don't you?" Grannie said with forced cheer. "A chance to get dressed up. Speak well of the deceased no matter how you feel. Mix and mingle. You know."

Helen smiled. "It was beautiful. The pies were just fabulous. And the weather. Perfect as usual. Couldn't ask for anything better. Just what I'd want, wouldn't you?" She included me in her gaze as well as their friend Grace who'd joined our group. I assured her it was exactly what I'd want.

"Except for the part where Bob passed out," Grace said. "Anyone hear how he's doing?"

"Hanna's going to take me to the hospital on her way home. It's the only way to get the facts from the horse's mouth, I mean the doctor's. Otherwise you just get the runaround. Especially if you're not family. It's just hearsay."

"How true," Helen said. She tilted her head to give Grannie a sharp look. She knows, I thought. She knows that Grannie is involved with this Bob. Why else would someone go to the hospital to check on someone if they weren't connected in some way or more than just a casual friend? "He should have someone he knows there when he wakes up. Otherwise it can be very disorienting," Helen added.

I liked Helen's optimistic attitude. After all, the last inhabitant of Heavenly Acres who was taken away did not wake up.

I looked around the patio. Helen and Grace both drifted away, after telling Grannie to call them from the hospital with any news. I noticed the chief had disappeared. Gone to the hospital as well? I didn't see any of Mary's family. Gone home? Too sad to hang around?

The Heavenly Acres administration had removed the cordon and the guests who were left were standing around in tight knots. They were drinking coffee, eating pie, and speaking in hushed tones as the afternoon sunlight filtered through the grove of heritage maple trees. Just the kind of occasion a pie-baker longed for. The more people who tasted my pies and associated my shop with a special occasion, be it funeral or wedding or holiday, the better. I confess hearing the compliments about my crust or filling filled me with a rich, creamy satisfying feeling. Kind of like eating a piece of coconut custard pie with a graham cracker crust.

"I'm really concerned about Bob," Grannie said, her good cheer seeming to have evaporated when her friends left. As if she no longer had to pretend or put on a happy face. I was almost glad she had someone else to worry about other than herself.

"Did he have any medical problem that you knew about?" I asked. "Taking any medication? Any dietary restrictions? Am I right in thinking he'd eaten a piece of coconut pie?" I didn't mean to overwhelm her with my rapid-fire questions, but I was a little worried too, for a different reason. All I needed was another pie-related death on these premises. Besides my business taking a hit, I already had one pie-type murder to solve. I didn't need another.

"Probably. He's on a low-fat diet, but he loves to eat. He was taking some pills and he had a weak heart. Otherwise, he's very fit and vigorous."

"Uh oh," I said. I hated to hear that about his diet and his weak heart. I could have made a low-cal pie with gelatin and yogurt, but I hated to go down that road.

"Don't blame yourself," Grannie said, putting one manicured hand on my shoulder. "People have to take responsibility for their own health."

"I know, but still … I'll be ready in a minute. Then I'll take you to the hospital if you still want to go."

She said she did, so I left her sitting on a stone bench looking pensively out at the view of the cove that no longer seemed to sparkle as it did earlier in the day. I went back to the kitchen where two women in black uniforms and white aprons were washing dishes at the huge industrial double stainless sink and dishing some dirt at the same time. When I heard them mention Mary Brandt, I stopped in the doorway and listened shamelessly.

"I gave the bitch back the earrings," the one said. At least I thought that's what she said. Maybe it was *witch* and not *bitch*. With the water running as she rinsed the dishes, I couldn't be sure. "Even though she told me I could keep them. Told me she didn't want them anymore, they reminded her of her dead husband. So I took them and then she tells everyone I stole them. Trying to get me fired. I'm on probation and I'd be out of a job if she was still here, the lying... You know she told me..."

I leaned forward but couldn't hear the rest of the sentence.

The other girl spoke up. "She was out of her mind. Everyone said she deserved to die. You're not the only one."

"Don't tell anyone I said that. Or they'll think..."

At that moment the one woman turned and saw me. She poked her friend, the one who'd given the bitch back her earrings, and they stopped talking.

"Just checking on the pies," I said lightly. "I want to leave the leftovers here and I'll be back later for the pie pans."

"Very good, Ma'am," the friend said like she was a servant out of some British drama. Nothing like being called Ma'am to make you feel old.

I left the extra pie on the counter with the empty pie pans and went back outside. I beckoned to Grannie on the patio and we walked out to the parking lot without speaking. I had a million questions for her, but she looked as if she'd been through the wringer, her forehead as wrinkled as her dress, so I didn't say anything during the twenty-minute ride to the Our Lady of Angels Hospital.

I parked in the emergency lot and we went in and asked at the Admissions Desk about Bob Barnett.

"Are you his wife?" the clerk said.

I poked Grannie in the ribs and said, "She's his sister."

"I'll tell the doctor. He'll want to have a word with you."

Grannie thanked her and we sat down in the waiting room.

"His sister?" Grannie asked me with a puzzled frown.

"You can't say you're just a friend, or they won't let you see him or tell you anything. You want to find out something, don't you?"

She nodded. "Sometimes you amaze me. You've got, what do they call it, street smarts."

"Thank you. That's a nice way of putting it."

Soon a doctor who was wearing a crisp white jacket and short gray hair like he was in a TV ad for a weight-loss program came out to the lobby. He explained to Bob's "sister" that Bob was resting comfortably.

"Then he wasn't poisoned?" she asked anxiously.

"Poisoned?" He took a step backward, shook his head and finally gave Grannie a reassuring smile. If he was surprised by her question, he recovered well. He acted like maybe everyone whose brother passed out might ask about the possibility of poison. "I didn't check for poison. Your brother suffered a mild heart attack from an overdose of his ED medication. It happens. He'll be fine."

I gave an inward sigh of relief. My pie had nothing to do with Bob's collapse. I shot a quizzical glance at Grannie because I wondered. Did she know ED stood for erectile dysfunction, or was she playing it cooler than I gave her credit for?

"Can I see him?" she asked.

"Just for a few minutes. He shouldn't be overly stimulated. The nurse is with him now taking his vital signs. We'll let you know when you can go in. Room thirty-six A."

"Thank you."

When the doctor left, Grannie turned to me and spoke softly. "I told you before. Between you and me, I'm glad Mary's dead."

"You said 'between you and me—' does that mean you didn't tell Sam how you felt about Mary? That morning in the station?"

"I think he knew."

"I hope he also knows you're not the only one who's glad Mary's dead."

"Bob for sure."

"How come?"

"She had her claws into him. He told me he was terrified of her. He'd do anything to get away from her clutches."

"Anything?" I asked, startled. Would he tamper with her medicine? Would he kill her?

"No, not anything. He didn't kill her, if that's what you're thinking."

"Well, who did?"

"I don't know, but I'm going to find out," she said.

I shouldn't have been surprised at her determination. That's the way she was. But I hoped she wouldn't put herself in danger trying to find out.

"I wouldn't blame Bob if he did. But I know he didn't. Do you know what the ratio of women to men is at Heavenly? Ten to one. Mary wanted a man. She went after Bob. She was ruthless."

"But he wanted you."

"Well …" She gave a modest little shrug.

Just then a nurse came and motioned for Grannie to follow her. She didn't jump up and run down the hall. Instead she seemed a little hesitant. Was she afraid just her presence would excite her boyfriend and cause a relapse? Or was she afraid she'd lost the power to excite him and didn't want to test it? Or was she going to ask him if this meant he had to give up his ED medication? And if so...

I balled my hands into fists as I tried to stop my runaway imagination from going berserk. It was none of my business what my grandmother did behind closed doors, as long as she wasn't plotting to get rid of a Bridge or romantic rival.

"You go ahead," I said to Grannie. "I'll wait here."

She nodded and finally walked away down the hall.

I picked up an old issue of *Sunset* magazine and perused the recipes. Grasshopper Pie. Now that was a blast from the past. Two kinds of liqueur and a cookie crumb crust. I could do that. Maybe have a nostalgic appeal to the older crowd that seemed to be my crowd these days.

I was stealthily and carefully ripping the recipe out of the magazine with one eye on the nurse behind the desk when I saw Sam come walking down the hall, this time with a leather jacket over his shirt and tie instead of his blazer. I wondered if he'd ever worn a uniform, but I was glad he didn't. Anyway, he looked better each time I saw him—even better than he did fifteen years ago, which isn't true of all of us, unfortunately. I just wondered, how did a policeman, even the Chief of Police on duty in a small town where nothing ever happens, afford to dress like he'd stepped right out of *GQ*? What had he been doing since high school besides the police academy?

He stopped at the desk and I overheard him asking about Bob Barnett. The clerk said something and nodded at me. Sam glanced over and showed no surprise to find me there. Did he ever show anything?

He walked over and sat down next to me on a small padded couch. He was so close the tangy scent of his leather jacket and a hint of aftershave hit me like one of those rogue waves the surfers in Crystal Cove have to deal with. While I took a deep breath and tried to think of something innocuous to say besides "Hi," he glanced at the ripped page in my hand. I smoothed it out and looked him in the eye with as much confidence as I could. "It's a pie recipe," I said.

"So that's how you do it."

"By stealing recipes, yes. I confess. But I prefer to call it research."

Would he arrest me on the spot for defacing a magazine? Or would he let me off with a warning? Maybe I could think up a good excuse. Then I decided cutting up an old magazine was not worth apologizing for, not when the Chief of Police was looking for a murderer.

"I hear Mr. Barnett's sister is visiting the patient," he said. "Is that true?"

"Not exactly."

"Then what are you doing here?" he asked. His gaze traveled over my black dress and my shoes. I was glad I'd painted my toenails. But I was sorry to see him. As much as I needed a man in my life, I didn't need the long arm of the law hanging around my grannie suspecting her of wrongdoing. I wished I could go home and get into a pair of jeans and start mixing, whipping, and baking and forgetting about old people being carted off to the local hospital after eating a piece of pie.

Nothing like work to offset the tension of a memorial service and the collapse of one of the mourners. I looked at my watch, then I looked down the hall. My shop was closed. Not that anyone noticed. Anyone who was anyone was at the service today, mourning the dead and eating my pie. Where was Grannie? I was stuck waiting for her. And I was nervous sitting next to Sam, wondering what he was thinking about me or my grandmother.

"I could ask you the same thing," I said. "What are you doing here? You don't think Bob had anything to do with Mary's death, do you?"

"I'm here to check up on him. I need to keep in touch with all the residents of Heavenly Acres, especially those who passed out at the memorial service. And those who were involved with Mary. It seems Bob fits into both categories."

"So you heard about Mary and Bob," I said. "They were an item at one time." If I had to, I would throw Bob to the wolves or on the lap of the law if it meant diverting suspicion away from Grannie. If Bob was desperate to disentangle himself from the tenacious Mary, it wasn't inconceivable that he'd done her in no matter what Grannie said.

"I have another confession," I said. "I lied to the nurse. Grannie wanted to check up on her friend Bob Barnett. I told the nurse she was a relative just in case his visitors were restricted. Go ahead, arrest me or sue me. It was my idea, not hers. She never lies." I threw that in at the end. He probably saw right through me, but who cared? She'd be here any minute and anyone could tell him who'd she'd been visiting.

82

"As one of the few single men at the retirement community, I imagine Mr. Barnett has many women friends who might want to visit him."

"I imagine he does," I said lightly. "So that's why you're here? Checking up to see who visits Bob?"

"Among other things."

"Are you sure you're not here to trap some helpless old woman into confessing she'd tried to murder him in a jealous rage? Wait a minute, if they're all after him, why try to kill him?"

"Come on, Hanna. It's jealousy. Do you know how common it is as a motive?"

"No, I don't. I didn't go to the Police Academy, you did."

"It doesn't mean I know everything. If I did I wouldn't be here. But I am here and so are you. Tell me your ideas. I know you have them," he said.

"As a matter of fact I do. I overheard something interesting this afternoon. It has nothing to do with my grandmother, but it does have something to do with a motive for murder."

"Really," Sam said. "I'm not surprised you're one step ahead of the law."

"You don't mind?"

"Not at all. As long as you share your findings with me," he said. "You always did have a good mind and an active imagination." One corner of his mouth twitched but no smile. I don't think he ever smiled in high school either, so why should I be surprised? This was one guy who'd changed a lot, but no one would say he'd mellowed.

"I guess you heard Bob is going to be okay," I said. "He wasn't murdered. Nobody even tried to murder him. As you know he had a mild heart attack. So I could ask you, what are you really doing here at the hospital? Did you think you had a serial killer on your hands? First Mary Brandt then poor Bob Barnett."

"Is that what you thought?"

"Is that what they taught you at the Police Academy? To answer a questions with a question? Anyway, I think I know the answer to my question. You're here in Crystal Cove and at the hospital so you can catch this killer before he kills again."

"So you assume it's a man."

"I should have said he or she."

"Catching killers is only one of my jobs. The other is to protect the populace from all kinds of crime. Not just homicides, which are rare around here. If I wanted to specialize in homicides, I would have stayed in San Francisco." He looked grim, and he must have remembered that I knew exactly why he hadn't stayed in the city after his partner was killed.

"I thought you might be glad to show the town how you go about finding a murderer. But what do I know? I'm just a simple pie baker, but people sometimes say things to me or around me when they don't know I'm listening."

"You may be a pie baker, but you've never been simple, Hanna," he said dryly with his sideways look of slight amusement. He stretched his long legs out in front of him and crossed them at the ankles. "You have a duty as a citizen to report any suspicious or illegal activity, you know. So spit it out," he said with an air of studied casual unconcern that didn't fool me for a minute. He was dying to know what I knew. Or was he pretending not to care so I wouldn't know he really did care?

"What I heard today was very interesting…"

At that moment Grannie came walking down the hall, her eyes popping at the sight of me with Sam. I saw her smooth her hair with one hand and adjust the neckline of her lace dress with the other.

"Why, Officer Genovese," she said. "Nice to see you again. What are you doing here?"

"Just checking up on Mr. Barnett," he said, standing up to tower over Grannie. "Can't afford to lose any more Crystal Cove citizens."

"You'll be glad to know he's on the mend. He told me just now he's anxious to leave and get back to Heavenly Acres. That's the way we all feel," she added. "We love it there."

"Heaven on earth," I murmured. I don't think either of them heard me.

"I won't keep you then," Sam said to Grannie. "But I am wondering if I could invite you two ladies to dinner tonight. I understand the old Seaside Grill has a nightly buffet."

I jumped to my feet and blinked rapidly. My mind was racing about sixty miles an hour, about ten miles faster than the speed limit on the winding coast highway. What was going on here? Was he going to ply us with cocktails and pump us for information, thinking we'd confess to Mary's murder since he had no luck last Saturday with his lie detector? Or maybe he'd get us to finger each other for the crime. Well, I wasn't going to play his game and neither was Grannie.

"You don't have to do that," I said. "We are more than happy to cooperate with your investigation without your bribing us."

Grannie shot me a warning look. "But we'd love to have dinner with you, wouldn't we, Hanna?" she said.

"Of course," I said. But I was thinking *of course not.* Whatever his motive for this bizarre invitation, I could not get involved with this guy in any way again. It would be the height of stupidity. I needed to concentrate on my new career. Inviting both of us might be just what it seemed, a chance to pump us for information and no reason to worry about Sam's hitting on me. Then why dinner? Why me? I didn't need to be pumped. I'd be happy to give him my theories if only he'd take me seriously.

"Aren't you afraid someone will see you having dinner with a suspect or a witness or an informant or all three rolled into one ... or two?" Grannie asked with a twinkle in her eye. She was amazing. Instead of withdrawing or turning a cold shoulder, which a normal person would do when confronted by the police, she was being her regular charming self. That should be enough to send Sam back to the drawing board.

I could have told her the Sam I knew wasn't afraid of anything. Not the school principal, not his father who was an abusive drunk, or ... or ...

"You do have a reputation to uphold," I suggested.

"I don't think it will be compromised by dinner with a senior citizen and a local businesswoman. Especially when they're the most attractive women in town. And the purpose is to talk business."

"In that case we'd be delighted," Grannie said, who obviously loved the part about the most attractive women in town. I opened my mouth to decline, but then I closed it. There was no chance there would be anything personal about this dinner with Grannie on hand.

But when she mysteriously came down with a bad headache that evening, I felt my own headache coming on.

FIVE

Look," I said when Sam came to the door of the bakery that night wearing dark pants and a white shirt that made him look like he'd never left town at all. For a moment I was swept back in time, fifteen years ago. He'd come to pick me up for a school picnic on the beach. That was weeks before the incident at the prom. Sounds harmless, doesn't it? But nothing with Sam ever was. Not then, and not now. He never looked that good then, or did he? Or was I so desperate to connect the dots I couldn't remember? I wiped my hands on my apron. I was deliberately wearing ripped jeans stained with peach juice and Nike running shoes to indicate I wasn't going anywhere. Not with him. Not without Grannie. "What is this about? Really."

"It's about my solving a murder," he said, walking right past me into my shop though I really hadn't invited him. The store was warm and the fragrance of baking pies hung in the air. The contrast with the atmosphere and his stark words was startling. I wasn't sure he even noticed. I had several excuses for not going out with Sam on tap besides the one about the headache, but first I needed to have a talk with him.

"That's what I thought you'd say. I know you're looking for a murderer. I know you gave Grannie a polygraph test, which I assume has convinced you she is not your murderer. Tell me you've taken her off your list of suspects."

"How can I? First, her test was inconclusive. Second, she told me in no uncertain terms she wanted Mary out of her way. She had the motive, the means, and the opportunity. That doesn't mean I don't find her charming. In fact, that's a characteristic of many famous criminal minds."

"Oh please. You're saying my grandmother is like Jeffrey Dahmer, Ted Bundy, and the Sundance Kid?" I asked incredulously. "I'm surprised you'd trust her across the dinner table. She might slip you a mickey."

"I'm not arresting her. Not yet. I'm taking both of you out to dinner. All I want to do is for the two of you to relax, let down your hair, and talk to me. Tell me about the people in town. You both know the people here better than I do. That's all."

Oh, sure that was all. If I believed that, he'd be the first to sell me the Golden Gate Bridge. "So you were planning to take us to dinner, ply us with wine and good food, and pick our brains and try to get my grandmother to incriminate herself. Is that right?"

"It beats bringing you into the station with her and sitting both of you down across a table in an examination room. Doesn't it?"

"Like you already did once with Grannie. How could you?" I demanded.

"I had to."

He stood in the semi-darkness of my shop, gripping the back of the chair at my new table. In the light from the overhead fixture he seemed to fill the small shop, towering over my new furniture and making it look like it belonged in a dollhouse. "Hanna, a woman died. Maybe nobody liked her. Maybe many people wanted her dead. It doesn't matter. What matters is that one person killed her. A person who had access to her medications. A person who fed her a cranberry pie."

"It wasn't Grannie," I said, crossing my arms across my apron and leaning against the wall. "I know it wasn't. I don't care what she said during the lie detector test. It's a well-known fact they're not that accurate. I don't know who killed Mary, but I do know it could have been anybody."

"No, it couldn't." He straightened. "Get dressed. We're going to dinner. We'll talk later."

"What about? I'm not going to spend the evening defending my grandmother."

"Fine, we'll talk about something else."

"Let's talk about some*one* else. Grannie isn't coming with us. She has a headache."

"I'm sorry to hear it," he said.

I turned and walked to the kitchen, knowing he probably thought she couldn't take being interrogated by him over dinner. Maybe I couldn't either. "We could talk now," I offered. If it would save Grannie, I would sing like the proverbial canary and tell him about Bob and his possible motive for getting rid of Mary.

"Later."

"This is blackmail," I called over my shoulder as I walked up the stairs to my tiny apartment. The sexiest man in town was buying me dinner and giving me a chance to clear my grandmother if I said the right things. Why should I object to an opportunity to exonerate my grandmother while eating an expensive dinner? A win-win deal, I told myself. Then why was I dawdling, trying on a long skirt, taking it off, then putting on a pair of skinny jeans with a tunic top that skimmed my knees, blowing my hair dry and slipping into a pair of Steve Madden flats? Maybe I was afraid of telling too much. Afraid Sam would pry into my past the way I'd done with his. Afraid he'd force me to come clean. Afraid of sounding defensive. Of being laughed at or even worse, afraid of being taken seriously and fingering the wrong person. Or giving too much away.

Most of all, I was afraid of letting down my guard and falling for Sam again. Falling for the man who was no longer a bad boy, but just as dangerous for me. It was bad enough to get mixed up with the town bad boy some fifteen years ago, worse to get mixed up now with a law man who had something to prove. Which he did. He had to prove to the town he was up to the job of protecting and serving. Why else was he back in Crystal Cove? Though you could ask me the same thing. In fact, he did ask me the same thing. I had terrible taste in men. That was obvious. But I would prefer to keep my problems to myself.

I told myself I was being ridiculous. It was only dinner. I hadn't had a date in months, and no serious boyfriend in years. Just a botched relationship that never should have happened. An attractive man asks me to dinner. Sure, he's only doing it to find out what I know so he can solve a murder, even if he suspects my own grandmother. I'd be crazy not to go. So I was going.

I wouldn't have hesitated so much if I'd known Sam had a Mazda Miata convertible. I've always had a weakness for cool cars, which is why I was happy to get Grannie's old Buick. Not everyone's idea of cool, but I liked it. We drove out of town along the coast highway with the wind in my hair and the setting sun slanting rays of golden light on the winding road with the sea on one side and the sheer cliffs on the other. I let my mind drift, trying to forget this was a business dinner and that I had my work cut out defending my grandmother and her friends from being charged with murder.

"Wait, this isn't the way to the Grill," I said, thinking of the noisy, crowded family restaurant I remembered from the old days.

"Too noisy and crowded," he said.

"Too noisy and crowded for you to get me to spill everything I know, is that what you mean?"

He slid a glance in my direction. "Something like that. Have you been to the Bohemian Beach Distillery?"

"I haven't been anywhere. I've been working round the clock, trying to get my business going. But I remember hearing about it. Hasn't it been around since Prohibition?"

"That's the one."

"I thought it was a tourist trap. They even claim a blue ghost who comes around for atmosphere."

"I haven't seen the ghost but the food is good and the view is worth the drive." What he meant was it was worth a drive to escape prying eyes and nosy neighbors. If it was a tourist trap, all the better for us to have a private conversation where no locals would hear us.

"So you've been there."

"A few times. It's quiet. We can talk there."

Of course, we could have talked quietly at the police station or at the pie shop, but I was here and we were on our way. Who else had he brought out here so they could talk quietly? Other suspects? I wouldn't put it past him. He'd been to Mary's family's house. And God knew where else. He wasn't sitting around the station waiting for someone to turn himself or herself in, that's for sure.

Maybe he'd been here with other women. Why hadn't Kate told me if she'd heard he was dating anyone in town? Wait, I thought I was the only single, eligible woman around. It didn't matter. This was not really a date. In fact, I should offer to pay for my dinner even though it was no doubt expensive. If I could persuade him of my grandmother's innocence, it was worth it.

We pulled into the driveway just as the sun was setting and filling the sky with streaks of violet and scarlet. Sam told the hostess we wanted to have drinks on the patio probably because it was deserted and the cool night air off the ocean was refreshing. The waiter brought glasses of Chardonnay and bowls of olives and cashews.

Instead of interrogating me, Sam asked if I knew the place had been a speakeasy. When I said no, he told me the story.

"During the twenties, the Canadian rum-runners landed on the beach below with illegal whiskey. Under cover of fog, the locals dragged it up the cliff here, and loaded it into cars for San Francisco."

"Is this all on their website?"

"Probably," he said. "It makes a good story. But I heard it from my grandfather, who was one of the guys who hauled the booze.

Of course, a few bottles always found their way to his basement. Unlike a lot of the other speakeasies along the coast, this place never got busted."

I leaned back in the padded chair facing the fading sunset. "How does he feel knowing you're on the other side of the law now?"

"He died a few years ago. It was actually his idea," he said. "He steered me toward law enforcement. He wanted me to have a better life than he did."

"Are you? Having a better life, I mean?"

He picked up his glass and studied it as if it held a clue to his life or the murder of Mary Brandt. I sensed a change in the atmosphere. The wind had shifted. It happens along this coast. Especially when you're dealing with an old boyfriend who is now a cop. Especially when the appearance of a blue ghost may be imminent. "We're here to talk about you," he said. "And what you know." I wondered if he was sorry he'd spilled his guts the other day about his past. Because he'd sure clammed up now. He looked around. There was no other customer in sight who'd braved the cold night air. Even the waiters had left us alone on the deck.

"I probably don't know anything that you don't know," I said to start the conversation he was interested in. "But if you're looking for murder suspects, I have to tell you there's a woman who works at the retirement home. She supposedly stole a pair of Mary's earrings, only she claims Mary gave them to her then changed her mind and got the poor woman put on probation. She was not happy, I can tell you."

"You say poor woman. But aren't you suggesting she killed Mary?"

"I don't know. You must know that many people thought she deserved to die. I know, you're not allowed to off someone just because they deserve it, so spare me any lectures. You're the cop. I'm just a concerned citizen. I'm telling you what I heard. If you don't like that theory, what about Mary's family? Anyone with a ton of money, especially if they're tightfisted, is prime material to be bumped off by a greedy family member who stands to inherit, which is why you dropped in on her grandson Blake, isn't it? Did you learn anything?"

He ignored my question. I guess you can do that if you're a cop. "How do you know Mary had a ton of money and that she was tightfisted?" he asked.

"Isn't it obvious, the part about the money, I mean? You saw her house. The one she lived in before she moved to Heavenly Acres, which you know is very expensive."

That's when the hostess came out to tell us our table was ready.

She showed us to a round table in the middle of the room but Sam asked for a booth in the corner. She smiled, no doubt thinking romantic get-together. Let them think what they wanted. I slid into my seat and was grateful for the candlelight and for the large elaborate menu to hide behind. When I looked up, Sam was staring at me. Waiting for me to incriminate myself or my grandmother? I'd starve to death first.

I looked around at the glowing fireplace and the old pine wide-planked floors, picturing rowdy customers waiting for the boats loaded with illegal whiskey to pull in so they could haul it up and quench their thirst.

"I can't decide if this feels like a twenties-style roadhouse or a French country inn," I said.

"Glad you like it," he said.

"Do you come here often?"

"Only when I have a debt to pay."

"You owe me?"

"For the pie."

"You paid me."

"Then we're even."

The waiter appeared, and since Sam was paying and there were no prices listed next to anything, I ordered the salad with bay shrimp, hearts of palm, and asparagus and a filet of sole Florentine.

Sam said he'd have the same. The waiter complimented our choice of entrees, then he refilled our wine glasses.

"I went back to Heavenly Acres this afternoon," Sam said, looking at me over his wine glass.

"Did you?" I said, uncomfortable with that probing gaze. "What did you find?" I carefully buttered a slice of warm homemade bread.

"Things have calmed down. Those people seemed to have resumed their normal lives."

"You shouldn't be surprised. They're a hardy bunch and they're not unaccustomed to someone 'Knockin' on Heaven's Door' at their age."

He smiled briefly at the mention of the Bob Dylan song, then got back to business. "I found this on the bulletin board," he said. He reached into his pocket for a sheet of paper and held it up. "It's a schedule for the Bridge tournament."

I squinted but I couldn't make out the names in the candlelight. "Old? New? Including Mary or not?"

"Someone has crossed Mary off the list," he said. "There's a blank space. Any idea who will fill in for her?"

"As Donna's partner? Oh, I see. Whoever it is may have bumped off Mary to get her spot. That sounds reasonable." I'd jump at anything that let Grannie off the hook.

"When I was up there, I talked with some of the help in the kitchen. One of the maids brought me a jewelry box she found in your grandmother's waste basket. She was going to ask Louise about it, but when she knocked on her door a few days ago she overheard your grandmother talking to someone. Something on the order of 'If you don't quit cheating, you're out of the tournament. You'll never play Bridge here again.' Know who she was talking to?"

"I can guess. I've heard that Mary cheated at Bridge. I'm sure you've heard the same thing in your interviews. Did you ask her while she was under oath?" I was still furious he'd given Grannie a polygraph test and no one else.

"Not yet."

"Not yet?" My face flamed with anger and indignation.

"I'm not sure they're that helpful. As you mentioned, they're not always accurate."

"Then why bother? No, don't tell me. It's your job."

He ignored my sarcastic tone and continued as if I hadn't spoken.

"What we do know from the autopsy report is that Mary died from an overdose of warfarin, which combined with a large dose of cranberries was enough to poison her."

"A large dose of cranberries? How many pieces of pie did she eat?" He didn't answer. Maybe he didn't know. Maybe I should be the one doing the asking of this kind of question. "You know, anybody could have changed her anti-clot medicine for something stronger. Her daughter, her son …"

"If it's her family members who killed her, then why are they so eager for this investigation?" he asked. "Why not just let her rest in peace and collect their inheritance?"

"She's got a big family. If I were investigating this crime …"

"You're not," he said curtly.

"I know, but if I were, I'd find out who had the most to gain from Mary's death."

"You can't deny your grandmother had a whole lot to gain by removing her main challenge. Or do you deny Bridge is an important part of her life?" He held up the printout of the playoff schedule. Without Mary and her partner Donna, Grannie and her partner had a clear shot at the title.

"Of course not." I realized Grannie had probably told him in all innocence how much Bridge meant to her. How important it was to collect points so she could move ahead. I sure wished she hadn't.

"Who else wanted her out of the way so badly?"

"Besides the maid and her family?" I asked. "I refuse to discount Mary's family. If I were her granddaughter and I needed money for something like a new kidney or something and she wouldn't give it to me, maybe I'd be tempted to kill her myself. And then I'd demand an investigation to send the long arm of the law in the wrong direction. Maybe there is no fortune. Or maybe she left it to someone else. And that person killed her because they couldn't wait for her to die. Let's face it, we all know she wasn't a lovable person."

"Is that what Blake told you?"

"No, he didn't. He didn't have to. You interviewed him. And you were at the memorial service. Was anyone crying, her daughter, her grandchildren, anyone except for poor Donna?"

"Hanna, if we arrested everyone who wasn't crying at Mary's service..."

"I'm just saying..."

"I know what you're saying."

I took a deep breath. I was getting desperate. "I didn't want to tell you this, but you ought to check out Bob Barnett."

"The guy in the hospital."

"Yes, he was terrified of Mary. She had her claws into him."

"I checked him out at the hospital," he said.

"And..."

"He's clean. He couldn't have done it."

I clamped my mouth shut to keep from protesting. If I had to bet, I'd put Bob on the top of my list. What did Sam know that I didn't?

Sam shook his head. "You'll do anything to point the finger somewhere besides at your grandmother, won't you?"

"Wouldn't you if it was your grandmother?"

He didn't answer. For all I knew he had no grandmother, just his grandfather. Fortunately the waiter brought our plates to the table and Sam let it drop.

"This looks amazing," I said, glad to change the subject. Glad I could appreciate a beautiful plate of sole poached in Chardonnay with shallots, lemon, and butter on a bed of spinach, even though I'd just fingered a poor guy who was simply in the wrong place at the wrong time. I was proud of myself for digging in with gusto knowing what I'd just done. In order to save my grandmother, I was willing to point the finger at anyone and everyone else.

After a few minutes, Sam was back on task. No way was I supposed to think this was a social occasion. He'd made that perfectly clear from the start. That's what I understood. A business dinner, that's all. I might as well have a sign hanging around my neck. "Will blab for food."

"I understand Mary's partner Donna is looking for a new partner," Sam said.

"Hope she finds someone good enough," I said. "Those girls are serious players. Donna is just as competitive as any one of them. Grannie always tried to teach me to play, but I'm hopeless. They play to win. Nothing wrong with that."

"I understand Donna had been grumbling about Mary Brandt, her poor sportsmanship and her foggy memory."

"I'm telling you that's what everyone says. Are you saying she could have poisoned Mary?"

"Maybe. The place is crawling with suspects."

"Maybe I can help you narrow it down."

"Go ahead. Although don't you think you're a little too close to the situation?"

"Are you saying I'm biased?" I tried to act affronted, but I'm not sure it came off that way.

"That's exactly what I'm saying."

"All I can say is if complaining about Mary is a crime, then you've got your work cut out for you."

"It's when complaining leads to murder. And yes, I know how much work I have."

"Look, Sam," I said, resting my elbows on the table after the waiter had cleared the plates. "I understand you need to solve this crime, and I need for you to solve it so I can get back to baking and not sleuthing, so let me help you. As you know, I'd especially like to help you clear my grandmother. I understand I know nothing about crimes or criminals, but I plan to keep my ears open. As a private citizen, of course. I hope you won't mind."

"I do mind. In fact I have to tell you in the strongest terms to keep out of this. I appreciate what you've told me tonight. And anytime you have something to say that's relevant, fine. Give me a call. But that's it. Everything is under control. We will find the murderer."

"By 'we' I assume you are not including me."

"That's right."

I took a deep breath. "I actually don't have much time to do any detecting, so don't worry. I have a business to run. Such as it is." No sense pretending customers were knocking down the door or standing in line to buy my pies. He knew they weren't.

"Good luck with that."

I assumed he was sincere, but it was hard to tell by the tone of his voice.

I thanked him for the dinner and we drove back to Crystal Cove. I wondered if he thought it was worthwhile, spending his money, or was it the city's money used on me to grill me then convince me to butt out of his investigation? Was there a certain allowance to bribe or pay off citizens for turning in their relatives and friends? If that's what he was after, this dinner must have been a bust.

He walked me up to the pie shop and braced one arm against the door, effectively trapping me between him and my shop.

"So what do you think?" he asked.

"About what? Your methods of investigation? Your return to the city you always wanted to escape from? Your car? Your job? Your past? Your future. Your..."

He put his hand over my mouth then. God knows what would have happened if he hadn't. Since my tongue was loosened by two glasses of wine and some rich delicious food, I could have gone on and on. His warm palm against my lips caused me to have a strange reaction. I laughed. Not hah hah, just a little chortle I couldn't contain or explain.

He took his hand away. "I meant what do you think about Crystal Cove?" he asked. "Are you glad you came back?"

"I'm very glad, and I'll be even gladder when you find out who the murderer is."

"You didn't tell me why you came back," he said.

"Neither did you," I reminded him.

He waited a long moment, then he said, "Good night, Hanna." That's one good thing about Sam—he knows when to quit.

I stood there shivering in the cool night air and watching him sprint out to his car and swing his long legs into the driver's seat without opening the door; then the engine roared and he was gone.

SIX

"I CALLED YOU LAST night," Kate said when she stopped in for coffee and a slice of warm pecan pie the next afternoon. Actually she didn't stop in for something to eat, or so she said. How could she know I was in a lazy Southern mood that called out for peekawn pie? Since she's my official taster, I persuaded her to try a slice.

She came by just to say hello, she said as I poured her a cup of coffee. Though she muttered something about watching her calories, I brought out the pie and scooped a dollop of whipped cream on top of a generous wedge. It's my feeling that the richness of the molasses, brown sugar, and eggs in the pie cries out to be offset with cool cream.

"I can't resist, you know I can't," she said with a little moan.

"Don't even try," I said and sat down across from her at Grannie's small wrought-iron table. "What's up?"

"I came to dish some dirt about the memorial service," she said.

"Lovely ceremony," I said.

"Until Bob Barnett passed out."

"Gave us all a scare, didn't it? Especially Grannie. But he's going to be fine."

She set her coffee cup down. "So it's true? They're an item?"

"She likes him. But I hear he plays the field. With the numbers in his favor, I guess he'd be crazy not to."

"You mean all those rich, attractive women at Heavenly Acres and so few men. If I were him, I'd definitely go with your grandmother. She's new, she's young at heart, and she's got a lot of money."

"You think he's after her for her money?" Did I have to worry about my grandmother being a target for money-hungry predators?

"No, of course not. She's lovely and she's a lot of fun."

"I'll tell her you said that."

"So what's the deal with Bob? Don't tell me the pie had anything to do with him passing out?"

"No, thank God. That's all I need is another suspicious pie incident." I wondered if I would be in order if I said anything about the real cause of his attack. I supposed it would violate patient/ doctor confidentiality, so I didn't. "I hear he's recuperating nicely. Should be out of the hospital soon, I imagine."

"Is that where you were last night when I called, visiting Bob at the hospital?"

"No."

She waited, fork in the air, for my explanation as to why I didn't answer the phone when she called.

"Up at Heavenly Acres with your grandmother?"

I sighed. What was the point of continuing this guessing game? Why pretend I had something to hide? "I went out to dinner with Sam to the Distillery on the Coast Highway."

"I knew it was just a matter of time before you two got back together," she said with a smug smile.

"We are not back together. We couldn't get *back* together because we never were together in the first place. Not for long."

"Okay, okay. Forget I said that. You went on a date with Sam. End of story."

"It wasn't a date," I said. "It was business. I took the opportunity to tell him I only knew two things about Mary's murder. It wasn't me and it wasn't Grannie."

Reassured, she said, "And the rest of the evening you talked about . . ." She raised her eyebrows and speared a piece of pie.

"Old times. New times. You know."

"How do you feel about Sam now?"

"He's changed."

"Obviously, or he wouldn't be Chief of Police. You've changed too. Has he noticed?"

"He didn't say."

She gave an exasperated sigh. "What *did* he say?"

"Besides telling me not to spy for him or play detective? Not much."

She raised her eyebrows. "What did you say?"

"I didn't have a choice. I agreed to butt out of police business."

She coughed. She didn't believe me, I could tell. "Just like that?"

"I had to."

"Come on."

"I had to *agree*. I don't have to actually do it as long as Sam doesn't know about it. He can't honestly expect me to sit on the sidelines while my grandmother is suspected of murder and questioned like a common criminal."

I thought she was going to choke on a pecan. "He really does suspect your grandmother … No way! He couldn't possibly."

"He does. He says she had the motive, the means, and the opportunity. Face it, Grannie threatened Mary, she hated Mary, and she's glad she's dead. Do you know Sam called her in and gave her a polygraph test?"

"Did she pass?"

"Inconclusive. But that doesn't mean she's off the hook as far as he's concerned. It doesn't look good. Otherwise, why wouldn't he take her off his list of prime suspects like he did Bob Barnett? In fact, I don't know if he has a list, even though I could give him one."

"But Sam won't let you, is that right?"

"Technically no, but I figure what he doesn't know won't hurt him. I'm going to make my list and I'm going to seek out everyone on it and make them talk. They might be more willing to talk to a simple baker than a cop. What have I got to lose?"

"Sam's good opinion of you?"

"Hah. Compared to clearing Grannie's name? That's a no-brainer."

"But what happens when you show him your list of suspects and tell him who's on top of the list?"

"Since I don't have a list, it seems premature. Besides, he won't take me seriously unless I've got an air-tight confession. He'll just brush me off like a pesky gnat. And I mean something in writing or … something."

"Wow, you don't mess around," Kate said.

"He's a cop. I understand where he's coming from. He can't let amateurs solve his crimes or he'd be out of a job. In every mystery I've ever read, the detective warns the amateur sleuth to get lost. To leave the mystery solving to him, the big macho hero. So I get it. But I can't go along with it. I will find out who killed Mary. One, because I have to save my grandmother from going to prison and two, because …"

"You need some excitement in your life?"

"I'm not looking for excitement. I'm looking for a calm, peaceful life baking pies. Is that too much to ask?" I didn't want to admit it would be a challenge to be in the middle of a murder investigation as long as no one I cared about got hurt, but this was not the case.

"So if there is no list, where do you even start?" Kate asked.

"In my humble opinion, the murderer is either someone from Heavenly Acres or someone in the family. Whoever had the most to gain from her inheritance."

"That's pretty general," Kate said. "Can you be more specific?"

"Just off the top of my head, I'm thinking her daughter because one, I'm assuming she's the main heir and two, from the way she glared at me. Then there's Bob, even though Sam doesn't agree. But Bob wanted to get rid of Mary, his own personal black widow."

"You really think Linda should be on your list? Rumor has it Mary gave all her money to a pit bull rescue mission."

"I'm not sure of anything. From what you say, I should be investigating the pit bulls that stand to benefit most from her death.

It's not what Sam wants, but I'm starting with the family. As it happens, your friend Blake called this morning and said he's coming by to give me a check for the pies I made for the service."

"So that's why you look so different. No apron and you even curled your hair."

"Don't get the wrong idea," I cautioned, feeling my face redden. "This is all in the interest of absolving Grannie by finding out who done it myself. If it weren't that Sam suspects Grannie, I'd be happy to call it an unsolved mystery and let Sam muddle through it. But I can't do that."

"Of course you can't. The good thing is there are two eligible guys in town and you are not hiding behind your apron and mixing dough. I'm proud of you. You're out looking and listening and selling pies and enticing the men into the shop."

"I am not enticing anyone," I protested, maybe a little too strongly. "They come to see me for one reason or another. I'm a professional baker and only an amateur sleuth. And I'm not interested in hooking up with anyone in town or out of town.

"I'm motivated to do one thing only. And you know what it is. Sure, Sam needs to solve the murder, that's his job, but that's nothing compared to saving your own grandmother. So after I have a little chat with Blake, I'm going up to Heavenly Acres and see what I can find out up there. At the same time hustling pie business."

"I like the way you hedge your bets. Keep a family member and one of the old folks both on your list. Just in case."

"What else can I do?"

"Now I see why you've decided to take my advice and kick up your image." She tilted her head to look over my leggings and long hip-hugging light-weight cotton sweater. "Green is a good color on you. Brings out the color of your eyes."

"Thanks."

"Let's hope it's not wasted on the senior citizens. Did you say Sam was going up there to interview everyone?"

"That's right, but …"

"I know you're not interested in hooking up with anyone. You're only interested in your career. What really happened while you were gone to make you so gun-shy?"

What could I say without giving a personal history of my past decade or so, including the partnership I was in with the guy who ditched me and left me broke and broken-hearted. Nobody, not even my best friend, or Sam, or my grandmother needed to know how dumb I'd been.

"It's a long story," I said. "And very boring."

"Maybe some other time," she said with a thoughtful look in my direction.

"Sure," I said, but I meant "Never."

"Speaking of guns," Kate said. "Aren't you afraid what might happen if you get too close to the murderer? Somebody might try to scare you off. Check the brakes in your car before you take off. Maybe you ought to be packing some heat just in case you hit a nerve."

"You're going overboard," I said, but I shuddered thinking of toting a concealed weapon under my apron. "I already have too much on my plate to worry about my own safety. I have to keep baking and selling and trying new recipes to tempt the populace. Besides keeping an eye on Grannie. I'm even thinking of joining the Bridge players, and sitting in on a game to hear the latest gossip. Does that show you that I'm serious about this? I know nothing about Bridge. I might even be murdered myself for bidding the wrong thing or showing my hand by mistake. What other reason could I have for hanging around the premises and asking a lot of questions?"

"How about giving lessons in pie baking?"

"Why would a bunch of seniors who get three square meals a day prepared by a staff want to make pies?"

Kate had to admit I had a point.

"Now if only I knew how to teach square dance or jitterbug, swing two-step or other fun dances. Though if that's what they wanted, they'd probably already have it."

"What about a book club?"

"I could put up a notice and see if anyone signs up. Then I have to read the books."

"Well, yes," Kate said. "Is that a problem?"

"I guess you're thinking I have plenty of time between customers to read books." I looked around. The shop was empty at the moment. The pies in the case and on the shelves were as appetizing as ever and ready to be eaten by anyone who popped in. "Another thing I thought of. I might hand out discount coupons for morning pie and coffee while I'm at the retirement home. Even though all the residents are richer than God, who doesn't love a bargain?"

"Good idea and it just might work." Kate gave me a thumbs up for my brilliant idea. "Coffee and pie special. Buy one, get one free. Eat in or take-away. Free refills. Happy Hour starts at ten—in the morning."

"I'll do it. The place could be filled with the older crowd mixing in with my core customers."

We both glanced around. Not a core customer in sight.

"I mean when I get my core customers."

"Which could be any moment," Kate assured me.

"By the way, are you going to that party Tammy and Lindsey are giving tonight?" I asked.

"Where they sell sex toys? I guess so. What else is there to do for excitement in this town? What about you?"

"They ordered pies for the party and I actually have filled their order already." I waved my hand at the pies in the case above the counter. "I'm going to deliver them, that's all."

"Parties you will always remember for nights you will never forget. That's what it said on the e-vite. So you should stay for the fun."

"I thought it was to spice up your sex life, and since I don't have one…"

"Not now, but I predict you will in the near future. Be prepared. That's what you have to do. A week ago you had no man in your life, now you've got two. If you wanted them, that is. Which you don't. For the possibility, you should thank Mary Brandt, may she rest in peace, for getting murdered. Who knows what will happen next week?"

"I thought nothing ever happened here."

"It didn't used to. Then you came back. Coincidence or … fate?" She wiped her sticky hands on a napkin. "You decide. I hope you decide to stay for the party. It's not your mother's Tupperware, you know."

"What are the products, exactly?"

"I don't know. This is my first time. Come and find out. Or are you afraid to tap into your latent sexuality?"

"I'm afraid of getting stuck in a room with a bunch of lascivious women I never wanted to see again trying out lotions and potions and lingerie …"

"I thought you didn't know what the products were."

"I'm guessing."

"You know who's going to be there? Blake's sister Melissa. I don't know if she's on your list, but you can ask her who she suspects of murdering her grandmother."

"Not a bad idea," I murmured. I'd bet anything Sam hadn't gotten to her yet.

"If Melissa turns bright red and drops the vibrating panties she's thinking of buying, you'll know she knows something. Then you can turn up the heat and do whatever those detectives do on TV, skillfully make her talk. If she says it was your grandmother, you've got a chance to talk her out of it after a few fancy drinks."

"Speaking of the Wilson family," I muttered, jumping to my feet as Blake pulled up in front of the shop in the family's Hummer. "There's Blake now."

Kate almost spilled her coffee, she was so eager to get a look at the former high school hero. First she beamed at him and greeted him like he was her long-lost brother. Then she paused at the door to say, "I'm so sorry to hear about your grandmother."

"Thanks," he said with an appropriate sober look of sadness. But was it real? Wasn't he really glad to pick up his own inheritance sooner rather than later?

"How is your family holding up?"

"Fine. I mean it's hard. Gram was such a … a …"

Cheater? That was one way to describe her.

"Great old lady," he said at last. "She'll be missed." He didn't say who would miss her. I had a feeling there wasn't a big crowd. "Good to see you, Blake," Kate said. "I hope you'll stick around for a while and not rush back to New York. I realize this is not the most exciting town in the world, but we do have a few things going for us. Great weather, beautiful beaches, old friends." She slanted a direct look in my direction. "Even Hanna has found her way back from the big city. You two have a lot in common." With that parting shot, she left. Probably convinced she'd subtly thrown us together and I'd owe her big-time for the favor.

"So right," he said, giving me the once-over. I was wondering if he noticed the green flecks in my hazel eyes and my new curly hair. I'd never admit I curled my hair for Blake, but Kate was right, it was time I stopped hiding behind my apron. I wasn't looking for a man, I was looking for a murderer. I just hoped they weren't one and the same.

"What can I get you?" I asked Blake. He looked at the refrigerated case and I looked at him. I didn't expect fireworks, but suddenly a loud boom filled the air followed by a huge whooshing sound. I jumped and my heart pounded. Alarmed, Blake jerked his head toward the kitchen at the rear of the shop.

"My pies," I shouted as I ran to the kitchen where I had a pan of apple turnovers baking in Grannie's vintage oven. Black smoke was creeping out from the closed oven door and filling the room. I blinked back tears that stung my eyes, bent over, and opened the oven door, which fell toward me with a thud, and yellow flames burst out. I reached for the knob to turn off the oven but it broke off in my hand. I screamed as my apron caught fire.

"Get the fire extinguisher," I shouted, pointing to the far corner of the kitchen with one hand and beating my apron with the other.

Blake found the red cylinder with the black handle and in seconds he was fumbling with the pin. Then he squeezed the lever and sprayed me with white powder. I coughed, I wheezed, but at least I was no longer on fire. But my apron was ruined. I was breathing hard and Blake was still clutching the fire extinguisher in his arms.

"Thanks," I said when I stopped coughing. "For saving my life." Although my turnovers were ruined.

He nodded, too overwhelmed with either smoke or emotion to speak. We staggered out to the shop and I opened the door and the windows. My legs wobbled. I fell into a chair and took huge gulps of fresh air.

"In all these years," I said weakly, "I don't think there's ever been an oven fire. Wonder what caused it?" Kate's words filtered through my smoke-filled brain. *Aren't you afraid what could happen if you get too close to the murderer? Somebody might try to scare you off.*

Blake shook his head. He was leaning against the wall, his bleached blond hair standing on end, his eyebrows singed and his face drained of that fabulous tan he had when he arrived. I could only imagine how I must look with a layer of soot on my face.

He looked so different from the suave guy I saw at his house over gin and tonics, that I started to laugh. I couldn't stop until I was almost hysterical. It was partly the shock of the explosion and partly the ridiculous situation of being blown up in my shop with Blake.

He looked at me and burst out laughing himself. My knees were so weak I couldn't get up. He took a handkerchief out of his pocket, leaned over and wiped my face with it. Who would have thought a rich, macho guy would have such a gentle touch? But he did. He looked at me with a crooked grin on his face. I grinned back.

"What caused it?" he repeated. "That's a question for the police chief or for your repair man."

"Police chief?" I said. I refused to see any connection between the faulty oven and the long arm of the law. It was a coincidence, that's all. "I'll call a guy I know to fix it." I'd call him as soon as I caught my breath and washed the soot off my face.

"Good idea. Officer Krupke has too much to do solving the murder of my grandmother."

"So you're sure..."

"I only know what they tell me," he said, shaking some ashes out of his hair. "Why else would the chief make another appointment to come out and ask my mother a lot of questions, like where was she the night Gram died? Who stands to inherit her money? I can tell you Mom isn't happy about that. She thinks she's under suspicion. For killing her own mother. Well, I'd better be off. Change my clothes before I see somebody I know. And here's your check." He reached into his back pocket and handed me a check on his mother's account for the memorial service pies. A glance told me it was a very generous amount.

"Thanks again," I said, standing up carefully for fear of collapsing. So I'd accomplished two things: I collected my money and heard that Linda was on Sam's list as well as mine.

"Next time you're in town this alleged murder will be forgotten. The motive will be discovered and the guilty party will be brought to justice," I said, though that would be small comfort if the guilty party was his mother.

He stood in the doorway, brushed some ashes from his sleeve and said, "I'm afraid money's the only motive that makes sense, especially when you're dealing with a rich woman like Gram. She was rich all right, and who doesn't need a little extra million or two or three. If she left me some money I might buy a little apartment in the Village. Won't know about that until we hear what's in her will."

"She had a will?"

"Of course. Let's face it, my grandmother was paranoid. She thought someone was trying to kill her so she made sure her will was up to date. Over and over, ad nauseum she called her lawyer in to discuss it or change it, who knows? The formal reading is Monday—I'll stick around for that and see. My mom told her to cool it and increased her meds. What really got to Mom was Gram's insistence on getting everything from that special pharmacy in San Francisco."

"How special?" I asked.

"They compound the drugs. I mean they combine them by hand, put your medicine mix in a little vial, cap it, then charge you an arm and a leg for the privilege."

I almost fell over. So that's how they did it. Whoever killed Mary added something to her "special mixture." It could have been anybody who had access to the card room, and who didn't? It wasn't locked. Obviously, Blake didn't realize he might have helped me in my search for Mary's murderer. Or not.

"Did you tell the police chief about this?" I asked.

He shrugged. "I don't think so. Why?"

"No reason." So I knew something Sam didn't know. Maybe more than I thought.

"I gotta go. Sorry about the blast. I'm serious about getting together under normal circumstances. After this murder business is cleared up." He grabbed my hands, pulled me up out of my chair, and looked down at me. "Anyone ever tell you you look good in soot?" he asked.

I shook my head.

He ran his fingers down my cheekbone and tilted my chin with his thumb. "Always good seeing you, Hanna. Glad we reconnected. I'll call you."

I watched him leave then sank back down in my chair, stunned and out of breath. I wished I'd had a moment to think. I would have said, "Wait, did you just finger your mother in the murder of your grandmother and why?" Or "I'd love to get together, especially after the reading of the will so you can tell me if your grandmother left all her money to some disadvantaged dogs? Or maybe you'll be celebrating because you'll never have to work another day in your life because of your cushy trust fund?" But it was too late. I didn't say a thing.

I watched him get into the family Hummer and wave as he pulled away. I felt like I was seventeen again, just as thrilled to have a guy like Blake stop by the pie shop. Sure I was older and wiser and I wanted to be able to trust a man again, but I wasn't quite ready for that. All I really wanted was to absolve my grandmother.

Back in the kitchen, I pulled the pan of blackened ruined turnovers out of the oven and called Ike, Grannie's faithful appliance repair man, who was now in business with his son Ike Junior.

"I told Louise she should get a new oven," Ike Senior grumbled. "Knew something like this would happen."

"Can you come right away? I've got more pies to bake. My inventory is shot."

"In an hour," he promised.

I was so busy scrubbing the ashes off the burners on the antique stove I didn't hear Sam come in. He looked even more surprised at my appearance. He stood staring for a long moment, then his mouth twitched in the way it does when he doesn't want to laugh or cry. I was thinking laugh. But I was laughed out. So I brushed my face with the back of my hand, knowing I must look like a zombie.

"Good God, what happened? An explosion?"

"A mishap."

"Yeah, I can see that."

"Ike the repair man is on his way. I'd rather Grannie didn't know about this ... event. She doesn't need anything else to worry about besides being a murder suspect."

"If you're referring to her polygraph test ..."

"I'd feel better knowing everyone was getting one."

"Everyone isn't, but I do want to show you something at the station you might find interesting. How about tomorrow?"

"I'm pretty busy," I said.

"At your convenience," he said.

"What if it isn't?"

"Then let's say nine and get it over with. It will just take a few minutes of your time."

"Come on, Sam, you're doing this to annoy me. Why can't you show me something here and now?"

"You'll see."

I sighed loudly. "Okay, I'll be there. Now if there's nothing I can get for you, you'll have to excuse me while I clean up the kitchen."

"Hold on while I get my camera."

"No photos until I wash my face and comb my hair."

"Stand next to the stove."

I reluctantly struck a pose next to the damaged oven and he took my picture. "I'm not going to file an insurance claim, you know."

"We'll need this in case the oven has been tampered with," he explained.

"Oh please. Not you too. There's no need to tamper with an old oven, they do funny things from time to time. Ike will fix it."

"Did it ever occur to you someone may not want you to meddle in this murder business? Someone besides me, that is?"

"And that someone sabotaged my oven?" I asked. I was a little worried but trying to act like I'd never heard of anything so ridiculous. "If you're trying to scare me..."

"I'm trying to make you aware of the danger out there."

"Is that why you're making me come to the station?"

"No, it isn't."

I couldn't imagine what he had to show me. And frankly I didn't want to think about it. It was late and I was exhausted, shaky, and yes, maybe a little scared.

I tried to ignore him while he looked around the kitchen, opening drawers and inspecting the cupboard while I called Grannie's cleaning lady. She said she had a key and promised to come by later with her crew. I knew I couldn't do it, and with Blake's check in my pocket I felt like I could afford a professional job.

"Okay," I told Sam, "take pictures of the damage while I go take a shower and change my clothes." I had planned to stop by Heavenly Acres after Blake left, but cleaning the oven had taken priority to solving a murder.

When I came downstairs, with the soot and ashes washed off and dressed for the party, Sam was still there taking pictures.

He took a step back when he saw me, studied my clean face and my white-washed skinny jeans, my flower-print cardigan over a Nile green T-shirt and a pair of Urban Outfitters strappy sandals in a neutral shade, and frowned as if he didn't like what he saw. Or maybe that was just my old insecurity cropping up. Then he held his camera up and snapped another picture.

"What's that for?" I asked. "Your files of suspects?"

"Evidence. To show how you've changed," he said. "Much better. Going someplace?" His tone was casual, but I thought he might really want to know. But why? For personal reasons or professional?

"To a sex toy party. All girls." I don't know why I said that. It was way too much information he didn't need to know. Maybe I wanted to shock him, to jolt him out of his complacency, or even make him pay attention to me. What was wrong with me?

He raised his eyebrows. "Really. How does that work?"

"I don't know. I've never been to one. But I'll let you know. I'm supplying the pies and, of course, I'll keep my ears open." I didn't say what for and he didn't ask. We both knew I had no intention of following his orders not to meddle.

He offered to help me load my station wagon with pies, and while we were outside Ike and his son arrived to fix the oven. Sam and I followed them back inside. Ike was already squatting on the tiles in front of the stove. He turned and held up a large cast iron part. "See this? It's the burner element. Fell out of place, who knows how come. One leg is missing. Looks like it's broken. It's an old stove. These things happen."

"Then you don't think someone was fooling with it?" I asked anxiously.

"Nah."

"But it could have been fooled with, couldn't it?" Sam said. He leaned over to survey the broken burner and take a picture of it.

"Sure. Who knows?" Ike said. "When it fell, the gas jet went straight out, must have been like a blow torch."

I nodded. "Yeah, it was."

"I'll have to weld this here cast iron burner and she'll be good as new," he said.

"I'm glad to hear you say that," I said, "because I hate to replace this old friend."

"She's good for another fifty years at least," he promised with a wink.

I wished I could say the same for myself.

SEVEN

I KNOW ENVY IS one of the seven deadly sins, but when I saw Lindsey's house I had to stifle the most horrendous case of jealousy I'd had since I coveted a pair of silver stilettos I saw in the window of a boutique in San Francisco. Not that I had anywhere to wear the shoes. Maybe that made the envy even worse. It was pointless. Better for me to envy and save up for a new stove and oven. No matter what Ike said about good as new, I'd probably need one sooner rather than later. Or if I had extra money, I could spring for a PR blitz with a pie-eating contest or a trip to Paris to study at the Cordon Bleu, where I would major in tarts.

Back to Lindsey's house. I so wanted her to live in a charmless cookie-cutter new house in one of the developments on the outskirts of town that I could tell myself was just as lacking in good taste as Lindsey was. But no such luck. It was an English Tudor–style house tucked away on a private lot a few minutes from downtown. Hedges along the driveway concealed the house from the street. I parked in the driveway and carried my pies stacked in an extra-large wicker basket up the winding path to a brick front porch. Peeking in the large paned window, I caught a glimpse of shining maple floors, high-coved ceilings, and a huge fireplace. Before I'd even entered, I could tell it oozed charm. What had Lindsey ever done to deserve to live here? Hang around and marry the man of her dreams, that's all.

I arrived early. If I hadn't been out to catch a murderer, I would have deposited the pies and left before the guests arrived and got into discussing the benefits of sexy beginner harness kits for couples. But not today. I realized this could be a golden opportunity to look and listen and nudge a few loose-mouthed women into dropping a hint or two in my direction. I planned to stick around long enough to see what I could find out as well as gracefully accept compliments and take orders for future pies. I decided not to dress like a baker tonight.

I was glad I'd made the effort to look halfway decent, because Lindsey herself was going for the gold with a pair of caramel-colored wide-legged silk pants, ankle-tie stilettos by Tory Burch, if I wasn't mistaken, and ropes of brushed gold metal necklaces over a stretchy knit sleeveless top.

She met me at the door and air-kissed me as if we were old friends, which we were, sort of. Then she stood back and gave me the once-over. I hoped I didn't look out of place, and I hoped she didn't think I was trying to out-do her, which I couldn't. She finally took my basket and invited me in.

"So glad you could come. Lots of old friends you haven't seen. Ever been to one of these things before?"

I shook my head. "I really can't stay long," I murmured.

"It should be a hoot. Wait till you see the merchandise and the party favors. You don't have to buy anything, although I get ten percent of the Passion Party sales plus a hostess gift. You could do it too, host a party in your shop. It's easy. They tell you how. First you serve drinks to calm any nervous guests, then show off the products. I'm telling you, they sell themselves."

What? A sex toy party in my pie shop? I shuddered to think what Grannie would say. Although after what Kate had hinted about Grannie's sex life, maybe she'd be the first to sign up.

"You have to stay," she said. "Some of the girls didn't even know you were back in town. This will be a chance for you to network."

"Sounds like fun," I said. She was right, after finding out who killed Mary Brandt, I could and I should network. Spread the word about pies in case they didn't know. Unless all attention was on the merchandise here and pies were too boring, even my "I'm too sexy for my crust" Italian Bittersweet Chocolate Silk Pie.

"I love your house," I said as I followed her to the kitchen. The Wolf range and the old Mexican tiles on the floor made me love it even more. A range like that wouldn't explode on me.

"It's old," Lindsey said, "but it's comfortable. And the neighborhood just got a big boost. Guess who's moving in next door?"

I didn't have to guess. She told me.

"Sam. Our Chief of Police." She nodded when she saw the look of surprise on my face. "I'll feel so much safer with him around."

"He bought the house next door?" I asked incredulously. Why hadn't he told me? Ever since he filled me in on his life story chapter two, he'd totally kept everything to himself as if he was sorry he'd let go that day and had promised himself never to do it again. Was it my fault? Had I turned him off by acting too cool or too interested? Or by keeping my own life story to myself? But buying a house? It sure sounded like he was planning to stick around for a while.

"Yes. Paid top dollar. Didn't even bargain. I can tell you the Sandlers were overjoyed. They got transferred to Houston and now they can buy a mansion there for what they got. It's a big house for one person, but maybe he's planning on getting married. Can't believe no one's caught someone like him by now, can you?"

Someone like him. She wouldn't have said that fifteen years ago when he was on probation.

"So he hasn't moved in yet?" I said.

"Not yet." She rubbed her hands together and smiled at me. "Even if there's no crime in Crystal Cove, it will be good to have the police chief next door."

"No crime? What about Mary Brandt's murder?" I asked. "Didn't you hear?"

"Oh, Melissa's grandmother up at Heavenly Acres? I did hear something about it. No wonder we never see Sam. He's got a murder to solve. Any idea who did it?"

Why did everyone keep asking me about Mary Brandt's murder? As if I was part of the police department. How ironic when I'd been told in no uncertain terms my help was not welcome. And now I was being dragged down to the station tomorrow morning for God only knew what. The thought made me livid. Not that that kept me from trying to solve the mystery. Just the opposite. I refused to let Sam stop me from saving my grandmother from being harassed. Or scare me into thinking someone was out to get me by sabotaging my oven. Or hooking me up to his electronic toy. No way was I sitting around too scared to move while waiting for him to solve this murder.

"It's always the next of kin," Lindsey said. "What about her husband?"

I shook my head. "Didn't have one."

"It couldn't be Melissa, I've known her forever."

I didn't want to say knowing someone forever doesn't necessarily mean they couldn't commit a crime. I wanted to tell her you had to drop all emotional attachments when you were looking for a criminal. Except of course when your attachment was to your beloved grandmother who wouldn't hurt a fly. I was tempted to tell Lindsey about Bob, Mary's erstwhile boyfriend who wanted to get rid of her, but I correctly held my tongue for once.

Lindsey's doorbell rang just then, and she left to answer it. I thought of how much I'd like to escape the sex toy scene, but I needed to stay. Already I'd made a tiny inroad into my quest for answers. Leaving now would be rude and it would look cowardly. Along with picking up clues, I still needed to network.

But I did sneak a look at the house next door, a stone Craftsman-style bungalow with an avocado grove behind it; it just cried out Single Professional Guy's house. What a change from the trailer park he grew up in. Whatever his shaky upbringing, he had landed on his feet. I guess you could say the same for me, although being brought up by my grandmother was far from shaky. It was comfortable, warm, safe, and secure. I owed her big-time for that. It wasn't her fault I went a little crazy in between times. She had nothing to do with my lack of judgment.

I owed her a safe, secure retirement where she didn't have to worry about the police knocking on her door and hauling her off for more questioning or a murder trial. The sooner I helped catch Mary's real murderer, the sooner we could all go back to our normal lives. Normal boring lives, some might say. Not me. I wouldn't mind a little boredom, especially if it came accompanied by an uptick in pie sales.

It wasn't long before the living room was filled with women and loud music. Music and booze in the form of little frothy fruit drinks that went down so easily, that was the formula. Then bring out food and the paraphernalia. Some of the women I knew from high school, like Tammy, others were new to town. When Kate came in she grinned and gave me a thumbs up. She took a frosted glass from a tray Lindsey was carrying and crossed the room to say hello.

"Be careful," I said. "The drinks are supposed to loosen you up so you'll buy more sex toys."

"Don't worry about me," she said, squinting and edging her face within inches of mine. "What happened to your eyelashes?"

"A run-in with an out-of-control gas flame in the old stove," I said. "Just one of the professional risks we bakers take. Nothing serious."

"Glad to hear it. Even more glad you decided to stick around."

"Why not? I'm here in my dual role as amateur sleuth and pie salesperson."

"Where are they?"

"The suspects or the pies?

"Both."

"Some in the kitchen, the others in the living room. Maybe Lindsey is saving the pies to serve when they bring out the arousal creams and performance enhancers."

Then I did a double take as a woman in a fuchsia-colored short dress walked through the room with a tray of cupcakes.

I gasped. "Did you see that?"

"Mmmmm," Kate said.

"Who's making cupcakes in this town?"

"Why?"

"I don't need any competition."

"Don't be ridiculous. Sure, cupcakes are the latest thing, but pies are historic. Pies are forever. Did you see the article I wrote?"

"No, but I heard about it."

"I have a copy in the car for you. You'll see, your sales will soar."

"I can't wait."

"Let's go sit down, Lindsey is bringing out the toys."

"Oh no, what are we going to do?"

"Relax and have a cupcake." I did have a cupcake. Just for re-search purposes. It was made with Meyer lemons and had a lus-cious fresh lemon filling. I had to admit it was pretty darn good. I just hoped no one else was thinking, "Cupcakes, I must order some for my next party." What if it occurred to them to conclude ... So much easier to eat than pie. I set my drink down on an end table, vowing to stay alert for clues to Mary's murder. After all, besides selling pies, that's why I was there.

Despite my concentration on the murder, the rest of the eve-ning was a blur. There were games. There were prizes. There were toys like bath balls; pleasure pearls; and rockets, rings, and tick-lers. There were books like *Great Sex (Secrets and Techniques to Keep Your Relationship Red-Hot)*; there was laughter, lots of laugh-ter. Several times I got up to leave, but I couldn't do it. Not until

I'd grilled at least one person and picked up a clue or two from a loose-mouthed addled guest.

Finally, when there was a break, I went to the kitchen and borrowed a knife to cut my pies into slices, since no one else was doing it. Lindsey came into the kitchen, flushed with the success of her party or too many margaritas in salty-rimmed special glasses. "Isn't this fun?" she asked.

I assured her it was a fabulous party, then I asked if she had a tray so I could serve the pie.

"Of course," she said and reached into her well-stocked dish cabinet for a beautiful bone china Royal Doulton tray. Armed with a selection of both the blueberry and the sexy chocolate pies cut in small pieces and served with small forks, I went back to the party. Working the room, hoping to get a chance to talk murder or at least to hear compliments, I stopped and handed a piece of blueberry pie to Melissa, Blake's sister, who was a younger version of her blond mother.

"I love all your pies," she gushed. "I had some of each at the memorial service."

"How is the family holding up?" I asked.

"Pretty well," she said. Her voice was a little unsteady and the glass in her hand even less so. How many of those little drinks had she had? "You know my grandmother had a good long, long, very long life. She was quite a character." I nodded. How could I disagree? "She will be missed," Melissa added. Only she said "mithed" instead of missed.

Now was the time to pump her, when she was not in complete control. I thought of the Bridge group and of the women I'd overheard in the kitchen the day of the memorial service. They'd "mith" her all right.

"I didn't know her," I said, "but I hear she was…" My mind went blank. What can you say about a woman who seemed to have no friends except perhaps her Bridge partner, Donna, and who knew how she really felt? Note to self. Talk to Donna. Talk to everyone at Heavenly Acres, which was what Sam was doing. But they might tell me things they wouldn't tell a cop. Finally I said, "Amazing. She must have been quite a lady."

"You can say that again," Melissa said. "I can't believe she's dead. Honestly we all thought she'd live forever. In fact, whenever we suggested her making a will or disposing of her valuables, she assured us she *would* live forever." She laughed a little too loudly.

I smiled politely. "She must have changed her mind."

"About living forever?" Melissa asked with another chortle, forking a piece of blueberry pie into her mouth at the same time.

"I mean about making a will. Your brother Blake said he was hanging around for the formal reading next week. Although isn't that something that only happens in the movies?"

"Probably. My mother could tell you that. She's a huge movie fan. She's the one who insisted Gram make a will. She sent her own lawyer up to Heavenly Acres to make sure Gram did it right. And that we all got what is coming to us. And what thanks does she get? The police think she killed Gram. Her own mother."

I blinked rapidly, partly in surprise and partly because I had so little eyelash left.

"Of course, Gram gave the lawyer a hard time, and told him she planned on taking it all with her." Again she laughed. "Even her jewelry, which she promised me as her only granddaughter."

"Lucky you," I said. What did she mean? Acres of diamonds? Or just a keepsake brooch only of sentimental value? "She must have had a good sense of humor," I suggested. "Which you've inherited." It was so hard to find something good to say about Mary.

"You think so? You didn't know her. That part about taking it with her? She was serious. You know something?"

I shook my head. I don't know anything, I wanted to say. That's why I'm here.

"She would have loved this party. She was quite the sexpot up at the old people's home there. She told me that sex was wasted on the young. What do you make of that?" She jabbed me in the ribs with her free hand.

What I made of it was that maybe Bob wasn't her only boyfriend. I would have to ask Grannie. Or that I really must give Bob a closer look as a suspect. Melissa took a big slug of her margarita. I told myself to dig deeper, get her to pull the rug out from under her guilty mother.

"Hope your mom gets more than the family jewels," I said frankly, hoping she was too drunk to think me rude.

"Oh, she will," Melissa said with a wink. "She's depressed now, but once this investigation is over, the murderer is found, and we get what's coming to us, she'll snap out of it. Don't worry about her."

I assured her I wouldn't worry about her mother. But I sure wished I could interview her. Fat chance of that. "I don't suppose you have any idea who would have wanted to murder your grandmother," I said, hoping she'd continue to say what was on her mind.

"It's too horrible to think about."

"Someone thought about it," I suggested.

Her eyes widened. Maybe I'd finally crossed the line. I couldn't worry about manners, not when murder was on the table. "Of course, thinking about killing someone is one thing, but that doesn't mean you'd actually do it," Melissa said. "Let's put it this way. I can't say anyone in the family is shedding any tears. Not my brother Blake—he hardly knew her. We hardly know him anymore since he moved to New York. He's a real player."

"Hmmm," I murmured. Of course Blake was a player. But a very attractive one at that. The perfect kind of guy for a girl who didn't want to get seriously involved.

"My grandmother was a handful," Melissa continued. "Always calling my mom asking her for something. Always ragging on my dad for not making enough money, never good enough for mom." Melissa took another big bite of pie and chewed slowly. "This is delicious," she said. "How's the pie business going?"

"Picking up nicely," I said as I digested this bit of information about her parents and their relationship to the deceased.

"Everyone loved them at Gram's memorial service. Too bad it was cut short when the ambulance arrived. How is that man doing, the old geezer who passed out that day?"

"He's better. A minor heart attack, but he should be fine."

"Gram liked him a lot. But she said somebody else was mooching on her territory. And she wasn't going to put up with that. Just as well, because he was suffering from some fatal disease so of course when the ambulance came we all thought..." She shook her head as if she couldn't bear to say the word dead or died.

"He must be in remission," I said. After I realized I'd probably gotten as much as possible from Melissa, I moved on, passing out pieces of pie and gracefully accepting compliments, glad that I had cards to hand out "The Upper Crust. 25 Ocean Avenue, Crystal Cove, California. Pies for every occasion. So warm, so welcome. Dangerously Delicious. We ship everywhere."

Of course I'd never shipped a pie anywhere, but there was bound to be a first.

I wondered how much money the old lady had now that I realized that Blake, Melissa, and their mother were all waiting anxiously for the distribution of her estate. Maybe all Melissa wanted was her jewelry for sentimental reasons. I tried to think about anything else the assistant in the kitchen had said about the earrings. Had Mary given away other pieces too? If so, Melissa wasn't going to be happy about that.

A few hours later, I walked out of the party with Kate. My empty pie pans were in the basket and my party favors in my purse.

"Now aren't you glad you came?" she asked. "I saw you talking to Melissa. She didn't look devastated by the loss of her grandmother tonight or at the memorial service. Is she a suspect?"

"I don't think so, although she said she wanted Mary's jewelry."

"She told you?"

"People open up and talk when they've had a few margaritas."

"You might suggest that to our police chief," Kate said, "liquoring up the suspects." Then she tripped over a brick in the walkway and grabbed my arm for support.

"Watch it," I said. "How many drinks did you have?"

"I lost count, but they were mostly lime juice, I think."

"Do you want a ride home? I think I'm more sober than you are."

"I can drive," she insisted.

"Better watch out. I'd hate to see Sam cite you for DUI."

"You'd get me off with a warning, wouldn't you? After all, you're his friend."

"Hah. I'm afraid I have no influence with him. Remember, I offered to help him solve Mary's murder, but he turned me down."

"So you're totally off the case?"

"With my grandmother as a chief suspect? I'm on the case in every way possible, only I'm strictly undercover. Speaking of which, I'm invited by Sam or rather commanded to appear at the police station to 'see something,' whatever that means. I have no idea what he's talking about, but it must be important to drag me from my place of work. Of course, anything I can do to help, right? Could you spare some time in the afternoon so I can do some undercover detecting up at Heavenly Acres? I'll make it worth your while."

"Sure. In exchange for a couple hours of babysitting? Jack and I need a night out."

"And a chance to try out your new sex toys," I suggested with a nudge of my elbow.

I'd be happy to babysit. After all, I had nothing to do in the evenings. But I needed some time during the day, and I couldn't leave the shop closed twice in one day. Hanging a "Closed" sign on the door discourages business.

She didn't bother to answer so I said, "It's a deal."

At nine the next morning I was ready to go in a pair of wide-leg cotton pants, a gauze tunic top, and flip-flops. My casual attire was meant to indicate this was no big deal and not worth the trouble to dress up. Just another day of interrogation in Paradise.

Sam was the only one there. I imagined his deputies were out patrolling the hills above town or helping old ladies cross the street. He took me into a small room and we sat down at a table with a control panel facing a small screen.

"How was the party?" he asked.

"Fine. If you're in the market for lubricants, vibrators, condoms, erotic books, or videos, it was definitely the place to be."

"Learn anything?" he asked.

"About sex toys or Mary Brandt?"

He leaned back in his chair. "Either."

"I'm not sure. I'll have to let you know," I said. Why should I share my info with him? He'd discredit it as being biased or take it and use it like he'd uncovered it.

"Fair enough," he conceded. "Now I want to show you what we picked up on our surveillance camera at Heavenly Acres."

"Where from, the parking lot? The front lobby?"

"The card room."

I felt a chill run up my spine. What was I going to see? I gave him a tight smile and said, "Is it on all the time?"

"Unfortunately, no. It seems one or some of the residents knew about it and turned it off at will. But we do have some footage from the day Mary Brandt died. Which you may be interested in."

"I'm sure I will. Did the accounts by the residents match up with what actually occurred?" I asked, trying not to sound overly concerned. Which I was.

"More or less. The interesting part is what happened before the Bridge game during which Mary Brandt collapsed."

"Ah."

He started the video. The camera panned across an empty card room. A woman entered the room. She was wearing fitted slacks, a sweater, and pearls. A popular combination. Almost a uniform. It could have been anybody's grandmother—mine, Blake's, whoever. I leaned forward. She had her back to the camera. She went to one of the tables, took a small item out of her pocket, and set it on the table. Sam stopped the machine and zoomed in on the table. The item was a pill bottle.

"Recognize that?" he asked.

I shook my head.

"Recognize her?"

I shrugged. He turned the video back on. The woman looked around the room, rather furtively I thought. Then she looked up straight at the camera. I swallowed hard. It was Grannie. She reached up and there was a click and the screen went black.

"I know what you're thinking," I told Sam. "Grannie substituted some strong medicine for Mary to get rid of her. But hear me out. Grannie takes pep pills—I'm not sure exactly what they are, but they sharpen her wits. But she's embarrassed to admit she needs any help. After all, she's been a Bridge fanatic for forty years. So I'm thinking she came early to put her pills at her place for the game."

"Then why turn off the camera?"

"I told you, she doesn't want anyone to know she's taking anything. It's a badge of honor to be pill-free at her age. Ask her."

"I did."

"And?"

"She said she doesn't take anything."

"There you go," I said with a relieved smile. "I told you she wouldn't admit it."

"She was under oath. I have to take her at her word. I have to assume those were the pills that killed Mary Brandt."

My heart sank, at least that's what it felt like. My grandmother had screwed herself out of pride. Did she even know it, or was Sam just waiting to pounce and arrest her?

"Did she see this video?"

"Not yet. I wanted to give you a chance to talk her into confessing."

"To what? Being a competitive card player? To being a kind, loving grandmother?"

He shook his head. "You know what I mean. Tell her to come down to the station, confess to killing Mary Brandt, and maybe we can work something out."

"Like what?"

"Reduced sentence for a confession."

I choked back the desire to snap "No way." Instead I said, "What's the alternative?"

"I arrest her at the residence, read her her rights, and take her away. That's what the DA advises."

I stood and glared at him. "You've told the DA about my grandmother?"

"I had to. I've got a murder here. Somebody has to pay."

"Well it's not going to be my grandmother. Give me forty-eight hours and I'll find your killer."

"Hanna, you're looking for trouble. You're vulnerable, you know. Look what happened already. You could have been blown away by the oven disaster."

"It was an accident. The oven has been fine for fifty years. Nothing lasts that long without a problem or two."

"Not only that, this is my job. I forbid you to try to help in this investigation. I'll handle it."

"I see the way you're handling it, and I don't like it," I said. "And if you think you're going to run for mayor of this town, you'd better watch out …"

"Why, you won't vote for me?"

I pressed my lips together to keep from exploding like my oven, then I turned and marched out of the room, out of the station, and across the street. I was so furious I almost ran into the mailman on his bicycle.

The rest of the day I spent thinking of how I'd absolve Grannie of the murder and how I'd run Sam out of town. By four o'clock when Kate came to relieve me, I'd helped the cleaning crew scrub down the whole kitchen and baked four pies. I was acting like I'd taken some of Grannie's uppers. Which is what I sincerely hoped had been in that pillbox.

"You look awful," I said to Kate, noting her pale face and red-rimmed eyes. "I told you not to drink so much."

"At least I've got eyelashes," she countered. "In my case having a few margaritas was worth it." She pressed her fingers against her temples. "You have to admit last night was a lot of fun. Besides, you got some good PR, word of mouth, pie in mouth. Here's your copy of my article."

I scanned the section titled "Personalities" and skimmed the article, which was studded with words like *mouth-watering, up-scale, all occasions, funerals,* and *weddings.*

"It's a good picture of you," she said. "You look cute."

"Compared to what? The Pillsbury Dough Boy?" I was determined to say nothing about my visit to the police station. So I changed the subject. "Hey, did you ever hear who was that woman with the cupcakes? Speaking of mysteries, there's one I have to solve."

"The one in the pink frou-frou dress, who looked like a cupcake herself? I don't know her name, but they sure were good. I had a peanut butter with chocolate ganache frosting and a passion fruit. Get it? Passion fruit?"

"I get it," I assured her. "Were they as good as my pie?" I knew she'd tell me my pie was better. Then why did I ask? A bout of insecurity.

"Different. I hear she does cupcake decorating parties. Like the sex toy parties only ... different."

"I could do pie parties. Sell pans and rolling pins and everybody takes home a pie that we bake in the shop. But then everyone would start baking their own pies and stop buying mine."

"Good point." She didn't seem as enthusiastic as my personal public relations agent should be.

"Actually I had a few calls today," I said. "A couple of solid orders, and other people calling to ask how much the pies cost and so forth."

"So leave me a price list with your specialties so I won't sound clueless."

I showed her where the list was, and I grabbed a pie and my swimsuit so I could join water aerobics with Grannie.

I noticed the official squad car in the Heavenly Acres parking lot, which must mean Sam was there conducting his interviews. No doubt hoping to cement his case against Grannie. Next to the black and white police car was a refinished postal van. It was painted silver and hot pink with a "Lurline's Luscious Cupcakes" sign on the door. Lurline. Was she the cupcake woman at the sex toy party? What was she doing there? I peeked in the window of the truck and saw cardboard boxes stacked behind the driver's seat. Empty or filled with Luscious cupcakes? I went in through the front door wondering where the cupcake lady was and how Sam's interviews were going. I knew Grannie was waiting for me in her room, so I didn't stop to ask questions.

"How do you like my new suit?" Grannie asked, turning slowly in the middle of her living room, one hand on her hip to show off her still-shapely body poured into a one-piece black maillot.

"You look terrific," I said. If Sam could see her now he'd never believe what he said he believed. I vowed I'd do anything in my power to keep her so happy and carefree and out of jail.

"None of those old-lady numbers with the skirts for me," she said, wrinkling her nose as if she might be mistaken for someone her age. "I ordered two new ones from the catalog and they came just in time for class." She donned a terrycloth cover-up, provided me with one too, and told me to get dressed and join her at the pool. "Hope you brought a bikini at least. I brag about you a lot, you know. How smart you are. What a great baker. But mostly what a catch you are. For some lucky guy. Some of my friends here have eligible grandsons. Don't let me down," she said with her hand on the doorknob.

"Speaking of lucky guys, how's Bob?" I asked. "Is he out of the hospital?"

"Yes, but he has to take it easy. Meals in his room. Even his interview with the police chief will be in his room. Everybody else goes to the office."

"When's your next interview?"

"Oh, I had it this morning."

"And you weren't going to mention it?"

"Nothing to mention. Just a formality. I'd already told him everything I know with that machine going."

"The polygraph?"

"That's the one. He had some follow-up questions and I assured him I'd do anything to help solve a mystery." She picked up a large colorful beach towel and tucked it under her arm. "I'm late for class. Hurry up."

I stood between her and the door. I wanted some kind of assurance, some hope to hold on to that she really wasn't the chief suspect. "So Sam didn't press you, make any demands, try to trick you into admitting anything you didn't want to?" I asked. Why was he going easy on her? Now I was getting even more worried. The only thing I could think was that he'd made up his mind. Which meant it was my job to change it.

"Of course not. I'd never admit to anything I didn't do, and I'm sure he wouldn't want me to. He's just trying to do his job, Hanna."

I couldn't believe she was being so fair. More than fair, she was acting like Sam was her grandchild instead of me. That's how it seemed to me. She refused to hear anything bad about him. Was this an act or was she really not that concerned?

I decided to change the subject for fear of freaking her out. "Do you know anything about the cupcake truck in the parking lot?"

"Somebody having a birthday party probably. I don't know. I wasn't invited."

She didn't seem to realize this cupcake truck was in direct competition with my pie shop. I got the message. She didn't want to talk about anything, not the investigation or the cupcakes. Was her second interview really just a formality? Didn't Sam ask her about the pillbox she'd put in the card room?

From the window I watched Grannie sashay down the path to the pool in her one-piece maillot as if she didn't have a care in the world. No wonder she expected me to be wearing a sexy bikini and a sign around my neck with my statistics indicating I was available. I wasn't wearing a sign or a bikini. It was a one-piece tank top suit with a hint of micro ruffles lining the edge. Probably not sexy enough for Grannie's taste, but it worked for swimming laps at the gym I'd belonged to in the city. I hated to disappoint her, but there was nothing daring about it.

I'd just wrapped up in the terrycloth robe she loaned me when there was a knock on the door. When Sam saw me standing there, he walked in and closed the door behind him. As if he knew I'd be there. Then he took a moment to look me over from head to toe. I'd like to believe he was blown away by my long, shapely legs and my sexy painted toenails, but maybe he was just taking inventory—robe, swimsuit, long legs, and sexy toes.

"If you're looking for Grannie, she's out at the pool. She hasn't left town, if that's what you're worried about." My voice was on edge just enough to let him know how I felt about her being treated like a common criminal.

"What are you doing here?" he asked with narrowed eyes.

"I'm joining the water aerobics class today. Why? Is that a crime? Kate's watching the store for me. I have something to show you if you have a minute."

I went to get my purse with the notes I'd made when I got home last night just in case I too had lapsed into a margarita fog.

When I reached into my capacious leather bag, the pink vibrating dildo called a speeding bullet I'd received as a door prize last night fell out on the floor. Before I could retrieve it, Sam picked it up and handed it to me with a knowing half smile on his face. Was it because he didn't know if I knew that he knew what it was? Or because he didn't know I needed one? Maybe he'd never seen one before. Not a hot pink one, anyway.

I felt my face turn the same color as the sex toy. "That's not what I meant to show you," I said. "This is the favor I got last night at the Passion Party. Everyone did. Although many people bought things. Not me though. Actually, it was at Lindsey Smith's house next door to where ..." I couldn't seem to stop rattling away nervously so it was good that he interrupted.

"I know where she lives."

"But you might not know she throws these parties."

"Is this relevant?"

"It could be. The reason I went ..."

"I don't have to know that."

"I just didn't want you to think ..."

"I don't."

"Good. I thought you might be interested to know Mary's granddaughter is expecting to inherit her jewelry."

"I don't think that's a crime," he said dryly.

"But it's a motive, isn't it?"

"I told you to leave the investigating to me and my department."

"After what you told me this morning?" I asked. "I can't do that. I have a duty as a citizen to tell you to pay more attention to Mary's family and less attention to the residents of Heavenly Acres."

"And why is that?" he asked with a slightly amused look.

"Because I have certain evidence. I know you don't take me or my observations seriously," I said. "But I'll tell you anyway that Mary's grandson Blake told me his grandmother was paranoid, and she thought someone was trying to kill her. His mother told her she was schizoid and she increased her meds so she wouldn't be delusional."

"Yes, I heard that."

"You did?"

"I spoke to Mrs. Wilson yesterday."

Damn, why hadn't I spoken to her? Because I didn't have the clout of the law behind me. I didn't wear a badge, but then neither did he. I should have walked right up to her car when I had a chance.

"So what did she say?" I asked. "What do you think? Or is that classified information?"

"I think you know the answer to that."

I refused to let him stop our conversation that way. "I know you believe that Mary's medication killed her," I said. "I just want to know if you've ruled out a connection to the pie she ate and I made. After all, since you haven't made an arrest, I think I have the right to know if I'm under suspicion too."

"Everyone who had access to Mary Brandt, her medicine, or her food is under suspicion."

I felt a sliver of relief. At least he said "everyone." "I assume you include Mrs. Wilson. And by food I assume you mean my pie. The point is everyone at the Bridge table ate pie and only one of them died. The one who was taking an overdose of her medication."

"Why would Blake tell you that his mother killed his grandmother? Somehow that surprises me."

"He didn't say that. Give me a little credit. I came to that conclusion on my own. Maybe Blake loved his grandmother and he hates his mother. I don't know. You're the detective. All I'm doing is…"

"I know what you're doing. And I want you to stop."

"Stop helping you find the murderer before he murders again?"

"Yes. Look, Hanna, you may think you're helping the police, but you're getting in our way. I don't want to accuse you of obstructing justice, but I will if I have to."

I frowned at him. "I'm surprised I haven't been hooked up to a lie detector machine yet myself. Doesn't seem fair. Then you'd know if I was lying or not."

"Don't push it."

"The least you can do is tell me if you'll give me the forty-eight hours I asked for before you… you know what. I've done everything I can to help you. You owe me."

"I'll keep that in mind," he said dryly. But he didn't say yes or no. He glanced at my chest as if he wanted to know if my heart was beating a little faster than usual under a layer of Lycra and terry-cloth. No way he could know that, could he?

"If you really want to help me, you'll go back to quietly baking pies," he said. "You're not exactly keeping a low profile. Sex parties, interviews, newspaper profiles."

"You saw that?"

"How could I miss it? Citizen of the Week. I didn't know you worked in the high-tech industry. Or that you formed your own company. Quite a change to baking pies."

"Not really. I was the marketing side of the business, my partner did the technical stuff. I'm still in marketing, only it's pie instead of data-based software."

"How did it work out?" he asked.

"What does this have to do with your current homicide investigation?" I asked.

"Nothing. I just wanted to know. Since we're getting caught up."

"Are we?" I asked edgily as I swiveled around in the chair he'd offered me. I shouldn't be so defensive. After all, in our previous conversation in which we got "caught up" I asked the questions and he answered them. Maybe it was my turn. As long as we didn't get too personal.

"Software," he said, "that's the cutting edge. And yet you came back to bake pies."

I sighed. "I think I told you, Grannie wanted to retire. I wanted a different life. I've got it."

"You must miss the high stakes in the computer business."

"Not any more than you miss the mean streets."

"What happened to your partner?"

"He left and …" I took a deep breath. There was no reason at all I had to tell Sam the sad story of my life and yet … and yet …

"He left and cleaned out our account. I don't know where Thad went. Or where our money went." At least I didn't have to tell Sam about my doomed personal relationship with Thad. The business part was bad enough.

"Did you try to find him?" he asked, his forehead creased in a frown.

"Of course. But there was nothing. He disappeared." I paused and tightened the sash on my terry robe. "I lost a lot of money, but I learned some valuable lessons, like 'Learn the rules and then play better.' I don't know if I'm playing any better, but I did learn the rules. It cost me plenty, but I can't complain. No, that's not true. I can complain, but I'm trying not to."

I walked toward the patio door. Sam was looking at me as if he'd never seen me before. Maybe I should have kept my mouth shut. But he's the one who was asking the questions. So I answered him. "Well, I'm going to water aerobics now. Strictly exercise. Nothing to do with anything else," I assured him.

Then, even though I knew I wasn't supposed to, I just couldn't resist asking, "How are the interviews going? I assume since you've made up your mind who's guilty and who's not, that they're just a formality."

"They're going fine," he said, his gaze steady. "I've actually learned quite a lot. The residents have been mostly forthcoming."

"Then you know by now that my grandmother couldn't have murdered Mary Brandt."

"I wish I could tell you more, but …"

"You can. I can keep a secret. Really."

"I'll keep that in mind," he said.

"Okay, I'm off to the pool," I said. I slipped into my rubber flip-flops and Sam held the door open for me. I felt his eyes on me as I walked out the door into the afternoon sunshine, grateful my grandmother was still free to participate in water exercise.

EIGHT

As I MADE MY way to the pool, I heard the loud beat of the music just when I was thinking water aerobics for senior citizens equals wimp city. When I got to the pool, the teacher or coach or whatever you call her was poised at the water's edge in a black Speedo, black tights, a pink headband around her forehead, and a whistle in her mouth. In the water at shoulder level, at least a dozen women faced her, waving their arms in time to the music.

Their leader shouted "Frog jump!" and they began jumping like frogs. I had to bite my lip to keep from laughing. Grannie saw me and beckoned to me to join them. I wiped the smile off my face. Piece of cake, I thought. I can kick like a frog.

The woman in the black tights turned her head and frowned at me. "You're late," she said.

"Sorry." I tossed my robe onto a chaise lounge, pulled my hair back in a rubber band, and jumped in the water. I joined the ladies in the back row, all in white rubber swim caps and goggles, one or two with floatation belts, and I tried to blend in with the crowd. I didn't want to show up anyone who was twice my age, like Grannie's friends Grace and Helen who waved to me.

I didn't need to worry about showing anyone up. I was panting after just a few minutes of frog kicking, followed by flutter kicking and finally egg-beater kicking. Worst of all, I wasn't able to keep up with the other women. Of course, it wasn't their first aerobics class. They'd been doing this for weeks.

Wait a minute. Contrary to what I'd just told Sam, I was there to spy, not kick. Of course, I needed the exercise too. After spending my days measuring flour, beating eggs, and rolling pie crust in the bakery, my thighs were crying out to be firmed up. Or crying out for some other reason. I told myself not to expect every activity I participated in to yield results on the muscle or murder front. I was not a detective. Besides, the class wasn't over. Surely there'd be time for talking with the gang during the cool-off period.

Cooling off meant swimming laps freestyle, which inhibited talking. Especially with the coach shouting instructions like "Rotate your hips." "Inhale, exhale." "Turn your head." "Breathe."

The woman was a tyrant, but the ladies seemed to love it. They thought they needed to be pushed and goaded into action. But I was a guest … she couldn't possibly have thought I was old enough to live there, could she? Since I was a guest, I didn't think I needed to be humiliated for my poor performance. I didn't even have to follow her instructions, but she obviously thought so. She kept blowing her whistle at me and shouting orders. I mostly ignored her and did my own freestyle stroke. If I tuned her out, it felt good to swim laps through the cool water in the afternoon sunshine and let my mind wander. This retirement business sure had its advantages.

"This is the life," I said to Grannie and her friends as we dried off around the pool. When Donna, Mary's Bridge partner, joined us, they greeted each other politely but it seemed to me there was a slight chill in the atmosphere. Did they believe Donna was just as big a cheater as Mary or at least an enabler? Or was that my imagination? The atmosphere thawed when Donna offered drinks from the thermos in her beach bag. "Happy Hour at the pool. My favorite time of day," she said.

"Delicious," Grace said, sipping from the paper cup Donna gave her. "What is it?"

"Cosmopolitans," Donna said. "Vodka and cranberry juice. I mixed them up earlier. Exercising always makes me thirsty."

I agreed that the exercise had definitely made me thirsty, but I couldn't help making the cranberry connection. Did anyone else? It was cranberries that killed Mary. Or rather the combination of cranberries with an overdose of her drugs. I looked around the circle of women wrapped in colorful beach towels or robes, but I saw nothing but polite smiles and heard nothing but gratitude for Donna's providing us with cocktails. I just hoped no one was taking an overdose of anything that would interact with cranberry juice.

Surely a mixed drink with just a shot of cranberry juice didn't threaten anyone, no matter what kind of meds they were on. It was when I saw Donna's hand tremble just slightly as she poured the drinks that I began to wonder. What did she have to be nervous about? Maybe worried the gang lumped her in the same category as her cheating partner. They probably did. How can one partner cheat and the other not be complicit?

But maybe I didn't understand her relationship with Mary. Maybe she wasn't a willing partner in the cheating scheme. Knowing what a dominant personality Mary had, that was a possibility.

Donna looked to be in good shape in her flirty ruffled see-through cover-up over her one-piece tummy-control bright red swimsuit. I wondered if she'd found a new partner. I wondered if she'd been dating Bob too. I also wondered if she'd been interviewed too. No hope of learning anything like that from Sam.

"So, how are the interviews going with the Chief of Police?" I asked, looking around the group with a casual air.

"He's so cute. Don't you just want to lock him up and keep him here with us?" Grace said.

"I feel so much safer with him around. Why can't he have a permanent office here?" Helen said.

"I know we're safer with him around, but he scared me," Donna said. Was that why her hands were shaking? "He asked me if I felt threatened. I said no, why should I? And he said if he didn't catch Mary's killer soon, he'd have to impose a curfew and have guards outside the main entrance. I think he suspects it's a serial killer." She pulled the sash of her beach cover-up tight around her waist and shivered. No wonder she was nervous if a serial killer was loose.

"A serial killer?" the ladies chorused. "At Heavenly Acres?"

"It's ridiculous," Grannie said.

"That's what I told him," Donna said.

"Me too," Helen said, and the others all nodded.

"He ought to concentrate on Mary's family instead of her friends here at Heavenly," Donna said. "They were her worst enemies. You should have heard what she told me."

"Did you tell the chief what she said?" I asked, dying to know what she'd said.

"You bet I did," she said, refilling everyone's paper cups from her thermos. "I gave him an earful. How Mary and her daughter were always fighting over her charity events. What to do with the money, how to divide it up. Who deserved it most. Mary wanted it to go to the dogs. Her daughter Linda was all for a new art museum with their names on it. Mary once said she felt like disinheriting them all." She shrugged. "Maybe she did. I wouldn't blame her. She had her lawyer up here about two weeks ago. Again."

"Who's that?" I asked with a casual I don't really care, just asking … manner.

"Seymour Evans, who works at the courthouse," she said. "Mary trusted him completely."

I wondered how rare that was for Mary to trust anyone. I felt like hugging Donna for giving me something to work on besides myself and my grandmother. Sam would be sorry he'd told me to drop my quest. He had all the resources of his office plus the right to barge in and ask questions anytime he wanted. But I planned to solve this mystery myself before he arrested my grandmother and made a fool of himself. Oh, yes, he'd be sorry he ever refused my help.

"Sam took notes too on his computer," Donna added. "He said I'd been very helpful." I didn't blame her for looking pleased. I'd be pleased to get a kind word out of our taciturn police chief. Then she screwed the top on her thermos and said she had a hair appointment in town.

After she left, there was a brief silence. I looked around the group, hoping to hear more details of their interviews, but no one said anything. I glanced at my waterproof watch. "I really have to get back to the shop. I've left my friend Kate minding the store."

"How's the pie business?" Grace asked.

"A little slow but I've got some ideas to perk up sales. I'm going to give out discount coupons for pie and coffee."

"That's brilliant," Grannie said with a proud smile. "Sales will go through the roof, you'll see."

I could have also said something about giving pie parties on the order of the sex toy party, but I didn't want to get into a description of sex toys with these women for fear they would tell me more than I wanted to know about their sex lives and their toys. Instead I said, "I'm thinking of going mobile." I didn't know I was going to say that. I wasn't thinking of going mobile until I saw that cupcake truck in the parking lot today.

No wonder Grannie looked surprised as she rubbed sun block on her arms, being ever vigilant against the late afternoon sunshine.

"Not that I'd give up the shop, but if I had a van I could drive around to where the action is."

"Action, in Crystal Cove?" Helen said, wrapping a beach towel around her shoulders.

"I know what you mean, but if people don't come to where the pie is, I've got to take the pie where the people are. For example, wedding receptions, retirement parties, barbecues." The more I thought about it, the more I liked the idea of getting out of the shop. I was not too proud to copy a success story. It would be good for me and my pies to hit the road occasionally.

"And memorial services," Grace said. "Your pie was such a hit at Mary's service. May she rest in peace."

"Why shouldn't she rest in peace?" Grannie asked.

Grace looked around. The pool was empty. None of Mary's friends around. If she'd had any friends. "I didn't want to say anything in front of poor Donna. She's suffered enough. No partner. But we all know Mary was a cheat and a conniving phony. She complained about everyone on the staff, her family, and her so-called friends. She bribed some of us and threatened the others." Grace lowered her voice. "Don't deny it. She's gone now and I'm not the only one who isn't sorry."

"I'm willing to forgive and forget," Grannie said. The others nodded. If Grannie could forgive Mary, why shouldn't they?

"We have a good life here with no worries and three gourmet meals a day," Grannie said. "It can be your life too," she told me, "in thirty, forty years. Heavenly Acres is a reward for a lifetime of hard work." I believe she spoke with tongue in cheek there. No more worries? When she was the chief murder suspect in her own hometown? She put up a good front, I'd give her that.

She should have added that Heavenly Acres was her reward for marrying a rich man who, although divorced from Grannie, had the goodness to leave his money to her in his will. I didn't say it. I didn't have to. She knew it as well as I did. I was happy for her. If he hadn't left her the money, she wouldn't have left me the shop, and if she hadn't left me the shop, I'd still be in the city, where everyone I knew either felt sorry for me or thought I'd gotten what I deserved. Here no one knew except Sam, and I didn't think he'd tell anyone. And so far he only knew the half of it.

I called Kate because I was running late and I wanted to stop in to see Sam. She said she'd sold three pies.

"I guess I just have the magic touch," she said proudly. "They came in because they'd read the article about you in the paper."

"I owe you," I said. I'd pay her back in babysitting.

I changed clothes in Grannie's room and stopped by the house-keeper's office next to the dining room where Sam was holding fort. The dining room was set up for dinner with crystal and silver and white tablecloths. Classical music filled the air. A delicious smell wafted from the kitchen. Lucky residents. Good company. Good food. Classy ambience. And an exciting murder investigation right in their midst. Better than those Solve a Murder Mystery parties you can host. This was real.

I raised my arm to knock on the door of the office when I heard voices from inside. I checked the interview schedule but there was no one listed for that time slot. Then I heard a light, feminine laugh. And a light, flirty, feminine voice say, "Go ahead and try one."

A few minutes later, a woman who looked like Lurline, the cupcake lady, wearing a pair of short shorts showing off firm slender thighs, high-heeled sandals, and a tight T-shirt came prancing out of Sam's temporary office. Her eyes were bright and her smile even brighter. She wasn't looking and bumped into me, sending a flat cardboard cake box flying and its contents of cupcakes dumped all over the floor.

"Watch where you're going," she said, bending down to scoop up her mini-cupcakes. I should have helped her, but I was in a kind of shocked state. Besides, she was younger and more agile than I was and it wasn't my fault she'd run into me.

"Oh, it's you," she said, doing a double-take when she was back on her feet. "I'm surprised you'd show up here after what you did."

Mystified, I stared at her. "What did I do?" Sure, I sold delicious pies, but she didn't seem to have any problem selling cupcakes.

"Don't pull the innocent act with me. Everyone knows you killed that old lady with your poison pie. Once everyone finds out you'll be out of business with your Upper Crust. Then I'll be the only sweet thing in this town."

She turned on her heels and walked down the hall and out the front door. I watched her go, feeling stunned. Suddenly I shivered. My muscles ached from a workout my grandmother did every other day. My hair was wet and straight and I hadn't reapplied any makeup. The contrast between Ms. Bright Eyes and myself was stark.

"What was she doing here?" I asked when Sam opened his door, told me to come in, and closed the door behind me. Then I saw a box of cupcakes on his desk and I knew. She'd come to tempt him with her wares.

"Lurline?" he said. "Delivering cupcakes for a birthday party. She has the residents decorate them. They seem to love it. She's very popular. Did you two meet? You have a lot in common."

"How do you figure?" I asked him. "She's ten years younger than I am, she has a van, and she makes cupcakes."

"You're both entrepreneurs and you both sell bakery goods."

I surveyed the cupcakes on his desk. Chocolate, caramel, coconut, banana, and that fabulous Meyer lemon, if I wasn't mistaken. They were all adorably decorated with sprinkles, twists of fruit or a ribbon of contrasting frosting, and I knew for a fact they tasted just divine.

"I thought you were on a fitness program," I said, sounding as crabby as I felt.

"I plan to leave them here. It's the least I can do. The staff has invited me to dinner. Crab Cioppino."

"How nice," I said. I tried not to sound bitter, but no one had invited me to dinner. I guessed I should just be grateful the conversation hadn't turned to murder for a change. "I suppose it's all in a day's work. I won't ask, but I assume it has something to do with your investigation."

He stood and stretched and towered over me. "You never know. My theory is that some people tend to speak more freely over dinner than in a small interrogation room."

"Yes I know. That's why you took me to dinner the other night. Was it worth it?"

"I think so. Sometimes it takes awhile for the payoff. Next time it's your turn."

I wasn't sure if it was my turn to buy him dinner or to grill him.

"Have a nice swim?" he asked.

"Very nice, thank you. Just FYI, at the pool this afternoon Donna told us Mary and her daughter had been fighting over the charity events. I suppose Mary's daughter filled you in on it."

"She did, " he said. "She has a different version than Donna does."

"Well, of course she does. But who has the most to gain money-wise by Mary's death? I assure you it isn't my grandmother. We won't know for sure until they read the will." He didn't say anything. "Or do you already know what's in it?"

"No matter who gets her money, you can't deny your grandmother has a lot to gain from Mary's dropping out of the Bridge tournament. Not money, but some things are more important."

"Like revenge or jealousy? I know all about the ten common murder motives, so don't patronize me. If what you mean by more important is Bridge, then you're right. But Grannie had nothing to fear from Mary at Bridge. Mary might have won a lot of games, scored a lot of points, but it was because she was cheating. Sooner or later she was going to be found out and kicked out. So why would Grannie kill her? She exposed her instead."

"It doesn't have to be either-or. She could expose her and then kill her."

"You just don't quit, do you?" I asked, exasperated.

"If I quit, I wouldn't have a job. I understand you're eager to clear your grandmother's name. I admire you for your loyalty, however misplaced it may be. You have a close relationship with your grandmother. She raised you. You owe her a lot."

"I don't owe her covering up a murder."

"Do you deny your grandmother is glad Mary's dead?"

"Who isn't? I've been talking to people. I know you don't want me to, but sometimes they talk to me. What am I supposed to do? Tell them to shut up? You know as well as I do that no one is sorry Mary's gone. Not Mary's daughter, her grandson, the hired help here at Heavenly, the Bridge players, or Bob Barnett. And that's just for starters." I was tired of protecting everyone. The only people I wanted to shield were myself and my grandmother. Everyone else was on their own.

Instead of grabbing a pen and making a list of the suspects I'd so generously given him the way I hoped, he just leaned back against the edge of the desk and stared at me, because he'd already made his own list and he was one step ahead of me. I had nothing more to say. Neither did he.

He finally opened the door to the office, and I got the message. He was tired of this whole mess. He wanted to close this case. So did I. It was too bad we couldn't work together, but that wasn't going to happen. I was free to go. For now.

Before I got to the front door to the building, Grannie caught up with me. "Where were you all this time?"

"Talking to Sam."

"Such an attractive man," she said. "I know he thinks a lot of you."

"Really? I'm glad to hear it. He doesn't want me to help him solve this murder, that's for sure."

"Don't let that stop you. And if there's anything I can do..."

"Nothing. Just try to forget about it."

She nodded, but I was sure neither one of us was going to forget about it until someone confessed. It wasn't going to be Grannie, and it wasn't going to be me.

"I forgot to invite you to dinner," she said. "Tonight is guest night. We're having Cioppino."

"I have to go home and close up the shop. Poor Kate has been sitting in for me all afternoon."

"Come back when you're done." She paused and gave me a long critical look. "And change into something nice. We dress up up here. I don't mean formal, I just mean ... nice."

"I noticed," I said with a glance at her wide-leg black silk pants, her bright green cardigan sweater, and her chunky gold necklace.

"I like bold, amusing things," she said, shaking the gold bracelets on both wrists as if I didn't know. Her silvery streaked hair was styled as if she'd just come back from a salon. I wished I had her stylist and her positive attitude. She had to be worried about being the prime murder suspect, but she sure hid it well.

When I got back to the shop, Kate was entertaining her two girls, Tenley and Emma, by letting them roll out dough in my kitchen. There was flour and water everywhere. But they were having a good time making little figures out of dough and baking them in the oven.

"How did it go?" Kate asked on her way out the door.

"I got my butt kicked in water aerobics," I said. "And I heard a lot of dirt about Mary's family. Oh, and the cupcake lady accused me of killing Mary."

Kate gasped.

"Shocking, isn't it? And this was right after she was in talking to Sam and plying him with her luscious cupcakes. And Grannie wants me to come back for dinner. It's guest night and the chef is making Crab Cioppino. I have to go."

Kate gave me a critical look not unlike the one I'd just gotten from my grandmother. "I'm changing my clothes, don't worry. I don't want to embarrass Grannie."

"What about Sam?"

"He told me I owe him a dinner. He's invited to guest night too. Even though he's there to investigate a murder and find one of them guilty, they all like him. They think he's adorable. They want him around to protect them from the serial murderer on the premises. Just in case there is one. The bad news is that he still thinks Grannie killed Mary Brandt and I'm covering for her." I felt like there must be steam coming out of the top of my head. "What do I have to do to prove we didn't?"

She didn't answer. She didn't need to. I knew the answer. Find the real killer.

I had an hour to get ready for dinner and I needed every minute to wash the chlorine out of my hair, blow it dry, slather lotion all over my body, and find something to wear that wouldn't embarrass Grannie. I kept thinking of the cupcake lady in her short shorts and her wild accusation. Where did that come from? The fog was drifting in off the ocean this evening as it often did in summer, so I needed something to wear that was warm yet summery. Back to my white pants, a stretchy black V-neck sweater, a silver necklace, and a big sweater shawl I wrapped around myself. I'd be glad to have it later when it got even cooler.

Then I filled a basket with an assortment of pies, thinking I'd offer them to the kitchen or serve them after dinner in the lounge. But would Lurline get there before me? I hung a "Closed" sign on the door just in case anyone came by. I could always hope. Tomorrow I'd get back to baking, punching up my business, and making money.

———

Crab season along the California coast starts in November and by summer is fading away. I was guessing that tonight's Crab Cioppino at Heavenly Acres might be made with frozen Dungeness crab in a traditional tomato-based sauce with wine and clam juice. It's a treat no matter what season or where you get it, down at the wharf or in the fanciest restaurant. Fresh crab right out of the water or frozen from the catch last winter.

I wasn't surprised to see there were huge paper bibs at every place. Grannie waved me to her table, but first I deposited my pies in the kitchen. In the dining room, I was seated between Grannie's friend Charline and her friend Debbie. The Chardonnay was already flowing, even before the salad course.

I knew Grannie had given my outfit the once-over when she spotted me at the door. I hoped I'd passed her test though I was way underdressed by her standards.

"Fortunately the dress code has changed," she said, probably thinking she'd make me feel better though I hadn't quite reached the Heavenly Acres standard. "When I first came up here a few years ago to see the place, women weren't allowed to wear pants in the dining room. The old-timers are still grumbling about the changes. They don't want Pilates, they don't want weight rooms. They want tea in the afternoon and the old dress code back."

"The ninety-somethings even try to censor the movies on Friday nights. No sex, no violence. That sums up their taste," Charline said.

"And their lives," Helen added. My table companions laughed appreciatively.

"These are the people twenty years older than us," Grace explained. "And they might as well be from another planet. Hope I don't turn into a crank when I get old."

"No chance," Grannie assured her, reaching across the table to squeeze her hand.

"I had no idea there was any tension here," I said. Except for the well-known tension around the Bridge table.

"Oh, it's nothing," Grannie said, taking a sip of Chardonnay. "Just a few old fogies trying to hold on to the past. They'll get over it."

"What about Mary?" I asked, ever on the alert for a new suspect or two. "I suppose she was on your side."

"Wasn't she!" Grace exclaimed. "I'll never forget the day her little grandson came to have lunch with Mary. He was wearing blue jeans. Not only did he get looks from old Mrs. Harms, Edward Vaughn grabbed him by the T-shirt and gave him a stern lecture. Mary hit the roof. Told him to take his hands off her grandson. I thought she was going to give him a karate chop. She could do it. She bragged she'd once been a first-degree Brown Belt. He had no business talking to Brandon that way."

"I remember that," Grannie said. "Then she formed the committee for change. Out with the old and in with the new. Happy hour. Hip Hop Dancing. Jazzercise. It worked. Now we're allowed to wear what we want in the dining room as long as it's in good taste, and we can eat with bibs tonight. Not dignified. That's what *they'd* say." Everyone nodded. She didn't have to explain who *they* were.

"Whatever you say about Mary," Charline said, "and I'd never speak ill of the dead. She was a pistol. You have to give her credit for doing what no one else had the guts to do."

Like cheating at Bridge, I thought.

"All so we girls have the privilege of wearing pants at the dinner table," Grace said. "And the men don't have to wear coats and ties anymore."

"She made a lot of enemies though," Helen said thoughtfully. "Besides old Edward Vaughn. He's still bitter. I didn't see him at Mary's memorial service. Not here tonight either. That group doesn't forget easily."

Charline nodded. "Like elephants."

I leaned forward, hoping to hear more. Perhaps a list of her enemies. Sam probably already had the list on his computer. As usual I was playing catch-up. If only he was at our table, I could gauge his reaction. I scanned the room again. I didn't see him.

"You notice they've all boycotted the dinner tonight. Mary wouldn't have been surprised. She'd say good riddance," Grannie said.

"Don't know what they're missing," a guest named Fred said. He was introduced as a friend of Grace's. "You can't live on the coast and not eat crab."

"You know the story of Cioppino?" Helen asked. Without waiting for an answer she said the fish dish was invented in San Francisco in the thirties on the wharf. "The fishermen would haul in their catch and everyone contributed something to the pot. So every day the Cioppino was different, but always delicious."

We all agreed and there was a moment of silence while everyone helped themselves to the warm sourdough bread baked there on the premises and served in the basket on the table.

Grannie paused and looked around the room. "No old-timers around tonight to make us feel guilty."

I studied her expression. I couldn't see a trace of guilt anywhere. How Sam could suspect her baffled me. Despite the video of her with the drugs in hand. She had innocent written all over her.

"I don't suppose they'll come to line dancing tonight either," Charline said.

"You can thank Mary that you didn't have to dress up tonight," Grannie told me with a pointed look at my casual sweater and pants. She seemed to be going overboard in her praise for Mary.

Trying very hard to say nice things about someone who wasn't very nice. As if Grannie was afraid someone was listening, someone who was trying to pin Mary's murder on her.

"But I do see some of the women in long dresses and men in jackets and ties," I noted.

"Sure. You can still dress up. If that's what floats your boat. Nobody says you can't. Old habits die hard," Helen said.

I could see that dinner here at Heavenly Acres was still an occasion. It was the highlight of the day, after a hard day of cards, stretching exercises, flower arranging, Ping-Pong, Yoga, Trivial Pursuit, and shuffleboard. Something to look forward to no matter what the menu.

"Crab Cioppino is a messy business. Put your bib on," Grannie instructed me, as if I was five years old again. Messy business or not, it didn't stop the residents from looking their best on all occasions.

Grannie's friends made a big thing out of my joining them for dinner. Said it was an honor to have me. As if I'd turned down a few dates to be there. I admit, it was flattering, but I cautioned myself not to get carried away. Not to get too comfortable hanging with the aged. This life was not for me. Not yet. Not for thirty-some years, as Grannie reminded me. And even then, how would I afford it? At the rate I was going, at seventy I'd be right where I am now, struggling to make ends meet by baking pies.

Hungry after my bout with the aerobics group, I dug into my Caesar salad with homemade croutons and grated aged Parmesan cheese. With food like this, no wonder the monthly fees were astronomical at Heavenly Acres.

"Do you eat like this every night?" I asked Charline who had brought a date, an attractive man about her age who she introduced as Kevin, "a good friend."

"It's always good," she said, "but the Crab Feed is special. The crab season is almost over, so this may be our last crab dinner. No matter what the menu, we all get two free guest invitations a month, the rest we have to pay for. I've never been so popular," she said, and she gave her friend Kevin a flirtatious smile. She turned to me and said, "Louise is thrilled to have you here."

"I'm thrilled to be here," I said. My attention was riveted by the waiters bringing huge steaming bowls of Cioppino to the tables. The smell of saffron, crab, and spicy tomato sauce made me salivate. The huge Dungeness crab claws were cracked, but it was necessary to pick up the claws and extract the chunks of sweet meat with your small crab fork or your fingers.

The waiters brought stacks of fresh napkins and wipe-n-dries.

"I brought a few pies with me," I told Grannie.

"Enough for everyone?"

"I think so."

"We'll have them in the lounge with coffee," she said. Then she stood and rapped on her glass with her knife.

"I want to invite everyone to the lounge after dinner for a slice of pie from my granddaughter Hanna's shop, The Upper Crust." she said. "Stand up, Hanna, and take a bow."

I stood and said a few words about how happy I was back in town carrying on the pie tradition. And that I hoped to see them at my shop for pie and coffee tomorrow morning. I was offering a Saturday morning Heavenly Acres special for all residents. They clapped enthusiastically.

NINE

After dinner I thanked them for their hospitality and I went to the lounge, where Grannie and her friends helped me serve pie. The kitchen staff had provided us with plates and forks and were pouring coffee. I realized that one of the young women might have been the one who Mary had accused of stealing her earrings. I was glad to see she still had a job here. I hoped Mary's family had not pursued her claim of being robbed by the poor girl. Why did I believe her and not Mary? I just did.

It was gratifying to hear so many compliments about my pie.

"This chocolate with the marshmallows. What do you call it?" a lady who was definitely not one of the ninety-something oldies asked me. I could tell by the quilted chambray vest she wore with a pair of tapered white silky slacks and some trendy wedge sandals.

"Rocky Road," I said.

"It's delicious," she said, introducing herself as Jenny Moller. "I must come by your shop. Are you open every day?"

"Every day but Sunday," I said. *Except for when I'm out playing detective.* "If you call ahead, I can make any kind of pie you like. Of course, berry pies are popular this summer. Or cherry crumb, or cherry peach crumb. Or deep-dish peach, my personal favorite, in an all-butter crust."

"I wonder... I'm having a little party in my apartment next week. Dessert and coffee."

"For how many?"

"Oh, ten or twelve."

"How about one fruit pie like California Raisin and Maple Crunch Pie. It's so different I guarantee you'll be the first to serve it at Heavenly Acres. And I guarantee everyone will like it or your money back. I suggest serving that along with a Rocky Road or a Black-Bottom Raspberry Cream Pie. It's got a crust made of crushed chocolate wafers, the chocolate filling is rich and decadent, and it's topped with fresh raspberries and whipped cream." She looked interested so I closed the deal by adding, "It's rich, creamy, and decadent." Then I reached into my pocket and gave her my card. She promised to call me with an order.

I glanced over my shoulder to make sure Grannie hadn't heard me guarantee she'd like the pie. She never guaranteed anything like it in her life. She didn't need to. Everyone loved her pies. She was an institution. Some day I would be too. Fortunately, no one knew I was implicated as an accessory to murder—never a good recommendation for a baker.

I finally caught a glimpse of Sam across the room with a cup of coffee in his hand. Was he eating a piece of my pie? No, he wasn't. He was staring at me though. He couldn't be surprised to see me there.

"Wherever there's pie, you're there," he said after making his way through the crowd to the table.

"Or vice versa. Maybe that could be my slogan," I said.

"Do you need one?"

"I'd like to sell more pies," I said. "Since I can't count on you and your police buddies. Guess what? Saturday is California pie day."

"What does that mean?"

"I'm not sure, since I just decided to celebrate it. Actually I just made it up. Some people need an excuse to eat pie. It's my job to give them one. I was thinking I might set up tables outside with umbrellas like in France and I'll have specials. I'll make savory pies like French Canadian meat pies as well as the old summer French favorites like quiche. I'd appreciate it if you'd spread the word. Or is that a conflict of interest?"

"How's that?" he asked. "What kind of conflict?"

"Between cupcakes and pie."

"Come on, Hanna, there's enough room in this town for both of you."

What about in your life, I wondered. How much room is there for someone else? I could ask myself the same thing.

"How did you like the dinner?" I asked. "I didn't see where you were sitting." What I really wanted to know was, who did you sit with and what did you learn?

"I was over by the windows," he said. "Are you here in your professional capacity?"

"Always," I said. "I just made a future sale. What about you? You don't have to worry about sales. You work for the county." I lowered my voice. "You get paid whether you arrest someone for the murder of Mary Brandt or not."

"I have a duty to solve crimes any day, anytime. Whatever it takes. I like my job. And I like the town."

"I know. I heard your speech, remember? You like the hills and the beaches and the safe small-town atmosphere."

"I want to keep that atmosphere. I can't do that if there's a dangerous murderer loose."

"What if there isn't one? Would you still feel necessary? Wanted? Appreciated?"

He ignored the questions. "There is," he said. "Don't worry. I'll find him or her. Don't take any chances. Leave it to me."

I didn't say I would. I didn't say anything. At an impasse, we walked out together without speaking. I saw Grannie's bright eyes following us and I knew what she was thinking. Hanna and Sam, together again. Hanna and Sam sneaking off for a quickie. Better she should think that than think *There goes Hanna defending me from murder charges*. I didn't want her to worry.

"I don't know what *you* talked about at dinner, but I heard Mary Brandt had formed a committee to change the rules around here, like the dress code."

I slanted a glance at his face. No reaction. Why was I not surprised? It struck me like a sledgehammer that Sam already knew everything I knew. He knew it earlier and he knew it better. What was the point of my sleuthing when he had an office here and he had the badge of authority behind him? Although he didn't wear a badge, everyone knew who he was. My shoulders slumped. I exhaled. All my confidence was eroding.

"I told you not to try to help me," he said.

"I know what you told me, but can I help it if people tell me things?" I was tired. I'd been up since five baking and I'd exercised and swam laps. As usual he didn't answer me. "All right. I'm not confiding in you again. Ever. You don't need me. I know that. You already know everything I know, don't you?"

"Probably. The point is that it's dangerous to go around poking into people's lives."

"I assume you're referring to my faulty oven. For your information, I'm not poking into anything or anyone. I'm listening, that's all. Isn't that what they teach you at the Police Academy?"

"That's right. But you're not at the Academy. You're a private citizen. Trust your public servants to do the job. That's what we're here for."

Why did I always have the feeling he was reading something out of a manual? That he didn't take anything I said seriously? Maybe he'd accuse me of killing Mary so I'd rat on my grandmother and vice versa. All he had to do was wait until I folded and charge me with murder. Until then we would both pretend to be looking for the real killer. I wished I could think of a way to quiz Blake's mother the way he had, but how to finagle a visit to her house without making her so mad she'd clam up? It was much easier to confine my investigation to the retirement home. I decided to zero in on old Edward and/or Bob. I didn't care which one of them did it, I'd take whatever I could get.

"If you continue to act like a detective, you're going to draw attention to yourself. You'll feel threatened, and you may actually be threatened, and I'll have to provide you twenty-four-hour, round-the-clock police protection," he said. "It's a tough job, but somebody has to do it," he said.

Was Sam actually lightening up? I could only hope. "Would that somebody be you?" I asked.

"Since we're understaffed," he said. "I'd have to volunteer."

I had a vision of Sam guarding the front door of the pie shop. I'd forget about Mary Brandt and I'd invite him in. We'd talk about old times. It would get late. I'd whip up a French Canadian Meat Pie, the savory tourtiere made with ground beef, pork, and chicken stock under an oven-browned pie crust. It's the kind they usually eat at Christmas, but delicious anytime, especially on a foggy California evening in a deserted pie shop. I'd pour two glasses of red wine. He'd forget he ever mentioned my grandmother or suspected me of anything except trying to be a modest success in this town. He'd follow me upstairs. I'd take off my apron—no he'd take it off for me. His hands would linger…

I shook my head and took a deep breath. I was getting too excited. Forget that vision. Face reality. Instead of any personal police protection, Sam would probably send one of his overweight deputies to stand at the door with strict instructions to lay off the pie, while Sam was out joy riding in Lurline's Cupcake Wagon.

"Or I'll put you into the witness protection program," he offered. "You'll have to change your identity, but you're good at that." He gave me a rare half smile and my knees buckled. I blamed it on fatigue, not leftover teenage lust.

"How do you mean?"

"You're not at all the same as you were in high school."

"You've changed too."

To be certain, I studied his face. I was wrong. Behind the lined forehead, the blue eyes, and the reluctant tight smile, there was the same Sam Genovese I'd once been madly in love with. Teenage love combined with angst and uncertainty and insecurity. It was still all there, no matter how hard I tried to convince myself I was over him.

"Well," I said, trying hard to project a mature, cool but friendly air. "I'm sold. You convinced me. No more sleuthing. Time to pack up my pie pans and head home."

"Good girl," he said, looking relieved. I bit back a smile of triumph. He believed me. I'd fooled him. He put both hands on my shoulders and leaned forward. The hall was empty. The voices inside the lounge faded away. I didn't know what he'd do next. I don't think he did either. I held my breath, knowing I should leave but unable to move.

Then I thought about any leftover pie and I decided to take a piece to old Edward Vaughn tonight, seeing as he didn't attend the dinner. Who would turn down a woman with a piece of pie in her hand? That way, I'd have a chance to talk to him before Sam did. And Sam would never know. I'd have a different attitude than a policeman. Non-threatening. I could do it. And if that worked out, next I'd stop in and see poor Bob, still recovering from his attack. He might like a slice of chocolate marshmallow pie, which would inspire him to tell me how he felt about Mary. I knew what Sam would say but he'd never find out, and if he did, well, my story was that I was only serving pie. Could I help it if people insisted on telling me they'd committed a crime?

"It was good to see you," I said to Sam. He looked a little surprised to see me step back and not give in to temptation. As if he thought I'd fall under his spell like I once did and follow him around town like a lovesick bullmoose crossing the highway, oblivious to the traffic.

"I'm printing out discount pie and coffee coupons for all the merchants to hand out," I said. "I'll put some in your mailbox tonight." I looked around. The crowd was thinning out. "Well, I'll collect my pies and say goodbye to Grannie."

"Not staying for line dancing?"

"Are you?"

He shook his head. "Need any help loading your car?"

"No thanks."

What was going on here? Sam hanging around, making small talk, offering to help me? Maybe he'd picked up on my independent vibes, and my overeager willingness to forget sleuthing. He seemed eager to make sure I left before I did something unapproved by himself. Which was almost everything I did, outside of pie baking.

"I hope you're not going to do anything unauthorized," he said. "Remember, no breaking and entering. You need a search warrant to enter anyone's dwelling unauthorized."

"I couldn't do that," I said earnestly, "anymore than you could bake pies. Did you even taste my pie tonight?" I knew the answer. He hadn't. "What do you have against marshmallows?"

"Those white blobs? They're made of sugar, aren't they?"

"You're hopeless. Fortunately I have other fans." I gave him my best cool smile. "Bye."

I was afraid he was going to wait and follow me to find out where I was going with my leftover pie. Knowing him, he might suspect I had plans. I said I'd forgotten something and went back to the lounge, where I watched something on television for five long minutes. When I couldn't wait another second, I walked slowly to the front desk. No Sam. I checked out a map of the facility with the residents' names printed next to their apartment. I jotted down Edward's number as well as Bob Barnett's. I just hoped I wouldn't send Bob into a relapse with a piece of pie and a few questions. Surely he'd be glad to help my efforts to remove him from the suspect list.

Then back in the small kitchen off the dining room I ignored the Rocky Road Pie, still hurt by Sam's "white blobs" description, and cut two slices of Butter Pecan Apple Crumb Pie. I could have offered a piece to Sam, but I couldn't take another of his refusals. He obviously wasn't a pie person and nothing I could do would change him so I decided to quit trying. Butter Pecan Apple Crumb is traditional and irresistible at the same time, in my opinion. It had been so popular tonight there wasn't much left. I was sliding the pieces on plates when Grannie startled me by bursting into the small kitchen.

"You're coming to line dancing, aren't you?"

"I don't think so. I'm just packing up."

"You have to stay. You know who's here? Mary's grandson Blake. He's just as nice and polite as he could be. Which proves to me that his grandmother wasn't murdered at all. She died of natural causes. I ought to know since I was there."

I frowned. But I didn't ask her to explain that bewildering piece of logic.

"He just asked me if I'd seen you," she said.

"You think he's worth staying for?" I asked with a knowing smile. Grannie was a sucker for a good-looking man, which is partly why she was married more than once. Each time to a strikingly handsome man. Her luck was that Husband Number Two was not only good looking but rich too.

"In case you haven't seen him since high school, he's a hunk, as you young people say. And soon he'll be rich."

"I guess you're referring to Mary's will, but I don't think anyone knows what's in it except her lawyer and I don't imagine he's talking. I thought we all agreed she'd left her fortune to the dogs."

"Whatever," Grannie said with a smile. How like her to be thinking about me and my future when hers was in peril. If I were her and accused of murder, I'd be holed up in my apartment sobbing myself to sleep at night. Not her.

"Mary might have set aside a few million for Blake," Grannie said. "He's the only one she ever had a good word for in the whole family. So I say you should stick around. Line dancing is fun and it's good exercise. And Blake needs a reason to stay in town a little longer, maybe for good." She stopped and looked at the two pieces of pie I'd sliced. "Or do you have other plans?"

"Just cleaning up here," I said airily.

"What were you and Sam talking about?"

"The usual. His job, my job. Life in Crystal Cove."

"How does he like his job?" She asked this as if she hadn't recently spent time with him in a job-related activity and wasn't the least bit worried about Sam's objectives.

"It seems he likes being back in the Cove. I guess he wishes no one would die on his watch. Then he could concentrate on crime prevention and set up his community outreach programs, like maybe a cop school for ordinary citizens. I understand it's all the rage these days." Actually I had no idea if it was all the rage, but it should be. And Sam was the perfect guy to bring it to Crystal Cove.

"That's a great idea," she said. "I've always wanted to learn to shoot a gun."

I didn't ask her who she wanted to shoot it at.

"How's your friend Bob doing?"

"He's better. He should be. You should see the line of visitors he has."

"All women?"

"That's only natural," she said. "Women are the usual caregivers. I just hope he isn't getting overtired."

I didn't mention his ED condition and I didn't ask about their relationship, though I wondered if it had survived his illness and Mary's interference and her demise. I didn't mention either that I intended to be one of his visitors tonight, if I could get in.

She finally gave up on trying to drag me to line dancing or set me up with Blake. When she left, I put the pie I'd cut into my basket and headed to the elevator. While waiting, I heard the honky-tonk music and saw flashing lights coming from the recreation room across the hall. A man named Big Dave was calling the steps. I tried to blend into the scenery so no one would drag me in to join them. I did wonder as I rode up to the third floor how these sophisticated rich oldsters had gotten into dancing to music like "Bus Stop" and "Electric Boogie." I was just glad it wasn't me.

I found Edward's apartment at the end of the hall on the corner, meaning he'd have a large place with two big balconies. I knocked but no one answered. I looked at my watch. It wasn't that late, unless you were ninety-something and you'd had a hard day of fighting off upsetting changes at your retirement home like weight-lifting classes and casino parties that threatened your genteel life style. On the other hand, if I lived here I might hide out in my quarters to escape line dancing too.

When he finally came to the door I was startled by his appearance. I'd pictured an old guy in flannel pajamas and a full set of dentures. This man was wearing a Playboy smoking jacket, belted at the waist, in red satin lined in black, and an ascot tie around his neck. I swear he looked like an older version of Hugh Hefner and just as dapper. This was the old fogie?

"Hello," I said cheerily. "I'm Hanna Denton. Louise Denton's granddaughter. We haven't met but I heard you weren't at the dinner this evening so I brought up a piece of pie. Butter Pecan Apple Crumb. I made it myself."

"How thoughtful," he said after taking a moment to digest my opening statement. "Won't you come in? I thought pie baking was a lost art."

"Not at all."

"That looks delicious," he said, taking the plate out of my hands. "Better than the usual dessert here."

I wished Sam could hear that. There were some things old people could teach the young. Like manners. It didn't matter if he liked pie, wanted any, or thought it was unhealthy. All that mattered was to act like you liked it. I might learn nothing about Mary's death from this old geezer who dressed like Cary Grant, but it was worth the trip to the third floor. I went in and sat down in a stiff-backed chair at his invitation. I noticed all the furniture was dark and heavy. There were windows on two sides of the room. The view of the cove and the golf course must be beautiful during the day.

"You've lived here quite a while then?" I asked.

"Twenty-odd years. I've seen people come and go, mostly go. Who did you say your grandmother was?"

"Louise Denton. She's relatively new. When she retired I took over her pie shop." I paused. "She plays Bridge."

"My wife and I played Bridge," he said. "She wasn't very good at it. So many women consider it as a social function. A chance to gossip. Which is why we lost so often." He shook his head. "She didn't understand that Bridge is much more than that. It's a way of life, a challenge, the last communal campfire before the end of life. If you get my meaning."

I nodded although I wasn't sure I got his meaning. "Do you still play?" I asked.

"Not anymore. I would if they'd take it seriously. But they don't. I'm not a people person and I try to avoid the women around here who only live to socialize."

"My grandmother takes Bridge seriously," I said, feeling like I had to stand up for her. "She plays either for money or for points to advance to the next level. She was playing with Mary Brandt the day she died at the Bridge table."

"That woman," he exclaimed. "Was she any good?"

"At Bridge? I don't know. I know she was suspected of cheating."

"Then she deserved to die," he said.

I thought it was a bit harsh of him, but I imagined he was thinking of the argument he'd had with Mary over the dress code. He didn't mention it.

"I understand the police are investigating Mrs. Brandt's death. They call it a murder. My grandmother is worried that they suspect her of killing Mary."

"Why is that?" he asked, leaning forward in his chair. "What would she have to gain?"

"They were playing against each other. Without Mary as an opponent, my grandmother would have a better chance to move ahead in the state tournament."

The Tiffany lamp on the table cast a shadow on his gaunt lined face so I couldn't tell what his expression was. Was he shocked? Sad? Oblivious? Or totally in agreement that eliminating a Bridge opponent was understandable and desirable?

"But you believe your grandmother is innocent."

"Yes, of course. My grandmother is very competitive but she's not a murderer. What really angered her was not that Mary Brandt was a superior player. It was the part about her cheating. For her and some of the others like yourself, it's more than just a game. Not just a social occasion," I said. "It was a very cutthroat game, and it was morally important to win and move ahead in the tournament." I didn't want him to think my grandmother was some flighty old lady who didn't take the game seriously, like his wife. Grannie was a serious contender and I wanted him and everyone else to respect that.

He laced his bony fingers together and fixed me with a steady stare.

I felt the need to expound on the situation. "So she called Mary out when her cheating became obvious, and accused her of transmitting signals to her partner. Then Mary passed out and never recovered."

"That doesn't sound like murder," he said. Of course he would say that if he was the one who did the murdering.

"No, not that part. But there's a question of poison. There were pills on the table. Mary might have been given the wrong ones along with a piece of pie I made. Cranberry, not apple. It sounds as if the combination did her in."

"Maybe it was her time to go. Do you believe in predestination?"

"I . . . I'm not sure."

"I do. That doesn't mean we can't choose our destiny. It just means that some people choose the wrong path. They can't help it. This Mary chose to cheat at cards. She also chose to allow her grandson to violate the dress code. Hence she was punished."

Aha. So he did remember who she was. "You really believe that's why she died?"

"It seems certain, since she expired at the Bridge table. A punishment made for the crime."

I nodded. What else could I do? Accuse him of dropping by the card room and substituting a stronger dose of her medication to hasten her death? Or putting a hex on her? All because her innocent grandson broke the dress code? I could ask him the same question, *What would you have to gain*? I didn't need to ask. The motive was so clearly revenge.

The phone rang and he picked it up from a small end table where it stood in its stand.

"What is it now?" he asked. "Yes, I will." He walked to the sideboard holding the phone at his ear and surveyed a selection of small plastic containers on a silver tray. "I have it right here in front of me along with some herbal supplements and my vitamins. And a piece of pie a kind lady has just brought me. You don't need to call every four hours," Edward said. "My body is weak but my brain is still intact." Then he hung up.

"I hope you don't bother your grandmother with reminders to take her pills," he said to me. "Just because we're old doesn't mean we need constant supervision. Now if you'll excuse me," he said. "It's past my bedtime."

"I'm sorry to keep you up," I said.

"If you have any more questions about predestination, stop by and see me. I play dominoes every afternoon. Do you play?"

"No, not really."

"Bridge?"

"No."

"That's too bad that you young people have no time or interest in it. Bridge is an excellent game. It's an old game that was once known as Whist. In the 1930s I began playing Contract Bridge, as it's known today. It's the greatest game ever invented. Making a beautiful play, executing a perfect defense. There's nothing like it. It stays in your mind until the next day, the next week, sometimes forever. Unfortunately, some people here at Heavenly Acres have spoiled it for the others. Perhaps you know who I mean. It has become corrupted. Not by your grandmother, if what you say is true. Once it was an oasis, an escape from the real world. A game of strategy. That was a long time ago before ... " He closed his eyes and he appeared to drift off.

I stood and prepared to leave. I noticed his medicine laid out on the sideboard. I walked over and scooped up a few pills from a tiny container marked Coumadin. When Edward opened his eyes I was startled and halfway to the door. I thought he was asleep.

"By the same token Bridge can be a very dangerous game," he continued as if no time had transpired and nothing had happened. "Hurt feelings, hard feelings, jealousies and hatred. Especially here on the premises these days. I wouldn't recommend it to you."

Wow, what a lot of ideas he'd unloaded on me. Maybe he didn't have many visitors. Maybe he'd been saving up his speech for the right moment. Then I knocked on his door looking for evidence to pin the crime on him. I didn't feel I'd gotten what I wanted. But I'd tried. Had Sam tried too? I should ask Edward if he'd had a visit from a cop. But I didn't. I'd find out from Sam.

I was left with the impression that for Edward's generation, it was important to be articulate as well as a good Bridge player.

"I'll remember that," I said and then I left. But I wasn't sure what to remember, that Bridge was a dangerous game or that it was too bad I didn't play this excellent and beautiful and dangerous game or that rule-breakers deserved to die. I was quite aware of just how dangerous Bridge was; it obviously led to the death of Mary Brandt. Unless Edward killed her because of what her grandson did. That had nothing to do with Bridge—or did it?

TEN

As I walked down the stairs to Bob Barnett's apartment, it occurred to me Edward might have been warning me not to play the "dangerous game" of Bridge or I'd meet the same fate as Mary Brandt. He had a whole arsenal of pills there on his sideboard, an overdose of which could be dangerous. Which was why his relative had called to make sure he took his medicine. But who here wasn't on some kind of drug at their age? Even if, like Grannie, her drugs were simply harmless but effective stimulants. Anyone who lived here at Heavenly Acres could have dropped by the card room with the usual kibitzers and substituted something lethal for Mary's stash of medicine in her little pillbox. Too bad they hadn't been caught on the surveillance camera for Sam to see instead of Grannie. If only she hadn't turned the damn thing off.

What old Edward had to gain by killing Mary was the satisfaction of seeing her pay a price for violating the rules of the house. Which was no small prize. He had plenty of pills to use if that's what killed her. He clearly didn't like her or what she'd done here at Heavenly. Was that enough of a motive?

I was hesitant to bother Bob Barnett, who I assumed was still recovering from his minor heart attack that had prevented him from attending the crab fest, but I had to give it a try. I was here. I had the opportunity and I had the motive, which was to find somebody other than Grannie to pin the murder on. If anybody asked, I was simply stopping by his place with the pie to see how he was. Grannie had mentioned a long line of female visitors. I hoped I could slip in with the others.

I stood outside his door and heard voices inside. If that was Grannie, she'd probably prefer that I left them alone. If it was another woman, Grannie would probably prefer that I interrupt whatever was going on inside. What would Bob want? He was not supposed to get excited. Was he allowed to eat pie?

I knocked softly. I listened for a long moment. Then I heard someone say, "Don't answer it." That's what got me. Nobody should be telling these oldsters what to do. I knocked again.

"Anyone interested in some pie?" I said.

A few minutes later Bob came to the door. He was wearing a dark blue terrycloth robe, striped pajamas under it, and a pair of leather slippers. Nothing on the order of Edward's outfit, but still nice. Still appropriate to receive visitors.

"Hi, I'm Hanna, Louise Denton's granddaughter. I noticed you weren't at dinner and I thought you might like some pie. Unless you're on a diet."

"How nice of you," he said with a smile. "I am on a diet, but pie is allowed. Definitely allowed. Do you know Charmaine?"

A youngish-looking blond woman in a long skirt and a black sweater looked a little nervous. Why? Wasn't she supposed to be there?

"Nice to meet you," I said.

She edged around us and went to the door. "I'll say goodnight." She paused as if hoping someone would insist that she stay. No one did. "See you tomorrow," she said and left.

"I hope I haven't interrupted anything," I said, searching Bob's face to see how disappointed he was I'd knocked on his door. I couldn't tell by his benign expression. Of course I hoped I had interrupted any kind of tête-à-tête with anyone besides Grannie.

"Ever since I've been ill, I've been more popular than before. It's rather bewildering," he said with a shy smile.

How modest, I thought. He has to know he's the hot ticket among the seventy-somethings, and no wonder. He looked much better than the last time I'd seen him lying on the patio after Mary's memorial service. He could be quite a knockout when he was completely well and had all his parts in working order. No wonder all the women were crazy about him.

"You're Louise's granddaughter," he said. "She's told me so much about you. How you're taking over the pie business. If you keep up the good work, some day you may be as good as she was."

I was taken aback for a moment. It was true, I probably wasn't as good as Grannie. How did he know? She probably told him. I preferred to think I wasn't worse, I was just different. Then I remembered the day he had his attack.

"I must apologize if my coconut cream pie was responsible for your … uh … illness the day of Mary Brandt's service."

"Not at all," he said graciously. "I'm allowed to eat anything I want, in moderation of course. The day in question I may have overdone it."

Overdone the ED pills, I thought, or the pie? Or both?

"Did you know Mrs. Brandt?" he asked.

"Not really, but I've heard a lot about her," I said cautiously.

"It's all true," he said wryly. "Believe me. I have a hard time believing she's really dead. Even now. My shrink has been treating me for something called Geriatric Depression. I hold her responsible."

Depression? He looked so cheerful.

"I have mood swings," he explained, as if he'd heard my unspoken question.

I was puzzled. "Mrs. Brandt is responsible?" I asked. "But she's dead."

"Is she? Did you see a coffin? A body? I didn't."

I had to admit I hadn't seen a body. But I wondered if Bob was manic or truly depressed or maybe a little deranged. If what Grannie said was true, wasn't it more likely he was just extremely happy that Mary was dead? He sure didn't look depressed to me.

"I know what you're thinking," he said. "Bob doesn't seem depressed. But the Bob Barnett you see is now on medication. And he will be until he knows for sure she's gone."

Now I was getting worried. He was referring to himself in the third person. Was it possible Mary wasn't dead or was Bob a little crazy?

He picked up a small bottle of pills from the small table at his side. I noticed they were in the same type of pillbox as Mary's pills. That special pharmacy was sure getting a lot of business from Heavenly Acres.

"My collapsing at the Brandt woman's memorial service was because I hadn't taken my medication that day. I was upset."

"Because you lost a good friend," I suggested, knowing that wasn't the case. At least not in Grannie's version. Maybe he was too embarrassed to talk about his ODing on his ED pills.

"No," he said loudly. "That woman was no friend of mine. I can say it now. I'm not sorry she died." He sat down and buried his head in his hands. Good thing he was on antidepressants. If he had a bipolar disorder, that would explain these sudden mood swings. I'd hate to see him if he wasn't on his medication.

"If she hadn't died, I would have had to move. I couldn't live under the same roof as that woman. Before I met her, I'd never seen a psychiatrist. Now I go every week. Without these little pills that are not commercially available, I'm a different person. Because here I'm what's known as a resident with unusual health needs."

I nodded as if I understood. All I could think of was how Mary died from some special pills.

"I don't even know what I was capable of before I got the right medication," he said.

Like murder? Like more sexual activity? I squinted trying to read the tiny print on the label. What were those pills?

"You're not the only one who had strong feelings about Mrs. Brandt. Either they loved her or they ... didn't."

He leaned back in his chair and crossed his legs. I remained standing, not knowing what else to do or what else to say. Of course, I wanted him to confess to her murder.

"Put me down in the 'didn't' column," he said. Then he looked up. "Thank you for the pie."

I took that as a dismissal, said goodnight, and tiptoed out, wondering if Grannie had noticed that Bob was … how to put it? A little off.

Before I collected the leftover pie from the pantry, I stood in the doorway of the rec room watching the residents move forward in a line facing the wall. They were listening to instructions from the teacher while the music blasted out into the hall. Laughter floated in the air along with the lyrics to "Achy Breaky Heart." I have to say it looked like they were having a good time. I couldn't make out any faces in particular, but I assumed Grannie and her pals were all in there dancing side by side, doing the same steps with flushed faces, breathless and giddy from all the exercise. I hoped Bob would be up to dancing one of these days. If only he could see Mary's dead body. Maybe that would make him feel better. Now I knew he had extra pills to substitute in Mary's pillbox and a strong motive for getting rid of her. I wanted to tell Sam what I found out, but what would he say? That was a no-brainer. He'd say "Stay out of it."

I spotted Grannie dancing and asked myself who would have thought when she was my age struggling to make a go of the pie business that she'd end up in a full-care facility, surrounded by new furniture, good food, good friends, and enough activities to keep an army fit and stimulated. All that and a boyfriend too. Unless Bob Barnett was fooling around with other women, like the one in his room tonight. It was possible. If she could cheer up the poor guy, who was I to complain? I didn't know whether to mention her to Grannie or not. Probably not. I loved seeing her dancing and having fun with her friends, forgetting at least temporarily about being a murder suspect.

When I left Heavenly Acres, the fog had crept in like a cool gray blanket that hugged the ground. I stood outside looking at the lights in the windows, hearing the music wafting out into the night air. And I bounced ideas around in my head. Bob or Edward? Mary's daughter or …? It had to be one of them. It just had to be.

I turned on the heater in Grannie's old car for the short ride home. The lights were on in one corner of the police station across the street. Sam working late? Why? Going over statements from residents and suspects? Otherwise, it was another typical quiet night in Crystal Cove. It was good to get back to the shop and my little apartment above the store. And as much as I resented his know-it-all attitude, it was good to know Sam was on duty in case he was right and someone wanted to harm me or my oven.

I went in and made up a stack of hand-printed discount coupons for pie and coffee, and cut them into strips so I could hand them out to anyone and everyone. I put some in an envelope and went across the street to deposit them in Sam's mailbox with a note thanking him for doing his part to beef up my business. I glanced at his lighted window and I thought I saw a shadow of a figure inside. I thought about tapping on his window, but I was afraid I'd be greeted with a firearm. Yes, even in this peaceful little town where nothing ever happens. So I went back home feeling a little let down.

Alone in bed with Grannie's giant scrapbook filled with pie recipes, I wondered if life here above the shop in Crystal Cove was a little too quiet. That's what Blake hinted at. Not that I wanted to go back to the city. Not that I was ready for communal life at Heavenly Acres either, but I was ready for a more active social life.

Not line dancing or Bridge, but something. Something besides sex parties and pie baking.

But first things first. Find out who killed Mary Brandt. I took out a blank sheet of typing paper from my desk and wrote a list of suspects. To be perfectly fair, I put Grannie's name on top just as Sam would have done. Her motive—ambition. Next I listed Melissa, Mary's granddaughter, and next to her name I put her motive—greed (jewelry). Number three was old Edward, who hated Mary—his classic motive was self-protection and revenge. Grannie's boyfriend Bob was next. I'd call his motive fear, desperation with a large helping of insanity. Of course, there was also the worker woman who wanted to get back at Mary too.

Now what? How was I going to find out which one of them did it and prove it to Sam's satisfaction? And did I really have all the suspects on this list? I added Linda, Blake's mother, and her motive—greed, but I thought she was a long shot and almost totally inaccessible to me.

I needed a break. I switched gears and started looking for recipes that would appeal to my new drop-in customers tomorrow for my Saturday morning specials. I found a recipe for Apple Pie Bars. I didn't remember Grannie ever making them, but there was a photo showing these gorgeous squares of apples sandwiched between a rich buttery crust and a crumbly topping. Not as overwhelming as a pie, not as ordinary as turnovers, which had gone up in smoke, but with the same homey goodness. I could almost smell the cinnamon and the sweet apples swimming in their juices. Okay, one down and two to go.

I had no idea how many would come to the shop tomorrow to celebrate pie day. Maybe I'd be overwhelmed. I could only hope. I sat up in bed in a pair of Victoria's Secret red and white cotton pajamas and bright pink terry flip-flops, looking through Grannie's notebook. I flipped past Pheasant, Cider and Chestnut Pie, especially after I read the first line of instructions: "Pheasants can be tricky birds to roast." No way was I roasting a pheasant, no matter how comforting and delicious a pheasant pie could be.

The next pie that caught my eye was called simply Spinach Pie. The picture got me. It showed an individual pie made with pizza dough and stuffed with a combination of frozen spinach, chopped black olives, shredded mozzarella cheese, pepperoni, and pepper. I immediately thought of adding mushrooms to the mixture. I could make the little pies as small as I wanted. Brushed with oil and baked at a high heat on a pizza stone until the crust was golden brown, they would be perfect for lunch or a snack.

Just one more item and I could go to bed. Reluctantly, I passed on a Shepherd's Pie. It looked fabulous with its crust of cheesy mashed potatoes baked in the oven until they were browned and crisp on top, soft and buttery underneath. Under the crust was a mixture of beef, carrots, onions, thyme, sage, and white wine. My mouth was watering, but I turned the page. A summer day was not the right time for Shepherd's Pie. A foggy summer evening was what it called for.

Then I saw it and I knew right away it was the right thing for tomorrow: Torta di Riso, Rice Tart from Italy. A savory pie from Italy by the way of British chef Jamie Oliver. I'd never had it, never made it. I wondered if Grannie had made Torta di Riso. I knew she'd come to my Saturday special tomorrow, and I'd have her taste all three of my pies. I shouldn't be so insecure, but so far she hadn't said a word of praise about my pies, which worried me.

Was it because she didn't like them but she didn't want to hurt my feelings by saying so, so she said nothing? If she wasn't going to come clean, I'd have to watch her carefully so I'd be able to tell how she really felt.

I read over my list of suspects, put the list under my pillow for inspiration, and went to sleep.

———

In the morning I wasn't any closer to narrowing the search. I got up at dawn, fired up the oven, hung a sign in the window touting California Pie Day, and started my baking. It was exciting to make something new and to have hopes that my efforts would be appreciated. At last. Even with the discount coupons I'd be making money.

By nine o'clock I was almost ready with a good selection of pies. I had just poured myself a glass of fresh orange juice left over from the Torta when Sam appeared at the door. He looked more serious than I liked to see him. That look had come to mean there was trouble. I hated to ask.

"You're early," I said. "My coffee and pie hour doesn't start until ten."

"This is not a social call. Where were you last night after the crab dinner?"

My heart sank. The old questions. The baseless accusations. "Why, what happened?"

"Answer the question."

"If it's not a social call, what is it? Should I get my lawyer?"

"Do you have one?"

"No."

"Then just tell me, where did you go after I saw you?"

"I was here."

"What time?"

"I don't know, maybe nine. I saw your light on across the street. I dropped off the coupons then I came back and went to bed. Now it's your turn. Why are you asking?"

"I just got a call from the coroner. Edward Vaughn died last night."

"Oh, no."

"Friend of yours?"

"I just met him last night."

"So you admit it."

"Of course. Why not?"

"Because there was a half-finished piece of pie in his apartment when the EMTs got there."

"I brought it to him because he wasn't at the dinner last night."

"Then why didn't you tell me?"

"I *am* telling you. And after I saw him, I went to see Bob Barnett."

"He's still alive," Sam said dryly. "So far."

"This is déjà vu all over again," I said hotly. "Every time someone eats a piece of pie and keels over, you blame me. If you think my pie is responsible for killing people, then half the residents would be dead today. That man Edward was old, he was taking medicine for whatever he's got. Have you asked his doctor what he's got and what caused his death?"

"I have. But as possibly the last person to see him alive, I don't think it's out of line to ask you some questions."

"Go ahead."

"Any idea if he had any enemies?"

I couldn't help it. I felt good that he was there asking for my opinion. Even if he did suspect me. "I think he had a lot of enemies. He was one of the Old Guard. They objected to the changes the new people brought. Like Mary Brandt and her shocking new ideas for making Heavenly Acres a more informal, casual place. He chewed out her grandson for violating the dress code. She got into a fight with him over that. They were definitely enemies. If you'd acted more swiftly, you could have pinned her murder on him or vice versa. Now it's too late. They're both dead." I can tell you I felt pretty smug trapping Sam that way. At least he hadn't accused Grannie or me of killing Edward Vaughn. Not yet. But give him time and I wouldn't be surprised if he came up with a motive, a means, and an opportunity for both of us. "But wouldn't it be perfect if Edward did kill Mary," I suggested. "That way he's been punished, which saves you from an expensive trial."

"And Edward? In your scenario did he die a natural death?"

"I think so. Yes. Because …" I said, pacing back and forth in my small shop while Sam stood just inside the door leaning against it with a frown on his face. I loved being asked for my opinion, whether it concerned culinary matters or murder. It made me feel like I had something to say that other people wanted to hear. Like Sam. "What possible motive would I have for knocking off this old codger? I was bringing him a piece of pie out of the goodness of my heart."

"Spare me," he said. "I'll admit I have no reason to think you killed him, but I have a strong suspicion you had some reason for visiting him last night, other than the goodness of your heart." Again he fixed his gaze on my breast as if he might detect a suspicious change in the rhythm of my heart. I was glad I was wearing an apron over my beat-up old sweater. "What was it?"

"As usual, I was only trying to help you," I said.

He took one of the small wrought-iron chairs and straddled it as if he was making himself comfortable for a long haul of interrogation. This was getting downright tiresome, his accusing me of breaking the law.

"I'm not accusing you of anything," he said as if he knew what I was thinking. "I just want to know if anyone else was with Edward Vaughn or how he seemed. Normal? Sick? Weak? Worried?"

"He was alone when I got there, and he was still alone when I left about ten minutes later. I gave him a piece of pie. He thanked me. We had a discussion about Bridge, what a fine challenging game it is and how women just don't take it seriously enough and that's why he doesn't play anymore. Then someone called to remind him to take his meds. He seemed fine. He was old and set in his ways. But that's not unusual, I understand. Some of us are *young* and set in our ways. He didn't look sick at all, if that's what you want to know. He seemed vigorous. He has, I mean, he had strong opinions." I paused while Sam wrote something in a small black book. What happened to his notebook computer? And was it wrong of me not to tell him I'd sneaked some of Edward's pills?

"What did he die of? Heart attack? Stroke?" I asked hopefully. Anything but poison.

"Don't know yet."

"I'd be interested in knowing. And now I have to get ready for my Saturday customers."

He sniffed the air. I thought I almost heard his stomach rumble.

"Would you like to try something just so you know I'm not trying to poison anyone? But you. I'm kidding," I assured him.

"What are you offering?" he asked.

"How about Butter Pecan Apple Crumb Pie, which is what I gave Edward Vaughn last night? No? I understand. How about I eat a piece while you watch so you'll know there's nothing wrong with it? For you, I have a Spinach Pie with a pizza crust." I didn't wait for him to answer; I went straight to the kitchen and slid a small savory pie from the baking sheet onto a small plate. I put the last slice of Butter Pecan Apple Crumb Pie on another plate for myself. After I poured two cups of fresh coffee laced with cream, I brought it all to the table on a worn olive wood tray that had been in the bakery as long as I could remember.

He looked at me, then at the tray on the table, as if he was weighing his options. To eat or not to eat? To trust me or not? If he walked out of there without eating anything, I swore I would never help him in his work again. Which probably was just what he wanted me to swear to. Call me overly sensitive or too proud, I didn't care. He could call me names, arrest me, or send me to jail. But he could NOT turn down the food I made. There was something so elemental about making food for someone and sharing it. It was a part of my psyche and my heritage.

If he walked away from that food on the table, I would do something desperate. I would start a petition to get him removed from office. On what grounds, incompetence? No, that wouldn't work. Indifference? He was the opposite. He was too eager to find crimes where none existed. Old people dying. What could be more normal, more organic? Why was it so hard for him to accept? Maybe it had something to do with that grandfather he told me about. Maybe he hadn't gotten over losing him. I knew how hard it was to get over a loss. I'd lost my partner and lover in one fell swoop. Not to death, but to desertion, which hurt almost as much.

The only thing I could fault Sam on was doing his job too well. He was working too hard.

"What?" he said giving me a sharp look. I must have been staring at him while I psychologically analyzed him, and the possibilities tumbled through my brain. How could I let him know I was near the breaking point?

"Nothing. You look like you've been up all night. You look hungry. Sit down and eat something."

We sat down at the same time. As if that was the plan all along. Because the table was so small we were only inches apart and our knees kept bumping.

"This is good," he said when he'd eaten half the spinach pie. "You're right, I was hungry."

My mouth full of apple pie, I nodded. When he finished his spinach pie and drained his coffee cup, he said, "Thanks," and went to the door. I heaved a sigh of relief. I don't know why. Nothing happened. Nothing was settled. He was still there. But he looked better; and when Sam looked better, I was in danger of losing my head. I had to give myself a stern warning. Never, ever fall for someone you're working with. It just leads to disaster.

"How many people do you expect?" he asked.

"I don't know. Just keeping my fingers crossed. Why don't you drop in?"

"I might do that," he said. "In case she didn't mention it, your grandmother has an appointment for a new polygraph this afternoon."

I sighed. "No, she hasn't mentioned it. I guess because she's not surprised. Whenever you need to do something, you call her in. What more can you ask her? What else can she tell you? She's not worried. You know why? Because she hasn't done anything wrong. This is her second visit to your station. Go ahead, give her all the tests you want, show her all the videos in your VCR and she'll still pass with flying colors."

"And if she doesn't?"

"I refuse to discuss it."

"That's up to you."

After those last terse words, he finally left the shop. To keep from dwelling on the problem of my grandmother being suspected of murder, I looked around at the meager furnishings and called Kate to ask if I could borrow a couple of small tables. This afternoon I would get to the bottom of the Mary Brandt murder and clear my grannie's name once and for all.

"I don't know why I didn't think of borrowing tables before," I told Kate. "I guess I was afraid I'd get overconfident and feel even worse when the place didn't fill up for the Saturday morning specials."

"I'll find something," she said. "Maybe card tables and chairs. This is exciting. What are you serving?"

"The usual seasonal fruit pies—cherry, berry, and apple. And some savories. I just tested the Spinach Pie with pizza crust on Sam and he seemed to like it."

"Sam, he came over to test your pie? That's some kind of professional tester you've got."

"Actually, he came over to accuse me of another murder."

"And stayed for the pie?" she said. "Only in Crystal Cove." I could tell she didn't take it seriously. I wished I didn't either.

"He didn't actually say it was murder," I conceded, "but I know him. I know what he was getting at. He came to ask me some questions. Because one of the Heavenly Acres old-timers, Edward Vaughn, died last night, and it seems I was the last person to see him alive. And because Sam is in the law-and-order business, and I brought the old man a piece of Butter Pecan Apple Crumb Pie, which he presumably ate before he died, I'm high on his suspect list."

"But why? Why is he so sure it is murder?"

"Because that's the way his mind works. Maybe it's a form of job security. The more murder victims, the more important his job is. That's not all. He's giving Grannie another lie detector test this afternoon and she didn't even tell me about it."

"She doesn't want you to worry. Anyway, doesn't it mean he's trying to clear her name?"

"I wish," I said. "I'm afraid it's the opposite. But don't say anything about it."

"Of course not. Could be you're just overreacting. Calm down. I'll be over soon with some furniture. I hope you'll have a big crowd."

"I'd better bake another pie," I said. My solution to all life's little problems, like my grandmother on trial for murder or my being under suspicion, was to just take butter, sugar ... flour ... mix, bake, eat. Unlike life, unlike my previous career, it's so simple. That's why I love it.

In a few hours, I had a selection of Three-Berry Deep Dish Pie, the apple slices, the Spinach Pie, the Torta di Riso, a cool Key Lime

Pie, and two pots of coffee, freshly brewed. Kate had come by in her husband's truck with two small tables and eight folding chairs. I covered the tables with Grannie's old lace tablecloths. Now all I needed was customers.

They came. Lots of them came: Grannie and her friends Helen and Grace along with Donna, her friends Sheryl and Candice, two men, and several other women I didn't know. They were talking nonstop about a senior citizen pro-am golf tournament to be held at their golf course this summer with some famous elder statesmen of the golf world. It was going to be televised on the Golf Channel and they were all either going to play or at least watch.

"Hanna, tell everyone how to make your wonderful crust," Grannie said, her eyes sparkling like Fourth of July firecrackers that I was sure Sam would outlaw as too dangerous.

Not only did I tell them, I gave a demonstration in the kitchen. Then I let anyone who wanted to try to roll out the dough. I tell you, the way they were hanging on every word, I felt like Julia Child.

"I was always afraid to make my own crust," Helen told me as she sprinkled ice water over the flour-butter mixture while I instructed. "Instead, I bought the kind in the refrigerator in the store. If only I'd known."

"You can see it's not that hard," I said, "and it's so much better." She was wearing one of my aprons over an Army-green lightweight vest, matching green pants, and top-of-the-line running shoes. These old people had an outfit for every occasion, even a trip to the pie shop.

When I finished my demonstration, they trooped out to the shop and helped themselves to coffee and the pie of their choice.

With the shop full of happy eaters, I had a glimpse of what life could be like if every day was like this.

I noticed Donna standing at the window, staring at the police station across the street.

"Does it make you nervous knowing they're over there watching you?" she asked me when I handed her a cup of coffee from a tray.

"I like to think they're watching over me," I said.

"Oh, of course they are," she said quickly.

"But I wish they were better customers. Our new police chief has put his staff on a diet. That doesn't help my business."

"Their loss," she said and took a bite of the Apple Pie Bar. "I just wonder what they do over there." She nodded at the station.

I didn't want to bring up the M word and neither did she.

"Oh, just the usual, I suppose. Traffic violations, lost dogs, cats up a tree. And I suppose they have to keep up their skills with target practice."

She nodded.

"Did you have your interview with the chief?"

"Yes, I hope I answered all the questions correctly."

"I don't think there're right or wrong answers," I said. "All you have to do is tell the truth."

"What about you?" she asked. "Have you been interviewed too?"

"Oh, definitely. More than once. I'll be glad when this investigation is over. Any luck finding a new Bridge partner to take Mary's place?"

"No one can take her place. We were partners since the day she came to Heavenly." Her lower lip quivered. "There will never be anyone like Mary."

I had to agree. Most people around there would say that wasn't a bad thing altogether.

I left her standing, gazing out the window, and I made the rounds refilling coffee and offering small pieces of pie. I wanted to give them all a big communal hug for coming in and eating and spending money. Most of them didn't even use their discount coupons Grannie had handed out.

They were having such a good time, I wished Sam could see them. Did he realize what a hit my pies were? If he saw them so relaxed and happy, he'd never suspect any one of them, especially my grandmother, of any kind of crime.

Strangely enough, the subject turned to our police chief. Most of them had had their interviews and they wanted to compare notes.

It seemed that after quizzing them on the Mary Brandt murder, Sam had asked all of them what the police department could do for them to make them feel safe or to enrich their lives.

"We told the chief we like to be active," Grace told me. "We want to learn martial arts to protect ourselves so we won't have to depend on the police."

"Chief Genovese is going to do a class in karate. Did you know he has a black belt?" Grannie asked.

I shook my head. I shouldn't be surprised. Next they were going to tell me how he was Officer of the Year, how he'd won the Medal of Valor, Paramedic Achievement, and the Medal of Honor. I wouldn't be surprised. That said a lot for his interview techniques where the older folks were concerned. Even Grannie didn't seem that upset about her lie detector tests. Was I the only one who was offended by Sam's methods?

Maybe I was too sensitive. Because he knew me, he thought he could let down his hair and say whatever was on his mind. The result was that I had to find Mary Brandt's murderer before he arrested my grandmother. It occurred to me maybe that was his plan. He'd insist I stay out of his way, but deep down he really wanted my help after all and couldn't admit it. He knew the way to get it. Which was to forbid me from helping him. Because I'm stubborn. I admit it. There's nothing like somebody telling me not to do something to motivate me.

"What about you, Hanna?" Grannie said as the oldsters finished their coffee, said nice things about the pie, and filled my vintage cash register with cash. "Don't you want to learn self-defense? It's very important for women, you know. Especially if you're not carrying heat."

"I'm not," I assured her. "And yes I do want to learn. I'll sign up just as soon as Sam starts a class."

Finally the group was outside waiting for the van to pick them up. Only Grannie was left in the shop.

"You don't need to wait for a class to get together with Sam," she said. "Why don't you invite him to dinner some night?"

I gave her a sharp look. What was she after? It was no secret she worried about me being single at my advanced age. Or did she just want me to influence Sam to turn his attention toward a different suspect, anyone who wasn't her?

"I've already fed him samples of my pie," I said.

"That's not dinner," she said. "Single men never eat properly."

"I'll keep that in mind," I said. I didn't tell her he'd told me it was my turn next. I didn't want her to get her hopes up about Sam and me. She'd only be disappointed. She'd often said she wanted to live long enough to have great-grandchildren and since I was her only grandchild, I sometimes felt the pressure.

"Where did you get the berries for the pie?" she asked.

"The Hollisters brought them by. Said you'd always ordered a flat every week during the season."

"They seemed a little tart. You could add a little more sugar," she said.

"I didn't want anyone to go into a diabetic shock from too much sugar, so I cut back. I don't think anyone else noticed. Nobody said anything," I said.

"They wouldn't. They're too polite. They know you're my granddaughter."

"I hear old Mr. Vaughn died last night," I remarked. "Nobody mentioned it."

"Really? How do you know that?" She didn't seem surprised or sad about it.

"Sam told me. He didn't say it was a secret."

"Hmmm," she said. "You know I never approved of Sam when he was a teenager."

"You weren't the only one. He was kicked out of school."

"But now he's a fine upstanding citizen and the Chief of Police."

"Yes, I know."

"And so good looking. You could do a lot worse."

"Grannie, you seem to have forgotten he suspects either one or both of us of murder. The reason I know about old Mr. Vaughn dying is because Sam was here this morning quizzing me about him."

"Maybe he just wanted to see you. He needed an excuse. You're a very attractive girl. All of my friends say so. Or maybe he was hungry. Why do you jump to conclusions about Sam's motives?" she asked me. This from the woman who was in line for a second polygraph test and who'd been videoed with pills in her hand at the Bridge table. I wished I had her attitude.

"Sam is not hiding behind any ulterior motives," I said. "He comes right out with his questions. In case you haven't noticed. No doubt about what he means. Or who he suspects of criminal activity. While he was here, I had to urge him to eat some of my Spinach Pie. I told him I went to see old Mr. Vaughn last night to take him a piece of pie, and it seems I was the last person to see him alive. And guess what? Now Sam is thinking pie equals murder."

"No, he doesn't," she said flatly. "Not necessarily."

I knew what she was thinking. There goes Hanna with her theories again. She spoke with so much conviction, I knew I would never convince her and I should never have mentioned it. One, she didn't believe me because she was very stubborn. A trait I had inherited. And two, I had no business dragging Grannie into yet another murder by pie scenario. It was not only ridiculous, it was heartless of me to even mention it. Grannie was in deep doo doo with Sam, whether she realized it or not, and didn't need to worry about me too. She should be enjoying the fruits of old age while I was still in the trenches, working hard to make a living while fighting off a hopeless attraction to a man who thought she and I were both murderers. I forced a smile.

"That was fun serving all that pie," I said brightly.

"It's just the beginning. Everyone who was here today will tell someone else about your pie. And they'll be back. We have vans that go downtown and everywhere." She looked out the door as a bright blue minivan pulled up in front of the shop. "There's ours now. See you tonight."

I gave her a blank look.

"Didn't you say you wanted to learn to play Bridge? I'm offering Bridge lessons after dinner tonight. Now that old Vaughny is gone, I'm not afraid of him coming around and telling me what to do."

"He did that?"

"He was obnoxious. And very good at Bridge. He went to the state championship one year."

"So you're not sorry he's dead."

"Should I be?"

"No, I don't care. Just don't tell Sam." It was a good idea for me to play Bridge with the residents so I could maybe find out what was really going on there. Specifically, who killed Mary. It was past time that I did it. It would be worth feeling stupid for a few evenings to listen and learn. Not that I'd learn how to play Bridge, that was not my goal. Nobody my age played Bridge. It was an older generation's game. It was Grannie's game.

If I didn't need to be there I'd ask myself, wasn't I already spending way too much time in the company of the older folks? If I wasn't hanging out with them, I was hanging out with Sam, which was stimulating, maddening, and infuriating at the same time and also led me nowhere. Worse than nowhere, it led me to a state of denial. All I did was think of ways not to answer his questions and accusations. Most of all, he made me become my grandmother's principal defendant.

"So you'll come? I told all my friends you'd come and bring a pie."

"After what's been happening, do you think that's wise?"

"Of course. We can't get freaked out by every little thing that happens. And don't stint on the sugar," she warned.

I was determined to cut back on sugar no matter what she said. Diabetes was rampant among old people. Besides, the fruit was so sweet and ripe this time of year, I wanted the flavors to jump out without being overly sweet. By "every little thing" she meant every little murder or accidental death or homicide. What could I say? She wanted me there as her wonderful granddaughter, and I needed to be on site with my ears open. Sam didn't have to know why, when, or where I was sleuthing on my own.

I told myself not to worry about seeming stupid. It was trivial compared to what Grannie was going through. No one expected me to catch on anytime soon to a difficult game like Bridge, so I wouldn't disappoint anyone. That was a good thing. I had a strong desire to please and impress people. Which is why I made pies. As Kate said, "Nobody doesn't like pie."

Maybe they don't, but why did they keep eating it and die soon after? It was enough to make a person hungry for a piece of you-know-what.

ELEVEN

"You're going to play Bridge tonight at Heavenly Acres?" Kate asked, not even trying to hide her surprise and her pity when she stopped by to see how the coffee klatch went over.

"I'm going to pretend to *learn* to play Bridge," I said. "Not because I want to. Or because I think I can. Or that I think it will be a barrel of laughs. But in the interest of finding out who killed Mary Brandt. As long as Sam thinks Grannie did it, I have my work cut out for me finding the real killer, who may or may not be a resident of Heavenly Acres. Playing cards gives me a good excuse to hang out and listen for clues. Mary Brandt played Bridge. She collapsed at the Bridge table. It seems likely she died as a result of playing Bridge. Ergo, the clue to her death can't be far from the Bridge table. Which is where I'll be tonight." I paused. "Unless the murderer is a family member. I guess I don't want it to be because how am I going to hang out with the Brandt/Wilson family when they don't like me?"

"Blake likes you."

"He seems to," I admitted. "And I have to admit I'm flattered by his attention. But he doesn't know me, not really. As for his family, I already know they wanted her dead, but who did it? I have no way of finding out."

"I hope for your sake it's one of her contemporaries. And I don't mean your grandmother," Kate said.

"Me too, although it's a little embarrassing to have a date to play Bridge with old people on Saturday night."

"I won't tell," she said.

I actually had a lot more to worry about than the plight of a lonely single woman hanging out with her grandmother on date night. I had a crime to solve. This was no time for me to worry about my self-image. Or worry about what anyone thought of my spending Saturday night at a retirement home.

"You don't have to hang out with the old crowd on Saturday night, do you? Instead of playing Bridge, you could come over for dinner and I'll invite someone else."

"Someone else like who?"

"Sam or Blake. You choose."

"Isn't it kind of last-minute?"

"You think they've got other options?"

"Maybe not."

"So who is it?"

"Neither. I'm going to Heavenly Acres."

"The easy way out," she said, her eyes narrowed.

"You think looking like a dummy at the Bridge table is easy?"

"Go ahead. I'll have a little dinner party another night. And I won't tell you who I'm inviting."

"Can I guess?"

She shook her head.

"Actually, I'm anxious to know what was in Mary Brandt's will so maybe if Blake was there..."

"He'd tell us what she left him," she said, her eyes popping open wide.

"Or didn't leave him," I said. "I want to know who benefits from her death. So yes, this is really a good idea of yours."

"Thank you. Just to be clear, if you find out Blake benefits, then he must have killed her?" Kate asked.

"It would give him a motive, but since he was in New York at the time, he didn't have much of an opportunity," I conceded.

"How do you know he was in New York?" she asked.

I grinned. "Now you're thinking like a detective. I *don't* know. But that's what he told me."

"And you believed him?"

"I did believe him. With him what you see is what you get. It's refreshing. I just wish I could find out now what was in that will. Blake said the reading is Monday."

"Then I'll invite him to dinner after that just in case you haven't cracked your case wide open. Of course, I'd rather not invite a murderer to dinner."

"I understand," I said. Being in that room when the lawyer read the will was the best way I could get close to the family. I so wanted to see the expressions on their faces. Who would be surprised? Who would be disappointed? Who would be happy? Who would not be surprised because he or she already knew? Failing that, next best way was to be there when they left the room. Would I hide in my car in front of the lawyer's office? Would I stand outside pretending to be hawking pies? No, I had a better idea.

When Kate left, I went to the Yellow Pages and found a number for Attorney Seymour Evans' "Specializing in Living Trusts and Avoiding Probate" office and made an appointment for Monday morning for a review of my finances and the possibility of making a will. The secretary said Evans could fit me in at eleven though he had another appointment earlier, and I knew it had to be the Brandt family. Believe me, I was congratulating myself right and left. I suggested to the woman maybe I was too young to think about writing a will, and she said to no one's surprise, "You're never too young to make out a will. Everyone should have one."

Seymour Evans sure had brainwashed her. Maybe he'd brainwash me too. Making out a will was a small price to pay for finding out who had a motive for knocking off Mary Brandt. But if I had to go through with it, who would I leave my things to? Who would want the pie shop?

Of course, if by some chance Mary had left me or my grandmother a substantial sum I'd be in big trouble. If you call having a sudden fortune dumped in your lap trouble. But wouldn't we be summoned by Lawyer Evans to attend the reading if that was the case? We hadn't been. It seemed to me my grandmother would be the last person to appear on Mary's list of behests, and since she didn't know me, I wouldn't be there either.

Feeling good after selling pie all morning as well as entertaining a few customers in the afternoon, I got ready for my Bridge lesson with Grannie. I was hitting this mystery hard. Of course, it was possible a family member had offed Mary because I heard that it's often the person who has the most to gain. But I was betting on the retirement community. So first I'd hit the Bridge table because it was accessible and I had an in there. Nothing I was doing was in defiance of Sam's orders not to take part in solving this crime. I was still glad there was little chance he would find out what I was up to tonight.

———

It turns out he did find out where I was headed; as I was packing three pies into the back of the Estate Wagon, he came out of the station and walked across the street. I could only hope he had many more crimes to solve or prevent than I knew about. Even on Saturday.

"You're working late," I said.

"Paperwork," he said. Then he looked at my basket. "A late delivery?"

"I have a Bridge class at Heavenly Acres. I'm taking a few pies."

"I thought you weren't interested in Bridge."

"Did I say that?" I asked, fluttering my eyelashes in a wild attempt to divert his attention. "I'm always interested in learning something new, whether it's cards or crime prevention. I confess, I'm a rank beginner and those old folks are sharks. I can only hope they'll be gentle with me because I don't know a Club from a Spade. Anyway, the Bridge table is where the action is on a Saturday night."

"And you love to be where the action is."

"Right." *Next to the action at the lawyer's office, I love the Bridge table action.*

I waited for him to say something like I told you to stay out of this, but how could he tell me not to play Bridge, so he didn't. He looked like he was going to say something else, but he just took my basket and lifted it into the back of the wagon.

"Besides, those residents are my biggest fans. I have no interest in learning to play Bridge. It's just one of the many sacrifices I make in order to hang on to my job and my lifestyle."

"And what is that?" he asked.

"My job and my lifestyle are one. Small-town baker. Early to bed and early to rise. That's it. I came back to the Cove for a radical change and I got it. I can't complain. I hope you have an exciting Saturday night planned," I said. What a lie. I hoped he had nothing to do but read *The Police Officer's Manual* all alone in that charming house next door to Lindsey's beautiful mansion. I imagined Lindsey looking over to see his light on and inviting him over for drinks or dinner. Maybe her husband wasn't there. She'd said he traveled a lot on business. Maybe she wanted to try out her new sex toys. Or maybe he had a date with Lurline.

"Seen Lurline lately?" I asked. I wanted to tell him how she'd accused me of poisoning Mary, but that kind of whining was beneath me. Unless he brought it up.

He hesitated a moment then he shook his head. "No, I haven't. I'm on my way to a meeting." Then he gave me a second look. "What's wrong?" he asked.

"Nothing," I assured him, my face flushed and my heart palpitating at the thought of Sam getting involved with Lurline or Lindsey or anyone. This town was too small. I'd have to see him everywhere with whoever it was. I reminded myself there were no other single women in town except for that hostile cupcake lady. I wondered where his meeting was. I wondered who else would be there. My stomach growled. I hadn't eaten dinner and at this hour I'd probably only get a Bridge mix of nuts and candy at Heavenly Acres. My fault.

I said goodbye, got in the car, and drove up to the retirement home on the hill. Again.

I put my pie basket in the small kitchen next to the card room, storing the coconut cream pie and the chocolate mousse pie in the refrigerator. I was glad I'd brought them along with the blueberry. That way, I could offer a selection to everyone in the room. Which was good because there was quite a crowd in the card room, several tables of players besides Grannie's group and her friends. She told me I'd be playing with Donna. It made me a little uneasy to be in Mary's old seat, considering the outcome of that previous fateful game.

"I hope you all know this is my first time. I have no idea how to play Bridge," I said, sliding into the chair opposite Donna. No one asked, "Why? Why now? Why don't you have anything better to do on a Saturday night?" That's the nice thing about people of a certain age.

Donna gave me an encouraging smile. "I know you'll catch on right away."

They all nodded in agreement. They assured me everyone has a first time. No one was born knowing how to bid, how to win tricks, or how to lead or what's trump.

"All I know is that I want to be the dummy," I said. "Then I can watch."

They laughed politely. Naturally, they assumed that was a joke. It wasn't. It was clear they disapproved of anyone who didn't want to be in the heat of the game. They were serious players. I knew that. They were going to make me into one too if it took all night. I had news for them. It would take longer than that. It would take years and nobody had that much time. Not even me.

They shuffled the cards, then the dealer, Grannie's partner, Hazel, a tall woman with dark hair streaked with gray who was wearing a lavender-colored velour track suit, dealt everyone thirteen cards. I hadn't met Hazel before, but I'd heard she was an excellent player who Grannie hoped would accompany her straight on to the championships.

"This is just for fun, right?" Donna asked anxiously. I knew how competitive she was. How competitive they all were. How every game was life or death. In Mary's case, it was death. That's what I had to remember. Why I was there. When would I get a chance to learn something besides how to tell a trump from a trick? "We're playing, but we're not really playing," Donna added.

"Right," Grannie said. "We're going to show Hanna how it's done. It's about time she learned how to play Bridge. I tried for years but finally she's shown an interest." She beamed proudly. I had to admit it was worth spending Saturday night here to see her so happy.

"First pies and now Bridge," Helen said, leaning over to kibitz from the next table. "Following in your footsteps, Louise."

Grannie opened her mouth to say something, then closed it. I could only imagine she was going to compare my pies to hers unfavorably but thought better of it.

"Wish I could get my grandchildren to play something besides video games. Even my kids think Bridge is old-fashioned," Hazel confessed.

I was glad no one suspected why I was really there. It was worth seeming like a loser who had nothing better to do on a Saturday night than to hang out with this crowd and learn a difficult game. I reached for a handful of mixed nuts. Then I remembered how Mary had expired right at this table after an innocent piece of pie. I looked around the room, the nuts still clutched in my hand. What if her murderer was here now? What if the group refused to eat my pie? Mary had so many enemies who all took Bridge seriously. Seriously enough to murder her? How easy it would be to tamper with the snacks on the table or with the pills that some trusting someone left out in the open on the table.

Back to the game. They didn't expect me to become an expert tonight, but they did expect me to pay attention.

Hazel turned to me. "The object is to win tricks for your side."

"What's a trick?"

"A trick is four cards, one from each player," Donna explained.

"Say a Spade is led," Grannie said.

I didn't want to ask what a Spade was but they guessed I didn't know. Grannie went on. "There are four suits—Spades, Hearts, Diamonds, and Clubs." She set her cards on the table to show me which was which and how she'd arranged them. I guessed this wasn't the usual way to play the game. "Spades are the highest," she said. "Then Hearts, Diamonds, and Clubs. I can't believe I never taught you this."

I began to wish for the first time in my life that she had forced me to learn to play years ago. "Spades are the highest?" What did that mean? I was afraid to ask too many questions. But I have to say they were very patient and it must have been hard watching me struggle to catch on to the basics.

"Maybe it's like learning a foreign language," I suggested. "If you don't learn when you're young, it's twice as hard and you never really get fluent."

Grannie shook her head. "It's not the same at all." They all joined in and assured me it wasn't too late for me. Then they took turns standing behind me and telling me what card to play. We played a few rounds, I think they call them hands. I was exhausted from concentrating and so far I hadn't learned a thing. I think everyone was relieved when I said I'd go get the pie I'd brought and someone else could sit in for me.

They took a break until I came back from the utility kitchen with a classic double-crust blueberry pie cut in small pieces as well as the towering coconut cream pie and chocolate mousse pie. When the other players in the room saw the pies, they decided to take a break too. They all raved about the pies, which made me feel good, but I had the feeling the women at my table would rather be playing Bridge nonstop, and not with me.

"Did you use fresh coconut for your pie?" Grannie asked. "I always did."

I had to admit I hadn't. Everyone but her said it was delicious with the rich creamy filling and the toasted coconut garnish.

Two of the women at the next table had a small slice of each kind of pie. My kind of pie eater. They asked how I made the crust of the chocolate mousse pie, which was lighter than some of my other dense chocolate pies. I told them I used chocolate cookie crumbs and butter. I saw Grannie frown at this admission, and I knew there was something wrong with that one too. I was sure she'd tell me later.

Riding on a wave of compliments, I reminded myself I would like to accomplish something tonight. Like finding out who killed Mary. Then I could forget infiltrating the family, which remained my backup plan.

While the other tables went back to Bridge, the four of us sat around the table eating pie and drinking coffee from the Cuisinart coffee machine Grannie brought down from her room. Now was my chance to ask questions. But what?

"I notice there aren't any men playing Bridge," I said.

"There used to be, but now they prefer something more lively, like shuffleboard," Donna said. "Or watching football in the lounge. Couch potatoes," she added disdainfully.

"What about Edward Vaughn?" I asked. "Wasn't he some kind of Bridge champion?"

"He was. At least that's what he claimed. But he quit playing here. Instead he took on computer Bridge. He wasn't much of a people person," Grannie said, wrinkling her nose. "He was such a hermit I don't think I would have recognized him if I ran into him in the hall. He died last night."

They nodded. No remarks.

"No service, no memorial?" I asked.

They shook their heads. Nobody had anything to say about him. Good or bad. "I believe his family is having a private service in his hometown," Hazel said.

"He wasn't very popular," Donna said finally, lowering her voice. "One of the old guard, if you know what I mean."

I knew what she meant but I wanted to know more. "Did they hang out together, the old guard, the ninety-somethings?"

"Some retreated to their apartments and holed up there having their meals sent up like Vaughn, others just go on about the way things were and complain about the way things are."

"Did they fly the flag at half-mast at least?" I asked.

"Oh yes," Grannie said. "That's the custom. We had a moment of silence before dinner in his memory. But I doubt if many of the new people even knew who he was. If I start hibernating like that, just shoot me," she said with her usual good-natured impish grin. I had to ask myself if she really knew what serious trouble she was in. I hoped she didn't. I hoped her irrepressible good nature could not be dampened by any small-town police chief and his faulty polygraph machine. Everyone knew she would never be the type to hibernate, not my gregarious Grannie. Not even if they put her in solitary confinement. They could accuse her of murder and take away her pie shop, but they couldn't crush her high spirits.

"Mary knew him," Donna said. "She stood up to him. He picked a fight with the wrong person. He told her he'd get back at her. I always wondered..."

All eyes were on Donna, waiting for her to finish her sentence.

"If he did," she said.

"If he killed her?" I asked breathlessly.

"Oh, no. Mary died from a stroke," Donna said firmly even though she knew full well the official word was murder. Talk about being delusional. "I always wondered what she did to him. She was fearless. She went after what she wanted and she'd never quit. All she said to me was, 'He won't bother my grandson again.'"

I looked around the table. No one said anything for a long moment while we imagined what Mary had done to him.

"The police asked us all if Mary had any enemies," Hazel explained. "So we figured if we told him she had nothing but enemies, he'd never figure out who killed her."

"If anyone did," Grannie said. "Which I personally doubt. We were there. We would have noticed if anyone was trying to kill her.

But what do we know, really? If Sam thinks she was murdered, she probably was. We're not in law enforcement. He is."

"You would have made a great policewoman," I said, a vision in my head of Grannie in a blue uniform and a matching hat perched on her head. "Frisking suspects. Giving lie detector tests. Reading them their rights. Instead, you were a great pie baker, so we can't feel too bad about what might have been." I was getting carried away with pies as usual. Back to the question of murder.

"So did you get a sense of who the police believe killed Mary?" I asked. I hoped no one would say it was Grannie. Or me. I hoped I'd hear a new name, a new suspect.

Suddenly the room was too quiet and my voice was too loud. Everyone in the room turned and looked at me with shock and amazement that I would ask them to pin the murder on one of them. They shook their heads and studied their cards.

Why did I bother to ask? I knew that if Donna ever admitted she thought it was murder she'd vote for Mary's family. Grannie just knew it wasn't her or any of her friends. A good number of people like Bob Barnett didn't care, as long as she was dead. I realized I hadn't told Grannie that I'd stopped in to see Bob.

"Well, ladies, I'll pick up my pie pans and go. Thank you so much for putting up with me."

"Don't go," they chorused.

"You're just catching on," Donna said, but I'm sure she and everyone else were relieved to go back to the real game.

"You'll have to come back soon for your next lesson," Hazel said.

"I'd love to, but you need a real player. Have you found someone to fill in for Mary? How will you ever find someone to take her place?"

I knew Donna missed her old partner terribly, whatever her foibles like cheating were. She must be auditioning players to see if they were up to her standards so she could continue playing and proceed into the finals toward the county championship. So it was really nice of her to let me play with them tonight. If you can call what I did "playing."

"We're looking," Grannie said vaguely. "But Donna can afford to be choosy. In the meantime, we play three-handed Bridge or we get someone to sit in with us."

I made the rounds of the card room, offering seconds on pie and coffee before I left. I hadn't made any headway into solving any crimes, but I'd done some good PR for my pie business and received many warm compliments on my baking skills before I left.

"That chocolate mousse was divine," one red-haired woman wearing Bakelite earrings with card suit symbols in red and black told me. "So light and smooth. Your grandmother must be so proud of you."

"She taught me everything I know," I said. "But I've still got a lot to learn." At least according to Grannie I did. She used fresh coconut in her cream pie, she used a prepared pudding for her chocolate pie and nothing else would do. I wondered what she thought of the crust on the blueberry pie or if she noticed I used frozen berries. She probably did and I'd probably hear about it. She didn't know why I had to change any recipes when they were all right there in her card files.

Maybe that's why I wasn't as successful as she was yet. But I couldn't give in on my principles. I had to use my creativity or I'd die of boredom baking pies the same way over and over. No matter how good they were. I had to find my own way. Where was the fun in making the same pie year after year? Where was the fun in following somebody else's plan? Of course, I was into the pie business for more than fun. I planned on making enough money to support myself too.

In the lobby, I paused to offer the night receptionist, whose name tag said "Monica," a slice of pie. She thanked me and I cut a piece of blueberry with its flaky double crust oozing with purple juice and gave it to her on a paper plate.

"Looks yummy," she said. "Did you make it yourself?"

I nodded.

"Even the crust?" she asked incredulously.

"I know, it's a lost art, but I don't cut corners," I told her, then handed her one of my Upper Crust cards. She said she'd stop by the shop to check it out.

I turned from the front desk and almost ran into a man in a San Francisco Giants jacket and straight-leg jeans. He had a suitcase in his hand and I overheard him tell Monica he was returning the key to his grandfather's apartment. Edward Vaughn's apartment? I wanted to know but I didn't want to ask. If I told him I was there the night he died, would he too suspect me of murder?

"Wait a minute," he said to me with an eye on the pie pan in my hand. I froze, expecting him to accuse me of something. "Are you the lady who makes the pies around here?"

I had a sinking feeling in the pit of my stomach. Here it comes, I thought. He's going to blame me for poisoning his grandfather.

I was getting used to it. I stiffened and took a deep breath. "That's me. I'm Hanna Denton."

"I'm Adam Vaughn. I talked to my grandfather the night he died. He told me you'd brought him a piece of pie. That was you, wasn't it?"

I nodded. Why try to deny it?

"You made his day," he said. I heaved a sigh of relief. He wasn't going to blame me for anything. That was enough to make my day.

"Me? Really?" I said modestly.

"He didn't have many friends."

Wonder why? Maybe because he stopped playing Bridge, boy-cotted fun dinner parties, and yelled at kids for wearing jeans like the ones you're wearing right now.

"I didn't know that," I said. "But I heard he hadn't come to dinner that night and I had some extra pie so I thought…" Of course, I didn't tell him what I really thought, that his grandfather had killed Mary Brandt. I hoped it was him; then justice would be done and we could all forget about it. All of us, including Sam.

"I owe you for making him feel good during his last few hours on earth. And allowing him to pontificate on the subject of Bridge and bend your ear on something, whatever it was. He said you were a good listener, which in his opinion is rare among the younger generation."

"It was my pleasure," I said, basking in the glow of the com-pliments. A good baker and a good listener. If only everyone felt that way about me. "When you're a baker like me, you're always looking for people who appreciate your efforts. I guess it's not only bakers—everyone wants their work to be valued. So I'm glad he enjoyed the pie. And I was interested in hearing his views on Bridge since I'm hopeless at it."

I realized with a start that Adam had said Edward had enjoyed the pie. Maybe just giving it to him was enough to make him happy. An unexpected visit from a good listener and an unexpected gift. Sometimes that's enough. Maybe when I'm in my nineties someone will knock on my door and listen patiently while I rattle on about some subject and knock the young seventy-somethings who were against the status quo. Until then, I'd remind myself I was lucky to have found a job I loved. I got to make people happy every day with every bite they ate. Not many business owners could say that. There was Lurline, of course. Maybe someday we could compare stories. Once this murder mess was over.

I saw Adam Vaughn looking at my wicker basket. Did he suspect I had leftover pie inside?

"I still have some pie left over from the Bridge game tonight. Can I interest you in a slice of blueberry or chocolate or ..."

His eyes lit up. Now that's the kind of reaction I liked to see when offering pie. No "I don't eat desserts" or anything. Just pure joy at the thought of a piece of fresh homemade pie. That's what I saw in this stranger's face.

"I've just been packing up my grandfather's clothes to give to charity," he said. "If you would join me for a cup of coffee, I'd gladly take you up on your offer."

All I could think of was finding out if his grandfather had killed Mary Brandt. Chances were he didn't, and even if he did, Adam didn't know about it. And even if he knew about it, he wouldn't tell me. But what the hell? Why not give it a chance?

I led the way to the TV lounge where coffee was always ready, and there were only two old codgers sitting in front of the wide-screen television watching Jeopardy and shouting out answers.

I poured coffee into two paper cups and cut two slices of coconut cream pie. Sometimes asking people to choose just throws them into confusion. So I chose the coconut. For one thing, it looked beautiful if I do say so myself with its towering peaks of whipped cream kept cool in the fridge. I stifled all memories of Bob Barnett and the day he passed out at Mary's memorial service with a smear of coconut on his lips. Coincidence, that's all. I knew what had caused his problem and it wasn't my pie. He didn't blame me either.

"Tell me about your grandfather," I said, noting with relief that the two oldsters had turned off the television set and left the room. "Was he happy here at Heavenly Acres?"

"At first he was, that was years ago. But lately he had a lot to complain about. The other residents, the staff, the food, the activities. You name it, he wasn't happy about it. There was one woman he really couldn't stand. Mary something. She epitomized everything he despised about the younger generation. Their lack of manners and consideration and their arrogance. I believe that's one reason he stayed in his room so much, so he wouldn't have to run into this woman by chance. In a way, she ruined his life."

"That's a shame," I murmured. I didn't know whether to tell him she'd died or assume he already knew. If she ruined his life, maybe he thought his grandfather was justified in taking hers. But how?

"That's why it was so refreshing to hear him say something nice about someone. Especially since he died later that night. I was hoping to get a chance to tell you that you made a difference. I'm going to spread the word to the rest of the family as well. Believe me, we've all had our problems with Grandfather."

"I hope the excitement of my visit didn't contribute to his death in any way," I said. I took a sip of coffee. "What was the cause of his death?"

"I'd say old age, but he had a weak heart and other problems. You might have seen his medicine tray in his apartment, a regular pharmacy. Coumadin for his heart, something for his blood pressure..."

He went on to list his grandfather's other medications, but he had me at Coumadin. That was the brand name for warfarin, the drug that supposedly killed Mary Brandt, in conjunction with the cranberries in the pie. Would an autopsy show that somehow my pie had contributed to another death? I wisely kept my mouth shut but I couldn't shut off my brain.

If only I could tell Sam. Not about the pie, but about the warfarin. But he'd just tell me it was none of my business. I drained my coffee cup, and Adam finished his pie and thanked me. I thanked him. We said goodbye in the parking lot. I loaded my car with the leftover pie and hurried down the hill in the fog, thinking I should order some new amber fog lights for the old Estate Wagon.

Unfortunately, there were no lights in the police station. Where did Sam live these days? Why hadn't I asked him? Had he moved in to the house next to Lindsey's? What did it matter, I didn't have his cell phone number. I'd forgotten to transfer the number from my arm to a piece of paper. And he wouldn't give me any credit for my information.

All the same, I called the police station and left a message. I had to tell him. No matter what he said. I tried to sound calm and reasonable, but I may have sounded desperate. I felt bursting with all kinds of information and theories and I had no one else to share them with other than Sam. Where was he?

TWELVE

I PUT AWAY THE pies and changed into a pair of Blue Angel duck flannel pajama pants, a gray T-shirt with a red Stanford logo, and a pair of white bunny slippers. Red, white, and blue. Maybe a little too patriotic; but one of the perks, maybe the only one, of living alone is that you can wear anything you want to bed. It was a comfortable outfit for a damp, cool summer evening and it was ten o'clock. I had no plans to go anywhere else tonight.

Too restless to go to bed even though I'd been up and running since five this morning, I sat down at Grannie's old kitchen table and wrote out a recipe. A recipe for murder. I was used to first listing ingredients, putting them together in a certain logical way, and anticipating a finished product. How different could it be to plan a murder than a pie?

First, I listed the victim or victims. Mary Brandt and Edward Vaughn. Should I list Bob Barnett too? Maybe his "accident" wasn't one at all. Then, the phone rang. My only hope was that it wasn't Grannie telling me about another mysterious death at

Heavenly Acres. Or they'd start calling it "On Your Way to Heaven Heavenly Acres." Or "Closer to Heaven at …" Or "The Next Step to Heaven …."

"What now?" Sam asked without even bothering for the usual "Hi, how are you?" Or "Is this an emergency?"

"Just wondered if you were in the neighborhood you might want to stop by. Are you on duty?"

"Always," he said. I couldn't tell if he was being sarcastic or not. "Are you at home?"

"Yes."

"Got any coffee?"

"Of course."

"I'll be by."

Ten minutes later, I opened the door to the shop and realized then I should have changed clothes, because Sam was still dressed to kill, so to speak, in a navy blazer, Oxford cloth blue shirt with plenty of cuff showing, khaki pants, and leather loafers. He kept staring at my shirt, then his gaze shifted to my flannels and on to my bunny slippers.

"Good to see you," he said, following me up the stairs to my tiny apartment. "I hope I'm not keeping you up."

"Are you referring to my flannels or my bunny slippers or the bags under my eyes?"

"None of the above. Your lifestyle, really. I've seen your light on at five in the morning."

"You noticed? I'm flattered. I thought you'd be busy analyzing fingerprints or whatever you do over there." I poured him a cup of coffee and we sat down at Grannie's old kitchen I'd refurnished my-self. I had a list of things to ask him, but somehow at that moment I couldn't remember one of them. For once I wanted to forget he was a cop and I was under suspicion. I just wanted to be me.

"I can do fingerprints if I have to," he said. Then he took off his blazer and laid it across the back of the chair. He rolled up his sleeves and looked around. It didn't take long to take in the whole apartment. When Grannie left, I had the wall between the bedrooms and the living room knocked down to make a bigger living space. I didn't ever entertain up here, and I was suddenly acutely aware that my queen-sized bed was visible from all corners, including the small kitchen. I didn't need a big kitchen when I had the one downstairs.

After a survey of the place and of me, he reached across the table and took my hand in his and studied it with an intent gaze. "Along with fingerprints, I also read palms." He spread my fingers out flat on the table and focused his gaze on the lines on my palm.

I swallowed hard. He was kidding, of course. Sam reading palms like a fortune teller? Impossible. Almost as impossible as Sam kidding. But there he was. And there I was.

"See this?" He traced a line across my palm. I nodded. "This is your heart line. Hmmm, long and curvy, like you."

I felt my face flush. "What does it mean?" I murmured.

"It means you express your feelings and emotions. You don't hold back."

"I guess that's true. I guess some people wish I would." I gave him a pointed look. He didn't seem to get the message. He smoothed my palm and my pulse sped up. I wondered if he could tell. "What else?" I asked. This was better than sparring with him. Much better. In fact, I'd forgotten why I'd called him. Or maybe I just didn't want to remember.

"The life line," he said, moving his chair closer to the table, so close I could smell the musky masculine scent that clung to his skin, his hair, and his clothes. He traced my life line across my palm with his index finger. Back and forth. I took a drink of coffee but it didn't help at all to calm my racing heart. This was not good. He was toying with me with some woo-woo witchcraft and I was enjoying it. Too much.

"See the way it swoops around in a semicircle?"

I nodded.

"It means strength and enthusiasm." He looked up and met my gaze. "That figures. That's you."

After all we'd been through, was this man paying me a compliment? I looked deep into those dark blue eyes and I wanted to believe it. I wanted to make up for the past. Forget what happened in high school. Make up for all those years in between where we both got hurt and were back here to recover. I wanted to find out who he was and, more than that, I wanted—I needed to—find out who I was. If I didn't do it now, then when?

After an eternity, he let go of my hand, leaned back in his chair, and closed his eyes. There were creases at the corner of his eyes and ridges in his forehead that had never been there before.

It's after ten o'clock at night, I wanted to say. You're tired. I'm tired.

"Where were you tonight?" I blurted, though it was none of my business. I couldn't believe he dressed like this to patrol the streets.

He ran his hand through his hair and pulled himself together, physically and mentally. "City Council meeting. Emergency. Or we wouldn't be meeting tonight. But there's a problem. I can't say anymore because it's top secret."

"You're on the City Council?"

He folded his arms over his chest and shook his head. "I was asked to appear."

"Why, what happened?" I asked.

"They're considering abolishing the police department," he said.

I dropped my fork. "The whole thing? Including you? Why? Because nothing ever happens here? What about Mary Brandt's murder? Who's supposed to solve that?"

"That's the interesting thing," he said. "Mary's son-in-law, your friend Blake's father, is the one who suggested it. He had some compelling reasons. One, the city can't afford a police department. And two, the city doesn't need a police department."

I jumped out of my seat and put my hands on my hips. "Because he knows someone in his family killed Mary. It could have even been him since everyone knows Mary made his life miserable. But he doesn't want the police to find out, so he's abolishing your department to get rid of you just like he got rid of Mary. The family gets her money and you and your men get sacked. Don't let him do it."

Sam tilted his chair back and looked at me like I'd blown a fuse. Maybe I had. "Calm down," he said. "Of course I don't want to close the station and lose my job. I like it here. But lots of small towns are getting rid of their police departments. Like soda fountains and barber shops, they're a dying breed. I knew that when I came here."

"I get that, but dumping the department in the middle of a murder investigation?" I asked.

"I admit that's rare. But let's not jump to conclusions about Mary's son-in-law. You're the one who said 'An old woman dies of a stroke...' No, 'A *paranoid* old woman tells her family someone's trying to kill her, then she has a stroke and dies at the hospital...' That is what you said, isn't it?" His eyes narrowed. Damn him for his perfect memory.

"Okay, I admit I said that, but you forced me to change my mind. I know you don't buy into Mary's family doing her in for her money. So after talking to Edward Vaughn's grandson, I have a new theory." I didn't wait for him to tell me to shut up. "It may help you keep your job because it involves a possible murder, which means the city needs you, but it boots me and Grannie and the family off the list of suspects."

"You've thought of everything," he said. He could have been sarcastic, but I hoped he wasn't.

"My position is the same as it always was. I didn't kill Mary and neither did my grandmother. I don't really care who did it, as long as nobody blames me or her. And justice is served, of course," I added as an afterthought. "As long as the murderer isn't some demented sociopath who's looking for his or her next victim. If it is, I'm scared. Not scared he'll kill me, but that he'll tie his next murder to my pies again. Like with Mary, like Bob, and now like Edward. If he does, nobody's going to buy pies anymore and I'll have to close the shop.

"But enough about my job," I continued. "If you lose your job, there would be nobody to patrol the streets, to investigate suspicious events and make us feel safe."

"Do I really make you feel safe?" he asked with a kind of intense expression I hadn't expected.

"You make me feel safe," I said. "And that's about all I can take now. Truthfully, you also scare me and you annoy me and you worry me."

He nodded. "Good," he said.

"But I owe you," I said, determined to finally say what I should have said sooner.

Puzzled, he asked, "For what?"

"That night of the prom. I know what you did."

"Yeah, I got into a fight and I cut out."

"You saved my life," I insisted.

"That's going a little far. Those guys wouldn't have killed you, they were just having a little fun."

"I don't think so and neither do you or you wouldn't have taken them on by yourself. It wasn't a fair fight." I'd never forget how my date, Ronnie Ferguson, ran the other way when he saw the gang from the other school approaching. Then out of the blue there was Sam. While I hid, he took them on.

"I would have thanked you but you were gone. I never saw you again. Until now. I never knew what happened to you and no one else did either." There were plenty of rumors, but no one knew for sure.

"That's the way I wanted it," he said.

"I owe you," I repeated. "I have to do something. What if I start a letter-writing campaign saying how much the community needs a local police department and a chief. You."

"That's not necessary. I'll take care of it," he said. As proud as ever. Did he ever let anyone do anything for him? Then he paused and focused his gaze on something far away, something nobody could see but him. "Maybe there's no need for a police department. Once we find out who killed Mary Brandt."

"You don't really believe that, do you? That you're not needed."

He didn't answer.

"As for me," I said, gearing up for a possible putdown and a lecture on how I was not allowed any theories or ideas. I simply had to take advantage of Sam's presence in my tiny apartment. The atmosphere had changed. We were back to being, I don't know, friends or colleagues or sometime adversaries. Maybe after this murder was solved, we could be something else. Or not.

"Here's my latest idea," I said. "I ran into Edward Vaughn's grandson tonight at Heavenly Acres and my latest theory is that he killed Mary Brandt."

"The grandson?" he asked with a puzzled frown.

"No, old Edward."

"For God's sake, Hanna, that's why I don't want you messing around in this investigation. You are once again stretching things to the limit. Even for you, this is preposterous. What possible reason…"

"I'm getting to that. When you hear the story, you'll be convinced, just like I was." I wasn't at all sure he'd be convinced, but I had to try.

"The grandson convinced you his grandfather was a murderer?"

"Of course not. He doesn't know his grandfather murdered Mary Brandt."

"But you do." Sam choked on the last dregs of his coffee and shook his head with disbelief. He even gave me a wry smile. He was that amused by my theory. But I didn't care. I'd have the last laugh. I knew what I knew. At least I thought I could build a good case.

"Don't laugh. You haven't even heard my theory."

"I have a feeling I'm going to."

I sat down again, propped my elbows on the table, and leaned forward.

"Edward Vaughn hated Mary Brandt. Everyone knew that. I heard it straight from his mouth the night he died when I went to take him a piece of pie. Of course, he wasn't the only one who hated her. But to Edward and the old guard, she represented changes that threatened the life they knew at Heavenly Acres. Substituting tea parties for academic lectures, jazz concerts for chamber music, jogging trails around the rose garden, and field trips to hear the San Francisco Gay Men's chorus. Yes, I saw a sign-up sheet for it on the bulletin board. They tried to stop her. But it was like trying to stop a tidal wave. The old people were dying off and there were fewer and fewer of them. So he retreated to his room. But…and here's what happened in my opinion…he bided his time until he could knock her off. He had the means."

I held up my hand, palm forward. "He was taking warfarin. I saw it in his room. He only had to read the warning label to know how it interacts with certain foods, and he could double her dose by opening the little vials provided by the compounding pharmacy she used and dumping more drugs inside. I have a couple of his pills here I took the night I went to see him. I bet they're the same as Mary's, easy to tamper with. I'm guessing when we have them analyzed, we'll see that's what killed Mary."

"You stole some of his pills? That's a misdemeanor."

"Arrest me, then. You would have done the same if you'd been me. The only reason you wouldn't is your badge. Am I right?"

"No, you aren't," he said.

Why was Sam being so difficult when I had just solved his crime for him?

"Stole is too strong a word. I removed some evidence, that's all. Just two pills. Believe me he had plenty. And I would have given them back, but ..."

"But he died before you could."

"He certainly had the motive and the method," I continued. "All he had to do was walk into the card room before the game, see the cranberry pie, and fiddle with her pills."

"Too bad he didn't get caught on the surveillance camera," Sam said.

"He couldn't because Grannie turned it off. You saw her."

"What good luck for him to find a cranberry pie on the premises," Sam said with obvious disbelief.

"Grannie ordered cranberry because somebody asked for it. Somebody put a note in the suggestion box asking specifically for cranberries. I wonder who that was?" I asked him. I paused to let the brilliance of my discovery sink in. "Now do you believe me?" How could he not?

"I can see why you like this scenario," Sam said. He got up, went to the small four-burner stove Grannie had used for thirty years and poured himself another cup of coffee. At least he hadn't rushed out of there. Not yet. At least he was still letting me rattle on while politely listening. Off topic, I wondered what he thought of the life I had here. Maybe nothing. Maybe I didn't figure as large in his thoughts as he did in mine. "Everything works out so neatly."

I nodded. It *was* neat. No need for a long, messy trial. "But I'm open minded," I insisted. "I want you to know that. In fact I'm going to the lawyer's office Monday morning to see what I can find out. Even though I strongly believe I have fingered your murderer, I want to be completely, absolutely sure."

"How did you manage to get into the law office?" I could tell he was impressed.

"I made an appointment with the lawyer to make out my own will right after the Brandt family has their appointment."

"You need a will?"

"Everyone needs a will. Even you. I thought you knew that. But that's not why I'm going. I'm going to be sitting in the waiting room as the family comes out of Seymour Evans' law office and observing their reactions and listening to what they have to say."

"Oh, God, what next? I thought you'd convinced yourself it was old Mr. Vaughn."

"I have. But I want to convince you too, so I'm not leaving any loose ends. I'm trying to keep an open mind. Just in case I'm wrong. If somebody walks out of the lawyer's office with a big smile planning on buying the yacht they always wanted, I might suspect them of murdering Mary for their inheritance."

"How?"

"The same way. Poisoning her with a combination of cranberries and the anti-clot medicine that interacts with it and causes internal bleeding."

"How did they know she'd be eating cranberries?"

"They could have put a note in the suggestion box. Anyone could have. That's why I made that pie; someone, not my grandmother, asked for it." I sat down again, hoping I'd convinced him I was an equal-opportunity accuser.

When Sam didn't say anything for a long time, I asked, "What would happen if the city closed the police department?"

"Various options," he said, looking past me toward the window. "Crystal Cove could merge with a few other small towns. Or have the sheriff handle everything in the county. It means there would be a slower response to an emergency. We can only hope there wouldn't be any emergencies. In any case, there would be no need for a Chief of Police."

"Where would you go?"

"I'd like to stay here."

"I understand that. I like it here too. But ..."

"You mean what would I do? I thought I might run for mayor."

"Seriously?" All I could think was if his being Chief of Police was a surprise; his being mayor of the city that once kicked him out was even more preposterous. I hid a smile but not very well.

"You think that's funny?"

"I think it's a great idea. That would show Mary Brandt's son-in-law."

"Especially if he ran against me."

"Using the money he inherits from Mary," I said, light bulbs going off over my head. "It would be a struggle of good versus evil. Of course, if he's guilty of murdering Mary, he wouldn't be much of an opponent. Now I hope it's him, for your sake."

"Thanks," he said dryly.

"You'll put him away and then you're a shoo-in. You run unopposed and bingo, you're the next mayor. What does the mayor do, by the way?"

"He sits in an office on the town square and hears complaints. Then he takes action. Cleans up the streets. Improves the schools. I don't know. I'll ask Clint Eastwood what he did when he was mayor of Carmel."

"So he's your role model." I wouldn't ever tell him, but Sam did have a certain chiseled Clint Eastwood look about him, complete with the narrowed eyes. The look that said, "Make my day." "Just curious. What kind of salary does the mayor of Crystal Cove get?"

"Something like one hundred a month."

"One hundred dollars a month?" My voice rose an octave or two.

"I wouldn't do it for the money."

"Obviously. Is it the power?"

"The power. The office. The desk. The name on the door. All those things."

I thought he was kidding. Sam wanting power and his name on the door? Unbelievable. And totally out of character. "Taking a job that pays one hundred dollars a month? I assume you don't need the money."

"That's right. I put some aside in my last job."

I waited with baited breath, but he didn't elaborate. Or say how much was "some." Must have been a big chunk if he could afford to take the mayor's job. Maybe it was time I stopped feeling sorry for Sam. Finally, I couldn't stand it any longer. "What were you in—real estate, fashion design, software, piracy?"

That time he almost laughed. Why? Were those jobs so off target? Then how else does someone make a lot of money these days? He didn't say. Instead he stood and grabbed his jacket.

"Let me know how it goes at the lawyer's office," he said.

I couldn't believe he said that instead of forbidding me to ever speak of my insane plan again. "Oh, I will. I'll be making out my will. Any ideas who I should leave my pies to?"

"I don't know about the pies, but you should leave your brain to medical science. It would be a service to mankind."

He left before I could ask what exactly he meant by that. Maybe it was just as well I didn't know.

———

On Sunday, I went to the beach by myself. I needed a break. Of course I packed a picnic lunch, and it was a gorgeous day. Low tide and big breakers.

The next day, I got Kate to sit in for me at the shop, just in case...

"I'm ready to sell pies," she assured me. "When customers come, I just hope you've got enough inventory. I made a sign I'm going to put in the window. I'll throw a net out the door. Because damn it, I will not let these pies go to waste." She waved a hand at the shelves with double-crust apple and at the refrigerated case with traditional lemon meringue. Nothing exotic today. Just good old reliable standard favorites.

"You're really going to write a will?" she asked. "Is that why you're dressed up?"

"That's the idea," I said. "I assume one should dress up to go to a lawyer's office. Even if it's only a few blocks away." I was wearing an actual suit. From the back of my closet I found an outfit I often wore to art gallery openings or concerts in San Francisco. A Calvin Klein single-button stretch black jacket with a skirt that hit me just below the knees, along with my black low-heeled, open-toed shoes. I thought I might never wear these clothes again. They were a symbol of everything I wanted to leave behind. But I didn't feel any bad memories clinging to the clothes. Surely that was a good sign. Maybe I'd crossed over an invisible barrier. If I could dress up again, maybe I could trust again and even love again. Or maybe I was getting carried away with the symbolism. Sometimes a black suit is just a black suit.

I was pleased to see everything still fit me after a month of pie baking and eating. I told myself I was lucky that my problems of making a living, my lack of funds, and the effort to fend off accusations of murder kept my nervous stomach from ingesting too much food. Some people eat a lot when they're under stress; others, like me, can't eat much at all. Except when there's a chance to taste something especially delicious; I can always make an exception.

I arrived a half hour early at Seymour Evans' office above the bank on the main square in town. His secretary, whose name plate on her desk said Marjorie Wilkins, looked startled to see me. Didn't she have an appointment book? Wasn't she the Keeper of the Gate?

"I have an appointment," I said.

"You're early," she said, looking at her watch. "He's in a meeting." She peered over her reading glasses at me, wondering what kind of a person would arrive a half hour early to write their will.

I just smiled and said I'd wait. Then I took a seat on a small leather couch in his lobby and picked up a recent *New Yorker* magazine from the table. The prints on the wall were reproductions of old masterpieces. Stodgy, but in keeping for a stodgy lawyer.

Maybe I hadn't yet caught on to the new improved demographics of my hometown.

If I strained my ears, I could actually hear voices coming from the conference room but I couldn't make out any individual words. If only someone would come out or go in. You'd think I'd had enough of citizens dying or passing out, but I wished someone would faint from hearing the news of their inheritance and have to be carried out. Thus giving me the opportunity to see who was in there and get a sense of who got what and how much it was worth them to knock off Mary Brandt.

Or maybe Marjorie would leave for a moment and I could press my ear to the door. But she just sat there as unmovable as one of the life oak trees outside, every gray hair in place, staring at a computer screen, her veined hands on the keyboard. I felt certain she knew exactly what was in Mary Brandt's will. What would it take to get her to tell me? Maybe I should have brought a pie. That would have loosened her tongue. The group would be served coffee if the stainless steel coffeemaker burbling on the small table was any indication. The aroma filled the air. A collection of mugs hung on a wooden rack. Would it kill her to offer me some? After all, I was a client bringing in business. But maybe she was saving it for the heirs of Mary Brandt of which I was not.

"I suppose Seymour is pretty busy these days," I said.

She looked up as startled as if a statue had come to life.

I continued. "What with people dying and all. Not that I'm planning to die anytime soon, but I hear it's a good idea to make out a will. I mean, you never know."

She gave me a condescending look as if I'd stated the obvious and she found it annoying when she was trying to work. With a sigh, she explained. "Mr. Evans is the only attorney in town. He handles everything. Wills and estates, property disputes, real estate, probate …."

"What about criminal defense?"

"What about it?"

"Does he defend criminals?"

"If he has to, but this is Crystal Cove," she explained with a pained expression on her face.

Oh, of course. No one ever commits a crime here.

"Am I the youngest person to ever have him write up my will?"

"I couldn't say," she said stiffly. "That's confidential information."

"I understand."

The minutes ticked by. Then it happened. Lurline came in wearing a short skirt, a tight pink T-shirt, a cardboard box in her hand, and a big smile on her face that faded when she saw me.

"You again," she hissed.

I gave her my sweetest smile and said nothing.

She set the box on Marjorie's desk and handed her a bill. "Four chocolate coconut, three chocolate caramel, six chocolate cherry Casablanca, and four chocolate marshmallow."

My mouth watered. I hated myself for it but I was dying to taste that chocolate marshmallow, for research purposes only, of course. I wanted to know how it compared to my S'Mores Pie. I wanted to know how this cupcake woman got all this business. Where was she from? Now was not the time to ask, so I just sat there silently fuming while Marjorie paid her and she left.

After a long moment I finally spoke. "Those look good," I said, just to show I had nothing against cupcakes, just against their baker.

She looked up as if she'd forgotten I was there. At least she was trying to forget I was there. "I wouldn't know," she said. Honestly, did the woman have a normal reaction to anything? "The clients ordered the cupcakes. No one asked me."

The clients? Who in the family ordered the cupcakes? Was it Blake? I stood up and went to the window and looked out at the town square. It was a bucolic scene. People were walking their dogs. Children ran through the sprinklers to keep cool on this warm summer day. The grass was like green velvet. I wished I was out there running through a sprinkler instead of dressed up playing a role in this stuffy office. I wondered how many pies Kate had sold. What was I doing here?

I thought about canceling my appointment. I watched Lurline get into her silver and hot pink converted van with Lurline's Luscious Cupcakes painted on the side. Okay, cupcakes were more portable than a piece of pie, not requiring a plate and fork, but still, I could make portable pies like apple squares and lemon tarts.

Marjorie set the box of cupcakes on top of a bookcase that was full of books like *Torts, General Edition*; *Constitutional Law*; and *Civil Procedure*. How Marjorie resisted the temptation to sample a cupcake, I don't know. If I worked there, I would have succumbed immediately. But that's me. I had no self-control.

After an eternity, Marjorie finally got up and went to the water cooler in the corner of the room. Not far enough for me to rush to the door and start listening or look at the cupcakes to see how they were decorated. But Seymour finally did open the door to his office just a crack. I craned my neck to see who was inside.

Marjorie flushed bright red as if she'd been caught playing computer Solitaire. She stood at attention like a soldier waiting for orders.

"I need the Brandt family transfer of ownership papers," he said.

She nodded and walked across the room to a huge file cabinet. Was this old small-town lawyer and his secretary who'd been here for ages still storing documents in a file cabinet? At least she had a computer on her desk. I heard voices from inside the office. Just a low murmur, no shouts, no screams. Had they gotten to the good part yet? Would someone faint? Would there be a fist fight? I prayed for some excitement. I wanted a breakthrough. Or I wanted assurance not one of them had a motive for killing Mary. That's why I was there. Seymour stood at the open door ignoring me. That was happening to me a lot.

Marjorie found what she was looking for and handed it to him.

"The cupcakes have arrived," she said with a nod at the box.

He put the file under his arm and took the box in his hands while I watched, fascinated. He closed the door behind him. Silence descended on the outer office.

"Quite a shock, Mrs. Brandt dying so unexpectedly," I said.

"I didn't know her," the secretary said.

"I didn't either. I hear she was quite a mover and shaker around here. Charities. Bridge." I waited. She said nothing.

"In fact that's why I'm here," I said. "To find out who hated her enough to wish she was dead."

Marjorie's eyes popped. She dropped her pen on the floor. Finally, I had her attention.

THIRTEEN

When Marjorie finally looked at me, it was as if I might possibly be someone worth noticing.

"I mean someone dying unexpectedly like that, it reminded me that all deaths are not accidental so it's important to have a will. None of us knows when we'll be taken away," I said. "By natural causes or otherwise." I was careful not to use the M word. "So I decided to write my will now, just in case. I don't suppose you have many other clients my age." It didn't do any good to reword the question I'd asked earlier. She still "couldn't say."

"Of course I don't have much to leave anyone," I continued. As if she cared. "Just my grandmother's pie shop. She lives up at Heavenly Acres."

"How nice." Marjorie reached into her drawer, took out a snap-top vial and shook a few pills into her hand. Then she tossed them into her mouth and washed them down with her coffee. Being interested in medication these days, I couldn't help but wonder what it was. I could only hope they were mood enhancers so she'd cheer up and start gossiping.

If I was a run-of-the-mill client of Seymour's, I never would have sat there chatting up the secretary, but her reticence was a challenge and an obstacle I was determined to overcome. As a legal secretary she must know a lot. As a legal secretary she was obviously sworn to secrecy. But couldn't she just share a tiny crumb of information with me that might save me and my grandmother from imprisonment? Or was I wasting my whole morning sitting here in this airless office listening to the rumble of voices that told me nothing? There was no possibility of my wasting time with Sam this close to arresting Grannie, especially after the video of her in the card room and her lie detector tests. I had to find the real murderer and I only had one more day to do it.

I wondered if Sam's job was really at stake, considering his casual attitude about closing the station. Why did he disapprove of my going out sleuthing for him? What harm could I do? Instead, he was always cautioning me to butt out of his investigation the way all the other policemen did with the amateurs who offered to help the local cops.

That story about running for mayor, which paid one hundred a month? I didn't believe that for a minute. Police chiefs make plenty. Even in small towns. If he didn't need the money, if he'd really made a bundle in the time between high school and now, why hadn't he told me how he'd done it? Instead of returning to a town he couldn't wait to escape from, why didn't he take his fortune, if he had one, and hit the road? He could buy a yacht and sail to the Mediterranean and thumb his nose at the town that kicked him out. That's what I'd do.

"It is nice," I said, trying to keep the conversation going. "They've got activities up the wazoo, like water aerobics and Bridge. Mary Brandt was a champion."

"That's not what I heard," she said.

I inched forward in my chair, trying not to look too eager.

"Her partner's cousin is a friend of my dentist."

"Dr. Klein, is he your dentist?"

"Dr. Klein retired years ago. His nephew Denny took over his practice. He took out my wisdom tooth on Saturday. I shouldn't even be here today, but Seymour had the big meeting so I had to come. I'm on Sodium Pentothal."

I nodded. Truth serum. If I couldn't get something out of her now, I never would. "What did you hear about Mary?"

"She cheated at cards."

Duh. I already knew that. I waited impatiently for her to tell me something I didn't know when the door to the office finally opened wide and Mary's relatives began drifting into the waiting area. I held my breath and tried to look invisible. I didn't have to worry. They didn't notice me. They were talking loudly to each other. Just what I'd hoped would happen.

"Can't believe it."

"All that money."

"What a waste."

"Gone to the dogs."

What did it mean? Had she really left it all to the pit bulls?

I recognized her son-in-law, Sam's nemesis, who muttered "Linda deserves better from her own mother" to a young man I'd never seen before.

When I spotted Blake's mother, Linda, standing in the doorway, she was actually smiling. Maybe she'd gotten more than she imagined. Or she was just glad she didn't have to deal with her mother anymore. I caught a glimpse of Blake looking gorgeous as usual in an Aloha shirt that showed off his East Coast tan and wrinkled khaki shorts showing the world that this was no big deal. I liked his attitude. I admired his legs too. He looked surprised to see me, but he came over to where I was waiting.

"Hey, what are you doing here?" he said.

"Just getting some legal advice," I said. "Seymour is the only game in town."

"He seems to know what he's doing."

"Good to know," I said. "So you're happy with his work?"

"Oh, yes," he said with a big smile.

I waited, hoping he'd go on and elaborate, but his mother called him over and he gave me a half wave and a wink and said he'd see me later.

My big surprise was seeing Donna, Mary's former partner, walk past me by herself. She looked a little dazed but well turned out in a white linen blazer over a frilly silk blouse, matching slacks, and Kate Spade black flats just made for a ceremony like this one. I only hoped that someday I'd have the cash for a wardrobe like Grannie's friends had. Because at that age, I'd need all the help I could get to look halfway decent. Had Donna known all along that Mary had left her something, or was she surprised to be invited as the only non-family member there? What had Mary left her? I couldn't tell by her expression. She didn't look happy or sad, just blah. Maybe she was still in shock from losing her Bridge partner. Maybe she was actually sadder than any family members. Losing Mary might mean losing her chance to move ahead to the big tournament.

I caught her eye before she left and gave her a little wave of recognition.

"Hanna, what are you doing here?" she asked, her blue eyes wide with surprise.

"I have an appointment with the lawyer," I said. "How did it go in there?" I wouldn't have been surprised to hear her say it was none of my business, but she didn't.

"No surprises," she said. She looked over her shoulder. The family had all left. "I told you how she felt about them," she said in a half whisper. "But they got what they deserved."

"What about you?" I asked.

She pressed her fingers to her lips, then she shook her head as the lawyer walked toward us carrying a stack of file folders.

"Mrs. Linton? I have a few papers for you to sign. Come into my office."

I watched as Donna followed Seymour into his office and closed the door behind them. Papers to sign? That must mean she got something. I'd find out one way or another.

The door to the large meeting room was wide open. I very casually stood in the doorway surveying the scene. Then I boldly walked into the empty room and looked around at the empty chairs, wishing the walls could talk. Coffee cups, cupcake crumbs, and a few leftover cupcakes were still in the box in the middle of the table.

Marjorie was talking on the phone in the waiting room, saying something about dying without a will wasn't a good idea. I was glad to hear her giving good advice and trying to bring in business. I assumed Mary Brandt's will and the division of her estate ought to be plenty lucrative for Crystal Cove's only estate lawyer. And only criminal lawyer and only family law lawyer.

I stood there at the end of the long oval cherry wood conference table trying to imagine what had gone on in this room. The veneer on the surface of the table was so shiny I could almost see my reflection.

I leaned over, curious as to which cupcakes were left. I wanted to know what flavors were most popular for the purposes of culinary research, of course. Without thinking I reached for one with a towering peak of coconut-dusted butter cream frosting. I held it up to my nose and inhaled the rich scent of vanilla. Then I couldn't resist. I bit into the cupcake. I closed my eyes to savor the taste and analyze the ingredients. Which is why I didn't notice Seymour had come into the conference room until he cleared his throat.

"Ms. Denton?" he said.

I whirled around and almost choked on my cupcake.

"Come into my office."

"Thank you," I said after I'd stuffed the rest of the cupcake into my purse and regained my composure.

"Have a seat," he said, pointing to the adjoining room. "I'll be with you in a moment."

Just what I wanted. A moment alone in his book-lined office with time to snoop around. There on his huge glass-topped desk was the stack of file folders Marjorie had given him. I sidled up to the desk and read upside down just in case I had no warning as to his return. Each folder had a different name on it. Most names were Wilson, for Mary's heirs, and there was one marked Brandt.

Right on top was the one with Linda Wilson's name neatly typed on the tab.

The absolute top of my wish list was to find out what Mary had left her daughter, Linda. I assumed she'd left nothing to Linda's husband if she really disapproved of him so strongly. I would love to find a motive for her to kill her mother. Very slowly and carefully I slid the folder toward me across the smooth glass surface of the desk. I flipped it open, and there in bold type was a list of items on the first page. At the bottom of the sheet was a sum of money that left me breathless. Could it be the amount of money Mary had left her daughter? Or a total of all the items?

When the door opened, I had time to slide the folder back in place and assume what I hoped was an innocent expression before Seymour told me to sit down in the chair facing his desk.

He sat behind the desk, straightened the folders several times in an obsessive manner, then set them aside. When he looked up at me, his eyes narrowed. I thought right away he knew I'd been snooping. Delving into matters that I had no right to. First the cupcake, then his file folders. In my opinion it was his own fault. He'd left the cupcakes on the table and he'd left the folders on his desk. He had to assume any normal person would first, eat a cupcake and second, look to see what was in the folders.

"Busy day," I said, licking my lips to remove any telltale cupcake crumbs.

"Yes indeed. Seeing as I'm the only lawyer in town I am always busy. Now, what can I do for you?"

"I want to make out a will. I know it might seem a little premature…"

"Not at all. It's never too early to think about the distribution of your estate. And you can always update your will when you marry and have children."

I frowned. "I'm not sure I'll get married or have children or that I have an estate. All I have is a pie shop and my grandmother's old car."

"You may think you don't have many assets, but you likely have more than you think." He took a yellow pad of legal-sized paper from a shelf and wrote something on it. I strained my eyes. It looked like he just wrote my name. Or maybe it was my name followed by "no assets" or "deadbeat." "What *is* required of someone making a will is that they be of sound mind," he added, tilting his head to one side as if he wasn't sure about me.

I smiled politely, hoping he wasn't going to insist I have some kind of psychiatric exam to prove my mind was sound.

"All we really need for a will is a list of your bequests and the name of your executor," he said.

"Ah," I said. "Then I'd like to leave my pie shop to my friend Kate Blaine."

"Take your time and think about it," he said, as if I'd suggested leaving everything to Lady Gaga. "You may want to also leave small items like jewelry or clothing to friends or family along with special messages. For example, Wear them in good health, or Enjoy these and think of me."

"Is that the custom?" I asked. I wanted to ask, *Is that what Mary Brandt did?*

"Some people take the opportunity to send a negative message with the bequest to someone they wish to hurt in some way, knowing they won't have to face the recipient or their friends and family again. Something they've always wanted to say but never did. It's a last chance sort of thing."

"I see. I never would have thought of that." Unlike Mary Brandt, I didn't have any enemies that I knew of. Except for Lurline. But after this murder was solved, I intended to make peace with her. Who wouldn't love a pie lady? I asked myself. Which is partly why I became a pie baker. Not just for the money. It was for the love.

He nodded. "That's why I'm here, to help you sort things out."

I took a deep breath. No harm in pushing the envelope. After all, I was paying him for his time. "I imagine someone like Mary Brandt had quite a lot more than myself to dispose of."

"Most old people do. That doesn't mean you shouldn't be writing your will now. You can always update it later after any significant life event." He wrote something on his yellow pad. "So. Jewelry?" He glanced at me, probably disappointed I wasn't wearing a diamond necklace or earrings. "Property such as a house or a business? What else?"

I didn't have anything else. It made me feel poor and out of place making a will when I had so little to leave behind. I sighed.

"You might want to go home and take an inventory of your valuables, then come back another day with a list of them and the beneficiaries."

"And the special messages," I said. "I suppose if one were the type to send a negative message, what would it be? Not that I would have any reason to do such a thing. I just wondered..."

"That would leave your heirs a bad impression of you, the departed," he said sternly.

"Yes, but you said it was a chance to say something you always wanted to say but never could."

"Whatever you wish," he said with a glance at the vintage walnut clock on the wall.

"Or I could leave nothing at all to certain parties I feel didn't deserve anything or who had wronged me. Has anyone ever done that?" I asked pointedly.

"I'm sure someone has. But I don't advise it."

"Did you advise Mary Brandt?"

He shifted in his high-back executive leather chair. "She was my client. I advise all my clients if they wish to be advised."

"I understand from her friends at the retirement home she didn't take advice kindly."

"As an attorney I can only offer my advice, I cannot force my clients to take it. You are in the pie business, I understand. Do your customers always take your advice?"

"Well…" What was he getting at? Every time I tried to interview someone they turned the tables and started peppering me with questions. Was it happening again? "I do make suggestions depending on what the occasion is or their preferences—savory or sweet pies, fruit or chocolate, a party or an intimate dinner, a Bridge game or…"

"Then you understand that although you may have a good option for the client, they do not always take your advice. If your business is anything like mine, you are dealing with humans and their frailties, such as stubbornness, denial, hope, greed, pride, and prejudice. I take my position very seriously. I assume you do too."

I crossed and uncrossed my legs. How did I get into a philosophical discussion with this lawyer about the similarities between pies and wills when there really weren't any?

I had to try one more time to find out something. Anything.

"If I wanted to punish someone after my death, what should I leave them so they would know how I felt? Nothing? Or something insignificant? Or something that only they would understand was an insult?"

His nostrils tightened as if I'd suggested leaving someone a dead skunk. "I can't advise you on anything like that. I wouldn't tell any of my clients to take revenge on someone. For one thing, revenge is a dish best served cold."

"Isn't that from *The Godfather*?" I asked.

"Actually it's an ancient Klingon proverb," he explained.

"Really?" I knew I should have paid more attention to those *Star Trek* movies. "I'm not sure what it means," I said. "Or how it applies to me and my will."

"It means that revenge is more satisfying when it's unexpected or long feared."

"As in after death. Just as I thought."

"If you are looking for revenge ..." he said with a frown.

"Not me. Just ... anyone. Like Mary Brandt, for example. Did she get her revenge after her death or before?"

He must be wondering why I was fixated on Mrs. Brandt.

"I am not aware that she was a vengeful person," he said with a slight telltale flush on his round face.

How could he say that? To know Mary was to know Vengeance was her middle name. Either he didn't know her or he couldn't violate the lawyer's code of secrecy. I thought I had my answer for all the good it did me. I decided to change the subject.

"Can you tell me if you think I should have a reading of the will like you did today? I understand it's not necessary, but call me a prima donna, I really like the idea of a little drama." I glanced at a painting on the wall. Under the frame was a small plaque. *1820. Oil on Canvas. Reading the Will. Sir David Wilkie.* It was a dramatic scene, full of color and action, with old people, babies, and children on the scene, and of course a lawyer reading from a manuscript. It looked like a valuable original painting. I wondered idly who Seymour was going to leave it to when he died.

"Quite right. In fact a reading of the will is very unusual these days. Usually left to scenes in paintings and movies. Most of the time, I send a copy of the will to each beneficiary and that's it. No drama. No tension."

"So they don't need to be present. And yet today..." I held my breath waiting to hear what the conditions were for today's exceptional occasion.

"Today only the family was here, with one exception."

"Donna Linton."

He didn't look happy that I noticed. From the sour look on his face he probably wished he'd kept his mouth shut and that I'd leave. Why? Was there something important he wasn't telling me? If only he'd tell me who'd been left out of the will or who was slighted. Who was angry? Her son-in-law? Who was pleasantly surprised? The Pit Bull Society? Who was disappointed? Donna? If he didn't tell me, I would find out one way or another. Because I was convinced someone who was in his office today killed Mary.

"If that's all..." he said, getting up from his posh super-sized chair. "I don't believe we can get any further until you've answered the questions about your beneficiaries."

"I'll get back to you with that," I said, standing and walking slowly to the door. Wracking my brain to come up with more questions. Never mind. I had an excuse to come back with the answers to the assignment he'd given me, though it would cost me. I didn't know how much lawyers like him charged by the hour, but if I could find out anything, it would be worth it.

Back at the shop, Kate was not alone. Sam was sitting at the little table drinking coffee, seeming as at home as if he did it every day. How had she lured him in when I had such a hard time doing that? Kate was standing in the middle of the shop, an apron around her waist and a smug smile on her face.

"How did it go?" she asked.

"I'm exhausted."

"Hope it was worth it."

"Time will tell. Anything happen here?"

Kate grinned. "Had a rush of customers after the will reading."

I glanced at the empty refrigerated case and the bare shelves behind the counter. There was hardly anything left. Just a half four-berry pie and a wedge of key lime. "I can't believe this. They served cupcakes at the lawyer's office and they still came here for pie. I'm speechless."

"That will be the day," Sam muttered.

"And where was I? Meeting with the lawyer so I can make out my will. When I should have been here. What did they say? Who was here, exactly?"

"Pretty much the whole family, I think. Her granddaughter, Melissa, was wearing the diamond necklace Mary had left her."

"How did they seem? What was the atmosphere?"

Sam said nothing. He just watched me and Kate going back and forth. Probably taking notes in his head. Or tuning out completely from this inane, useless chatter.

"It was far from funereal," Kate said. "No tears, I can tell you that. If Mary left anyone out of her will, I couldn't tell. If you and Sam are trying to figure out who had reason to kill Mary for their inheritance, it seems they all qualify. They were here to celebrate. And since there's no place like a pie shop for a celebration, they piled in. I found some folding chairs in your closet upstairs."

"The biggest sales day of the year so far and I missed it," I said, shaking my head. Not to mention all the gossip I didn't hear.

"Sit down," I told Kate. "And tell me everything."

"Can't do it," she said. "Gotta run. By the way, I invited Sam to dinner tonight."

"Sam?" I said, as surprised as if she'd invited Jack the Ripper. Hadn't she said she was inviting Blake? Had he turned her down?

"Is that a problem?" he asked.

"Of course not," I said.

"Dinner's at seven. Hope you can come too. But no murder mystery talk allowed. From either of you. Understand?"

"Wait," I said, but she'd tossed her apron on the chair and she was out the door.

I glanced at Sam. "What did she mean, no murder mystery talk?"

"Why don't you ask her? She's your friend."

"What are you doing here chatting up *my* friend then? I know you didn't come for the pie. Did you learn anything from the Brandt heirs, or did they clam up when they saw you?" I knew he wouldn't tell me anything important, but I was getting desperate.

The clock was ticking. I had to pin this murder on someone and I wanted it to hold up.

"I don't think they noticed me. That's the way I like it. They were high on sugar and caffeine and on their inheritance."

Not notice Sam? Sure, he didn't wear a uniform, but with his height, his cool demeanor, and his casual Brooks Brothers shirt and blazer he hardly blended into the local landscape.

"Did you zero in on anyone special in the crowd? Which I assume is why you're here." I said. "Or are they all under suspicion?"

He didn't say anything for a long moment, and my heart sank. I was afraid he was going to tell me it was none of my business or that none of them were under suspicion, not when he had me and my grandmother to focus on.

"If you don't want to share your information, I understand. Though if I were you I'd be glad to get help from myself. Especially since you've given me a deadline."

"What kind of help would that be?" he asked, standing and bracing his hands on the wrought-iron chair he'd been sitting on.

"Snooping where even the long arm of the law can't reach."

"I can't condone snooping," he said. "Or breaking privacy laws."

"But you can't forbid it either." I ran my hand through my hair. "I've got to get busy. My shelves are empty."

He got the message and went to the door. "Want a ride to the Blaines' tonight?"

"Sure. I'll be here."

To keep my mind off the scene at the lawyer's office in which I learned practically nothing, and the scene at my own pie shop that

I'd missed out on, and the dinner at Kate's I was committed to, I headed to the kitchen.

How was I supposed to act tonight when my best friend was engaging in an act of blatant and devious behavior, trying to throw me and Sam together? Did he notice? Did he care? Obviously not, or he would have turned her down. If we couldn't talk about the murder, then what would we talk about? Old times? I couldn't afford a strictly social evening when the clock was ticking and I still didn't have my proof.

To calm my overactive mind, I changed into my baking clothes —stretch pants, a blue and white University of California T-shirt, and my clogs—and started a frenzy of activity in the kitchen. I trusted my repaired oven would hold up for another forty years and decided to go with something savory. Not just because Sam didn't eat sugar, or so he said. There are others who might also enjoy an Asparagus Tart with Vacherin Cheese. I hadn't asked Kate what she was serving tonight or what I should bring, so I'd make whatever I felt like.

I would use this downtime to stop thinking about murder victims or suspects or inheritances and just focus on pie before I burned out. I made my tart and it looked and smelled wonderful, but I didn't stop there. I was filled with a restless kind of energy.

I pressed onward, flipping through my files looking for something challenging, something I'd never made before. I was anxious to keep my mind from dwelling on Mary's greedy family, or the vision of dapper old Edward looking far from death's door when I saw him. Death. Always around the corner, whether you're expecting it or not. Whether you're twenty, fifty, or ninety-five. Despite the heat that billowed from the old oven, I felt a cold shiver run up my spine. Was that death sending me a message? Don't waste a moment. Live every day as if it is your last. Grab happiness and hold on to it.

FOURTEEN

When I forced myself to stop thinking about death, I glanced out into the shop. There was Blake, looking totally different but just as gorgeous as ever, this time in an East Coast uniform of suit and tie. I was so involved in my recipe search, I hadn't heard the door.

I closed the big black loose-leaf notebook and went out into the shop.

"More pie?" I asked.

"The only thing that's more tempting than your pie is you," he said, a devilish glint in his blue eyes. "I'm leaving tonight. I came to say goodbye. I wish I didn't have to go so soon. If I'd known you were back in town, I would have taken some vacation days." He looked out the window. "I forgot how the town can get into your blood, grab you, and won't let you go. Know what I mean?"

I wasn't sure I did but I nodded anyway. "Maybe you'll come back more often."

"Now that I know you're here, I definitely will do that. And you're coming to New York, remember? And don't say you can't come because of your shop. Everybody needs a vacation. The town will just have to get along without pie for a week or two."

"You're right." I would need a vacation after this murder was solved.

"How did it go this morning?" I asked. I wasn't ready to promise to close up and go visit Blake in New York.

"No surprises in Gram's will. She left a token to each one of us. My sister got a necklace, I got her father's watch." He rolled up his sleeve to show off an antique Swiss timepiece set in platinum.

"Wow," I said.

"Kind of a drag having to wind it manually," he said, "but I remember now she told me I could have it one day. I guess it's worth a lot. Mom says Gram definitely wanted me to have it, but just in case another will is found I'm taking off today with my watch. Just kidding," he added with a grin that showed off his perfect white teeth.

"You don't really think there's another will, do you?" I asked.

"Rumor has it Gram wasn't happy with her lawyer, old Seymour. Can't understand why, he seemed okay to me. But you know her. Or maybe you didn't know her."

"Not really."

"So she threatened to update her will herself, but no one's found it if she did."

"I guess they've searched her apartment at Heavenly Acres."

"For now the police have it cordoned off until the complete autopsy report comes back from the coroner. Nobody goes in or out."

"Really?" Why hadn't anyone told me that? Anyone like my friend the Chief of Police or one of the other residents like Grannie. Maybe that's what Sam meant by forbidding me to snoop. I tried not to act too excited. But I was. If I was going to snoop, that was the place to do it.

Was one of Sam's officers posted outside the door with a gun in his holster? If not, since when did just a cordon keep me from going where I wanted to go? Never. I was so excited about the possibility of discovering something, I was hardly listening as Blake was talking about his trip back to New York and the weekend he had planned on Long Island. Finally, he shook my hand, kissed me on the cheek, and walked out.

"Safe trip," I called as he loped toward a black BMW. He turned and waved, blew me a kiss and drove away.

Before I closed the shop, I turned off the oven and changed into khaki slacks and a tank top, hoping I wouldn't run into Grannie at Heavenly Acres, who would doubtless criticize my appearance as not being smart enough for a visit to her upscale digs. A truck was parked at the retirement home's front entrance with the words Petrelli's Flowers painted in the side. So someone was having fresh flowers delivered to their door. What a life these old folks lived.

Once inside, I saw some residents in tennis whites, some in visor caps, shorts, and Lacoste shirts, but not my grandmother. They all looked like they had stepped out of an ad for an over-fifty-five luxury retirement community. I couldn't help thinking of Edward. Where were the ninety-somethings? Holed up in their apartments waiting for something to happen?

I walked down the hall, smiling brightly and saying hello to everyone I met until I came to Mary Brandt's apartment. No possibility of missing it with that yellow tape across the door. Once I realized there was no overweight or even normal-sized officer on duty, I thought it would be easy to just lift the "Crime Scene Do Not Enter" tape from her doorway, but it wasn't. For one thing, there were people in the hallway. No one I knew personally, thank heavens, but other residents on their way to high tea in the lounge or a favorite sport.

They walked past the door, some women like Grannie in capri pants and matching shirts and light-scented floral perfume, men in T-shirts and shorts on their way out to play miniature golf or shuffleboard, as if having a crime scene in the neighborhood was not a downer, just an everyday event.

When I got a chance, I casually leaned against Mary's door and tried the knob. As I suspected, it was locked. So I stood staring at the door until someone walked by and said hello as if I was waiting for something or someone.

I was momentarily tempted to break the door down or go outside and climb a ladder to the second floor. But I remembered from when Grannie was choosing her place that these second-floor balconies were shared with the next-door neighbor, which was why Grannie chose the first floor unit with the private patio. All I had to do was get into the next apartment. I tried that door and it was unlocked. That's why they liked it here. The residents felt safe and secure enough to leave their doors unlocked. At least some of them did.

I knocked on the door next door. A woman walked by and said, "Maxine is playing golf today."

"Thanks," I said. Then when the woman left I quickly entered Maxine's apartment. I assumed she wouldn't mind since it was all in the interest of solving a crime and making her home safe from more murders. Furthermore, if I was careful, she'd never know. I went straight through the apartment to the oversized balcony with the view of the spacious lawn below, closed the patio door behind me, and crossed quickly over to Mary's place before someone spotted me and thought, "What's she doing up there in that dead woman's apartment?"

Amazingly, Mary's sliding glass door was unlocked. But inside Mary's living room with the pale gray walls and the neutral wall-to-wall carpet, it looked like someone had been there before me and swept the place clean. Not a personal item to be seen. It looked like it was for sale already. Maybe it was. Then why did the police bother to cordon off the entrance?

I went into her bedroom. The walls were pale peach with re-productions of two famous paintings hung over the king-sized bed. The bed was made up as if for a photo shoot or a real estate open house, with cream-colored sheets, a café au lait–colored blanket, and a raft of pillows. In the middle of the bed was a tray set up with a small plate, a glass, a bud vase with a rose in it, a cup and saucer, and a large cloth napkin. Just waiting for the occupant to wake up, smell the rose, and eat breakfast. Only the former oc-cupant wasn't going to wake up. I desperately wanted to believe she died a natural death like Grannie and Donna said she did. But even they were going to come around to the murder verdict, if they hadn't already. Everyone else was sure she'd been killed.

I immediately checked the huge walk-in closet. Nothing but empty rods and drawers, shoe racks, and shelves. Somebody had removed all of Mary's clothes, and done what with them? Given them to the Good Will? Or tossed them in the dumpster behind the main building? The kitchen was next. It was even more upscale than Grannie's with granite counters, a stainless steel refrigerator, and a pale natural oak floor. I wondered if Mary had entertained anyone here, perhaps even Bob. Maybe she was into whipping up food for an intimate dinner or two and baking it in her convection oven mounted on the wall. But the cool perfection of the room made it look like no one had ever so much as brewed a cup of coffee there. Why bother, when it was available downstairs twenty-four/seven?

That's when I heard the front door open. And voices. I ran back to the bedroom and had a split second to decide whether to leave by the deck from which I'd come or drop to my knees on the plush carpet and crawl under the bed. I chose the latter. I hadn't found anything, but after all, I hadn't quite finished looking.

It was a man and a woman. I could tell by their voices and by their shoes, which I saw from my vantage point under the bed when they entered the bedroom. How did they get in when I couldn't? Staff members? Family?

"There's nothing left," the woman said. "The place is empty."

"It must be here. There might be a wall safe. Look behind the pictures. I can't believe she forgot about it," the man said.

"She didn't forget. She gave it to someone else."

"But she promised..."

"She promised to make it worth your while if you'd buy her a deck of marked cards and the luminous sunglasses that go with it."

I had to clamp my lips together to keep from shouting out, "So she *was* cheating."

"I did that. I didn't want to but I did it. I ordered it over the Internet. She said she'd do anything to win at Bridge. How could I say no when it meant so much to her?"

"You helped her cheat because you knew she'd make it worth your while, didn't you?"

"Not exactly. She said I'd get my reward when she got her marching papers."

"Marching papers? Oh, is that a euphemism for croaking?"

"Which is a euphemism for 'bite the dust.'"

"Or buying the farm."

"Stop talking and start looking. We haven't got much time."

"There's nowhere to look. The place is gutted. She left it somewhere else."

"The lawyer said it was in her final will and testament."

"They always say that. What did he know? It's got to be here."

My heart pounded. Whatever they wanted to find, I did too.

"Okay, I'll look behind the pictures. But I'm sure she didn't have a wall safe. She kept everything in her safe-deposit box at the bank."

"Before you look, get rid of that stuff on the bed."

"Yeah, yeah." she said. The whole bed shook as the woman stood on the bed and presumably took the pictures down one at a time.

"Nothing," she said and she jumped off the bed with a thud. "Are you happy now?"

"No, I'm not happy," he said. "I kept my promise, she got her cards. She said she'd leave me something. Something big. She let me down. I got nothing."

"Nothing? You got her car."

"That pile of junk."

"It's an antique."

"Let's go. There's nothing here."

I breathed a sigh of relief. When I heard the front door close, I edged my way out from under the bed, gripping the edge of the mattress. Just to be sure I'd covered all the bases I slid my hand between the box spring and the mattress. I gasped. There was something there. Why was I so surprised? Everyone hides their valuables under the mattress. Then why hadn't those two looked there? I grabbed the small, slim leather-covered booklet, got up, and looked back at the bed with the footprints on the quilt they hadn't bothered to smooth out.

I was dying to look inside to see what I'd found. But I knew it had to be worth something if Mary had gone to all the trouble to hide it. I tucked it under my arm and headed back to the deck. But when I crossed the balcony to the door I'd come from, I saw a woman inside, wearing only a pair of floppy shorts and a bra and doing exercises in front of a television set. She looked up, saw me, and screamed. I dashed back toward Mary's place, hoping she wouldn't follow me. Even more important, I hoped she didn't recognize me. I looked down. Too far to jump. I went back to Mary's apartment, ran through it, and left through the front door the way the other couple had, crashing through the tape across the door just as they must have done.

I was panting but forced myself to walk slowly down the corridor as if I belonged there and wasn't on the run with a valuable document under my arm. I was hoping it was what I thought it was. A new and revised will. Or was it an old will written before the one in the lawyer's office? Or was it Mary's diary filled with salacious details of her sex life? Or a list of people she feared might be after her? That might be the best thing for me because it might lead to her murderer. I could only hope.

Finally, out in my car I was afraid to take time to look at my treasure. I was also afraid the woman next door who'd screamed had called security, who were now looking for me.

I drove back to the shop, determined to fulfill my obligations before I went back to being an amateur sleuth. I had to make a pie for dessert even though I only had an hour before dinner. Even though Kate hadn't asked for anything, if you have a pie shop everyone expects you to show up at any social occasion with something you've made. I couldn't let her down, and I had to admit I hadn't given up trying to tempt Sam to break his "no sugar" diet restriction.

I kept the notebook in my purse but deliberately didn't look at it. First things first. The notebook could wait, but the pie couldn't. I turned my attention to dessert. Being it was summer, I knew I should make something light and fruity. I came up with a simple fresh raspberry pie I could serve with either whipped cream or homemade vanilla ice cream, but no time for the latter, so I stuck to the former. I hadn't had time to change clothes when Sam came to the door to pick me up.

I yelled down the stairs, telling him I'd be there in a minute. I knew I'd better dress carefully, or I'd get into trouble with Kate for not making an effort to look good when she'd made the effort to invite me over, along with the only remaining single man in town. I knew exactly what she was up to. I could only hope Sam didn't suspect he was being set up as my date. I plugged my curling iron into the outlet in the bathroom to try to work some magic on my hair. But what to wear? What was in my closet that Kate would approve of? All I had were my city clothes.

I chose a pair of pale, off-white Isaac Mizrahi linen-blend pants I used to wear to work in the office, which seemed like a million years ago. Then I slipped into a pair of gladiator sandals that went with everything. Next I pawed through my drawer and found a cashmere pullover in a luscious raspberry sherbet color that matched my pie. I shook my hair down over my face, then divided it into three sections. I pulled one over the other until I had a pretty decent loose braid hanging down my neck and fastened it with a rubber band. I took out a few loose strands of hair at the nape of my neck and one at my temples and gave them the treatment with the curling iron for a more feminine touch. All to impress Kate, of course. As for Sam, who knew what would impress him? It wasn't my brilliant analytical mind and it wasn't my baking of any product that contained sugar.

With my brilliant analytical mind, I should have no trouble deciphering Mary's diary or whatever it was I'd taken. I just didn't have time right now. Whatever it was, it was still in my purse and burning a hole in my arm as I flung my bag over my shoulder on my way down the stairs. I was afraid to leave it anywhere.

"Sorry to keep you waiting," I said breathlessly. Breathless from rushing to get ready and breathless at the sight of the man who looked better than ever in designer jeans and a blue Lacoste T-shirt.

Sam was sitting at one of my small tables, staring at his notebook computer. He closed it when he saw me; and did a double take. "New hair?"

"Kind of." My face flushed as I felt a wave of pleasure that he'd noticed. "Still working?" I asked with a glance at his computer.

"Of course."

"How can anyone imagine Crystal Cove doesn't need a police chief?" I asked. "Your work is never done. Protecting the populace."

"Almost as important as you feeding the populace."

"I wish."

I took my savory pie from the oven and my raspberry pie from the refrigerator and loaded them into my old reliable wicker basket, along with the dough figures Kate's girls had molded the day they came to the bakery.

Sam sniffed the air but said nothing. Would it kill him to tell me something smelled good and he was looking forward to my pies? If we weren't going to talk about pie and we were forbidden to talk murder or mystery, what would we talk about at Kate's?

Sam parked in Kate's driveway, but before we got out of the car, he put his hand on my shoulder. "You may think I'm being hard on you and on your grandmother."

"Whatever gave you that idea?" I asked.

"I know what you think, but I'm asking you to have faith in the system. It works. I know it seems unfair that you can't go off snooping as you call it, but you really have to leave it to us. The guilty will be punished and the innocent will be free to go back to doing whatever it is they were doing."

"Like baking pies or playing Bridge."

"Exactly."

"Now I feel a lot better," I said.

He picked up on the tinge of sarcasm in my voice, and he narrowed his gaze. Then he came around, opening my door and taking my pie basket out of the trunk.

Kate was at her front door waiting as we walked through a veritable forest of stately pines, eucalyptus, and oak trees in front of their three-bedroom, two-bath ranch-style house. She was smiling broadly, no doubt at the coup she'd pulled off: getting Sam and me together for a purely social occasion. Her husband, Jack, seemed glad to see Sam. It turned out they were both on the wrestling team in high school, and they went out to the flagstone patio to have a few drinks and a few laughs about their coach and various rivals.

Kate took the pies and beckoned to me from the kitchen window. Obediently, I went inside and poured myself a glass of wine. I knew what she was thinking. "See what fun we can all have together once you realize you and Sam are meant for each other?

"This looks fabulous," she said, taking my asparagus tart out of the basket.

"I didn't know what you were having," I said. "So I took a chance and made something new."

"Jack's barbecuing a butterflied leg of lamb."

"Yum. That's what I smelled out there." I looked around. "Where are the kids? I brought their dough figures."

"Thanks. They're spending the night at Grandma's house. Speaking of grandmothers ... How's Louise? Have things calmed down up at Heavenly Acres?"

"As far as I know. Maybe you'd better ask Sam. He's the one doing the investigation. But I thought we weren't going to talk about anything like murder or mystery."

"We're not. I just wondered how she's doing."

"I haven't heard from her. But I worry about her. It can't be easy to be dragged down to the police station and questioned under oath."

"She probably passed with flying colors," Kate said.

"I'm afraid to ask. But we have to have faith in the system. Faith that the guilty will be punished."

She gave me a funny look. "Do you really believe that?"

"I have to. For now."

I guess I misunderstood the rules for that night, because when we went into the dining room to eat a gorgeous barbecued leg of lamb, herb crusted on the outside and juicy and pink on the inside, Kate turned to Sam and asked how his work was going.

"Never a dull moment," he said.

"Really? I thought a policeman's life in Crystal Cove would be the epitome of dull," Jack said to Sam. "But who would have guessed there'd be a murder for you to solve? I'm glad to hear you've got a handle on the job. Maybe you'll stick around. We need you here."

"What did you mean by never a dull moment?" Kate asked. "Are you referring to the murder or has something else happened?"

"I thought we weren't going to discuss murder tonight," I said. "But since you brought it up ..." I looked hopefully at my friend Kate. "I could be wrong, but in my opinion the reason it's so hard to solve the crime is that almost everyone wanted to kill Mary Brandt, present company excepted, of course."

"Today's excitement had nothing to do with Mary Brandt except that it happened to the woman who lives next door to Mary's apartment," Sam said with a glance at me.

I looked down and concentrated on cutting my meat. Had I been recognized? Or did Sam automatically suspect me when something unusual happened? If he knew anything for sure, he would have said something earlier.

Kate leaned forward across the table and licked her lips in anticipation. And she was the one who didn't want to talk shop. I tell you, it's addictive. "Next door to Mary," she mused. "Coincidence or…?"

"I don't know," Sam said. "But the poor woman was scared to death, though not literally, thank God. She's still alive. All we need is another suspicious death at that place and they'll want to hire extra security guards. She said she saw someone on her balcony. If she hadn't screamed, she thought she could have been *murdered*. That's her word not mine," Sam said. "Just like Mary Brandt."

"Maybe it was just the window washer," I said.

"It didn't look like a window washer from the video camera we had mounted in the kitchen."

I smiled as if I wasn't a bit worried I'd been caught on camera. If I had, he surely would have mentioned it earlier. I should have kept my mouth shut but I couldn't resist. "I don't blame the poor woman for being scared. You've got your investigation going right there at Heavenly Acres. Doesn't that mean you suspect one of the residents?"

"I can't tell you that," Sam said.

"Well, who cares anyway?" I asked. "Certainly not her family from what I can tell. They all had their problems with her and now they've got what they wanted." I looked around the table. "Don't they?" Jack refilled my wine glass, probably hoping I'd drink more and talk less.

"The will is being contested," Sam said.

"What?" I said. "Not by her grandson Blake. He came by to say goodbye, pleased as punch with his grandfather's antique watch he inherited. Said his sister got a necklace. Never mentioned his mother wasn't happy with her bequest. Or anyone else." My unspoken question was who exactly was contesting her will. No one at the dinner table asked, and no one told.

Kate changed the subject. Not surprising, since she's the one who said we couldn't talk about murder tonight. She served wedges of the asparagus tart and everyone said it was the best asparagus and leek tart they'd ever had. I was glad to see the vegetables had a little crunch left and that it wasn't eggy or mushy the way some combination vegetable pies are. When they'd finished praising the tart, Kate asked Sam how he liked being back in town.

"Couldn't be better," he said. "I bought a house and I'm here to stay."

Kate looked at me quizzically as if I'd been holding out on her.

"I told Hanna after I clean up the town I might run for mayor."

"You think our town needs cleaning up?" I said lightly. "Just because an old person has hallucinations on her balcony?"

"I take every complaint seriously," he said, looking more like a pillar of the community than ever. "And I have to investigate."

I suspected he meant it as a threat to me personally, but I decided to treat it as just a job description.

"You take your job just as seriously as Hanna does hers," Kate said with a warm smile for both of us. "Which brings us to dessert. Hanna brought a raspberry pie that looks absolutely fabulous."

She didn't wait for Sam to say he didn't eat desserts, she just got up from the table, motioned to me to follow her and went into the kitchen while the men discussed Sam's running for mayor. I heard Jack volunteer to be his campaign manager.

"Did you have anything to do with that balcony thing at Heavenly Acres?" Kate asked in a half whisper as she cut slices of the pie.

"Who, me?" I asked.

"I thought so," she said shaking her head. "I hope you don't get into trouble."

"I'm permanently in trouble according to Sam. He even thought I had something to do with Mary Brandt's demise or that I was protecting someone else, I think you know who. But I don't care what he thinks or thought. I found something today that could be important."

"Important how?"

"In figuring out who killed Mary."

"Did you tell Sam?"

"Of course not. He would have confiscated it immediately because I got it under, how shall I say, unusual circumstances."

"This is exciting. He'll be grateful to you someday."

"Either that or he'll arrest me for tampering with the evidence."

"He'd never do that. He likes you."

"Uh huh."

"No, really. I saw the way he looked at you."

"Like he wanted to put me in jail?"

"Like he wanted to haul you off and make you Mrs. Police Chief, or would you rather be Mrs. Mayor?"

"I'd rather be the Queen of Tarts."

"That's a no-brainer. You've got that title nailed. This looks wonderful."

After I whipped the cream, we served the raspberry pie in the dining room. I held my breath but Sam didn't turn it down. After

Kate served coffee, she asked me who had invented pies. An obvious way to change the subject from murder to something I could go on and on about for hours. If anyone would listen.

"Pies have been around forever," I said. "Ever since man or woman could put water and flour together to make a pastry shell. No sweet pies though. The ancient Romans filled the crust with meat or seafood. Like wild duck, mussels, or pigeon, and spiced them with currants and pepper."

"Sounds good," Jack said. What a great guy, I thought. Someone who appreciates the effort that goes into baking.

"The Romans made a pie with rye crust and filled it with goat cheese and honey. I've been thinking of making my own version of that one."

I glanced at Sam. I had the feeling he wasn't listening to me. Was Kate right? Was he looking at me as if he'd like to haul me off and make me forget about baking pies for a living? That would be a refreshing change, one I could handle. Or did his look only indicate he'd heard more than enough about the history of pies? On the plus side, he'd made the supreme sacrifice and eaten his piece of raspberry pie. I felt good about that. So good I got a second wind and finished up the history of pie with a final chapter on the American colonists' contribution to our modern-day pie.

"The colonists baked many pies, all savory," I said. "They used the crust as a preservative, a way to keep the filling fresh during the winter months. But not to eat. Crusts were like the pan or the dish. They were only the receptacle to contain the meats or fish. They were called coffins, because their only purpose was to hold the filling."

I paused, afraid I'd introduced the subject of death when it was a no-no. "In England, they eat pork pie and steak and kidney pie. Served with gravy, pickles, and mushy peas."

"I don't think Crystal Cove is ready for mushy peas," Sam said. "Not yet."

"What about good old American apple pie? Who made that, Betsy Ross?" Jack asked.

"Apple pies have been around since the Middle Ages. But the first ones didn't have sugar or a crust."

"That's not really a pie then," Kate said.

"Not until the fifteen hundreds did they make apple pie with sugar and spices. It was so good a poet said his lover's breath was 'like the steam of apple pies.'"

"That was sweet," Kate said.

The rest of the evening we talked about old times and laughed about our high school teachers, like Miss Oggel, who made us memorize the first fourteen lines of the *Canterbury Tales* and recite them in front of the class. We reminisced about former classmates like Lindsey, Tammy, and even Blake. No one mentioned Sam's getting kicked out of school. I was wondering if Sam felt comfortable enough to tell my friends what had happened to him these past years, but he didn't. They didn't ask. Maybe they already knew or they thought it wasn't polite to bring it up. Or they thought if he wanted us to know, he'd tell us. Same with me. I did not want to talk about the mistakes I'd made in my past. I'd learned from them. I thought I'd put them behind me. Time would tell. I was here to get a new start. So far, so good.

We left about ten o'clock and drove slowly through the quiet streets.

"No crime. No vagrants. No break-ins," I remarked. "You've managed to clean up an already squeaky-clean town."

"You're welcome," he said.

"So clean you may have worked yourself out of a job."

"Not until I catch Mary Brandt's murderer."

"Not that again." I said.

"Is there something you want to tell me?" he said as he pulled up in front of my shop and cut the fog lights of his car.

I assumed he meant do you want to tell me you broke into a crime scene and stole some important evidence. "I don't think so," I said after a pause.

"Look me in the eye and tell me you're not guilty of breaking and entering."

Hah. Easy as pie, as they say. Nothing I like better than a challenge. Because it was dark in the car I had to get up quite close to look him in the eyes, and suddenly murder was the farthest thing from my mind. Maybe it was the way his face was half in shadows, making him look dangerously sexy. Maybe it was the rich smell of leather from his custom car seats. Whatever it was, I wasn't able to do much thinking about anything except how he had the power to turn my insides to custard and melt away my resolve to keep my distance like a stick of butter on a low flame.

When he tipped my chin with his thumb and kissed me, the memories came flooding back. It was fifteen years ago and we were in a car on this same street, frantic to take our clothes off and get our hands on each other when Grannie came out and beamed her flashlight at us.

Just like last time, I kissed him back. It was easier than answering his question.

This time there was no Grannie to stop us, just a modicum of common sense I'd acquired over the years. And a wall around my heart I'd constructed very carefully. I pulled away, took a deep breath, reached behind me, grabbed the door handle, and opened it. I slid out of the car seat, my heart pounding.

I didn't turn around or say a word as I walked unsteadily up to the front door of the shop, and he didn't speak or come after me. I didn't expect him to.

I had a long, hot soak in Grannie's claw-foot bathtub while I deliberately turned off my brain and let my body relax. What was the point? I'd already thought and rethought my new career here in town, my sophomoric attraction to the former town bad boy, and my role in solving this mystery. Of all my problems, I knew I had to solve the murder first, then worry about the rest of my life.

A kiss is just a kiss, I reminded myself, sinking deeper into the rose-scented hot water and leaning back against the porcelain headrest. It meant nothing to Sam except maybe he thought he'd soften me up so I'd confess to breaking and entering, contaminating the evidence, or just plain annoying the hell out of the police chief by stretching the truth or avoiding questions I didn't want to answer. Therefore, it should mean nothing to me either.

I got out of the tub, dried off with an extra-large velvety Turkish towel, and got into my cotton lounger pajamas. Propping my head against a half-dozen pillows on my bed, I finally opened the leather-covered booklet. It was Mary Brandt's diary.

_____

After I finished reading, I could say without hesitation that the woman had an enemy's list a mile long. At first I was overwhelmed, as I copied names on a sheet of typing paper until I ran out of space. Not only Grannie and her friends, but the whole Bridge crowd, the exercise group, and her family. You name it, Mary had a problem with them. You had to ask yourself, *Who wouldn't want to kill her?* But want is very different than did. Who did kill her?

I finally closed the diary at one o'clock in the morning with a pounding headache and a plan in mind.

FIFTEEN

I CALLED GRANNIE THE next morning and told her I needed another Bridge lesson. I lied and said I'd been studying up and playing online Bridge, and I thought maybe I was getting pretty good.

She sounded surprised. Surprised I was getting good and even more surprised I'd brag about it. I asked if I could come by for a practice session with her, her partner, and Donna that evening. Would Donna be willing to put up with me again?

Grannie assured me she would.

With my computer on the kitchen counter, I actually played a few online Bridge games on sites like Bridge Doctor, Bridge for Dummies, and Bridge Tutorial in between rolling, chopping, and mixing for something called Sawdust Pie, which I'd never made before.

Just my luck that the only person who came by was Sam. The look on his face indicated he'd forgotten everything that happened last night. Well, not everything. He remembered that he had to find the trespasser who'd frightened the resident next door to

Mary Brandt's place yesterday. He said he was having a lineup so she could identify the home-invader and asked me to appear the next day. I agreed. By that time, I intended to have this murder wrapped up. What was the point of protesting now? Then I closed the door of the shop, telling him I had a full schedule. He looked like he was going to say something, no doubt a warning of some sort, but I didn't give him a chance.

I couldn't eat anything that night because my stomach was in knots. I packed my new Sawdust Pie as well as a kind of a quiche called Spinach and Feta Pie I threw together at the last minute. My mind kept turning over quotes from Bridge for Dummies like "Length before strength" and "Learn to play before learning to bid." After a day of cramming, I hadn't learned much more than "Bridge is the greatest card game of all," and that it's "complicated and challenging." Tell me about it.

The card room was full as usual with the post-dinner card crowd. They seemed happy to see me, but it could have been because I came bearing pies. When you're a baker, you never know if it's you or your pies, unless it's someone who refuses to eat desserts and only reluctantly tries something new. Grannie got up to help me unload my pies in the pantry. She explained she and Hazel and Donna were playing three-handed Bridge until I got there.

"So Donna hasn't found another partner?"

Grannie shook her head. "Not yet."

"No one as good as Mary?"

"I wouldn't say that," she said.

"What would you say?"

"You can't just have anyone. She has to fit in. She has to have steady nerves. And be an excellent player. We take Bridge very seriously."

"Yes, I know. I got that. Maybe I shouldn't have come. Maybe I'm taking up your time, taking the place of someone who might work out as Donna's new partner."

Grannie rolled her eyes. "I'm not sure anyone will ever be good enough for Donna."

"Maybe she's suffering from separation anxiety. Afraid without Mary she'll never win again."

"Don't tell anyone I said this, but Mary wasn't that good," Grannie said softly.

"Maybe no one's good enough."

"Don't worry about it. It's not your problem," Grannie said, squeezing my arm.

"Not yours either. In fact, isn't it to your advantage if Donna doesn't find anyone good enough, you keep winning, then you speed ahead and progress to the finals?"

"As of now I promised Sam I wouldn't leave town."

"Not now, but we'll have this thing wrapped up in plenty of time for your tournament," I said with more confidence than I felt.

"Who's we? You mean you and your policeman boyfriend?" she said with a little smile.

"Right now it's just me and he's not my boyfriend. I do have a plan."

Her eyes widened. "What do you mean?"

"Louise," her partner, Hazel, called from the card room. "We've already shuffled and dealt."

I set down my pies and followed Grannie out to the card room.

"You don't mind, do you, Hanna?" Donna said, pointing to my cards already face down at my place. "We've been waiting for you."

"I'm sorry. It's so good of you all to let me play with you. I promise to try harder tonight not to do anything too dumb, but I can't guarantee it."

"It's just a game," Hazel said.

Donna smiled briefly, then she focused on her cards. I arranged mine and then looked around the table. Even though this wasn't a real game, and they couldn't earn points toward the tournament, the other three looked intent and focused. No wonder they were in contention for the county, then perhaps even the state, prize. I felt a little guilty taking up their time with my own agenda.

Donna led with the ten of Spades. Grannie played a nine, I played a three, and Hazel played a Jack. Donna grimaced when she saw Hazel's card. She frowned at me as if she knew I had the King, which I did, but she didn't say anything. We played a few more hands during which I withheld the winning card on purpose. Donna's face turned pink then red. After a while it was almost purple. No one seemed to notice but me. But the only way she could know I was deliberately holding back the high card was if she'd looked at my hand. She'd never admit to that, would she?

We did win a couple of tricks during the game, but it was no thanks to me. It was thanks to Donna, who glared at me and snatched up the cards when we won. It wasn't enough.

Finally, Donna couldn't take it any longer.

"Hanna, let me see your cards," she said tightly.

Startled, Grannie and Hazel looked up as I put my cards down on the table.

"How could you?" she demanded.

"I'm sorry, did I do something wrong?" I asked.

"Yes, you did something wrong," Donna said.

"You don't even know which card to play, do you? I don't expect you to be as good as Mary, but you're not even trying."

"Now Donna," Grannie said.

"Don't 'Now Donna' me," she said, swiveling her head in Grannie's direction. "At least Mary had an excuse for making mistakes. She had dementia. Yes, she did."

Everyone stopped talking. Cards were forgotten. Silence blanketed the rest of the room like whipped cream over pie. "She didn't want anyone to know. Even though it wasn't fair to me," Donna continued, her voice rising. "She wouldn't give up. She was like a dog with a bone. I told her that and she laughed. I gave her a jeweled dog collar for her birthday. She thanked me. She didn't get it." Donna looked at Grannie. "You know it's true. She'd forget what was trump, she'd play the wrong card ... just like your granddaughter here. I thought I'd gotten rid of her, then Hanna comes and does the same thing. She has no excuse. She's young. She could learn but she doesn't even try. It's not that hard. A King is higher than a Jack. A ten is higher than a seven. Why can't I find a partner who can count? I can't take it anymore."

Her hands shaking, Donna threw her cards on the table and stood up.

"Donna, Hanna *is* trying," Grannie said firmly. I felt terrible about tricking my own grandmother, but it was the only way I knew to keep her from being charged with a murder she didn't commit.

I stood too. "I didn't know Mary," I said. "And I don't play Bridge. But I know how challenging a game it is, especially if your partner is falling down on the job."

"No," Donna said, her voice as taut as a violin string. "You don't know because you didn't know Mary. She thought she was fine. She said everyone makes mistakes. Not like that, I told her. She should have quit. I begged her to quit. But she wouldn't. There was only one way to make her leave."

I looked around the room. The expressions on the faces went from shock to disbelief to embarrassment. "Just between us in the room, how many people are not sorry Mary Brandt is gone?" I asked.

Slowly everyone in the room except Donna raised their hand. Surprising after what I'd read in Mary's diary. Mary had bribed, pleaded, and hounded all the Bridge players as she looked for another partner. Of all the ironies, Mary thought Donna wasn't good enough for her. But she couldn't drop her because no one else would play with her. And Donna knew it.

"Every one of you in the room, everyone in the whole place, had some reason to dislike Mary," I said. "She wasn't easy to like with her obsession for winning at all costs. She cheated, she covered up, she did everything but play fair. But only one person here hated her. Hated her enough to kill her. Some of you, maybe all of you, think she's a hero, but I'm afraid she's a murderer." There was a murmur of "Oh no's," and "Who is it's," in the room. Everyone but Donna said something. Instead she held her head high.

"I did it," she said. "I did what no one else had the guts to do. You ought to thank me. I got rid of the monster in our midst. She not only terrified her family, her friends, and the staff of this place, she took away my chance of winning the Bridge tournament. Every one of you in this room understands why I wanted to get rid of

Mary. Yes, I switched her pills. I filled those little gelatin capsules with extra warfarin. I ordered the cranberry pie because I thought she'd have a reaction to the drug. She had one, all right. I didn't mean to kill her, I just wanted to make her sick so she'd have to drop out." She heaved a sigh and sat down in her chair with a thud and buried her head in her hands.

I went to the pantry to call Sam to come and get Donna. I said I had witnesses to her confession. He said to be careful, but there was no danger. When I got back to the card room, everyone was hugging Donna saying they understood. Some of the women who'd had bad run-ins with Mary even thanked her. Grannie told her they'd all testify for her in court and visit her in jail and bring her a computer with a Bridge program.

When Sam came, everyone was having pie and coffee, even Donna. She looked relieved to have finally confessed. She especially liked all the attention she was getting.

"Where is she? You didn't leave her alone, did you?" he muttered to me when I met him at the front door of the high-class institution.

"Alone? No, she's with her friends. She's a hero who got rid of the town bully. There's got to be a special category for criminals like that."

"Why didn't you tell me?" he said, speed-walking through the hall with me at his side.

"I wanted to be sure."

"You wanted to show me you could find out who did it."

I nodded.

He didn't cuff Donna. He just read her her rights and quietly walked her out to the unmarked squad car. No one gave them a second look as they passed the reception desk. But Donna's friends stood on the front steps waving and blowing kisses as they drove away.

Grannie and I had a quiet cup of cocoa in her kitchen after we watched Sam and Donna disappear into the night.

"I can't believe it," Grannie said, setting her cup on her small glass-topped kitchen table.

"What can't you believe, that Donna killed her partner? Surely it's happened before. I can't imagine a more powerful motive for a Bridge player."

"I can't believe you uncovered this whole thing," she said, staring at me as if I'd morphed into Miss Marple, her own personal favorite sleuth she always watched on PBS's *Mystery* series.

"I had to do something," I said modestly. "To keep you from another bout with the lie detector and to keep us both from going to prison."

"Do they have Bridge in prison?" she asked.

"I hope so, for Donna's sake," I said. "At least you can get her a computer so she can play online."

"It's the least we can do," she said. "We owe Donna big time for getting rid of Mary. I don't know how we can repay her. I was thinking we should name the card room after her with a bronze plaque on the door."

"Good idea," I said. "Tell me, were you surprised that it was Donna who did it? I remember at one point you were sure it was an accident."

"Nah," Grannie said. "I just said that. Knowing how we all felt about Mary, I could see someone crossing the line."

"Even you?"

"You know, I actually had a better chance of winning playing against Mary and Donna. I don't know how I'll do with a new couple."

"Here's to a winning hand and a better Bridge game," I said, lifting my cup. I put it down when I noticed my hand was shaking. "I'm out of here," I said. "One mystery solved and I've had it. I don't know how Sam can do this for a living."

Grannie kissed me on the cheek and followed me out to the car. "Drive safely," she said. Then she went back inside. Probably not nearly as shaken as I was. She had her friends, and they'd be waiting to hear all the gory details.

———

"Maybe Donna will get off early for good behavior," I suggested to Sam the next day as he sat at one of my tables drinking coffee and eating a slice of Spinach and Feta Pie. "Especially if she gets a good lawyer."

"Hanna, she murdered her Bridge partner. If she gets off, who will be next?"

"You mean who will be the next murderer or the next victim?"

"Either. Both. Finding Donna guilty should send a message. You can't just off your partner."

"Even if she's cheating? Even if she's demented? Can't remember what's trump?"

He shook his head. "Even if she's the most unpopular woman in the whole place. Even if everyone wanted her dead. Only one person went so far as to actually take action."

"Shouldn't she get something for guts? For sneaking the extra meds in Mary's pillbox?"

"She has got something. She's got everyone's thanks. Even Mary's family, if what you say is true."

"I'll let you read Mary's diary," I offered.

"That's stolen property. I'd be in trouble along with you," he said. "Breaking and entering. Petty theft. Frightening an old woman. By the way, the lineup is cancelled."

"Thank you. But I thought you wanted me to line up, be identified as a common thief and illegal trespasser, and suitably punished."

"I did," he said with a flicker of amusement in his eyes, "but Gayle next door didn't want to cause you any trouble. You can thank your grandmother for that. I understand she intervened on your behalf. Gayle has dropped the charges. As far as she's concerned, she saw a ghost on her deck or her own reflection in the glass patio doors."

"Whew." I wiped my hands on my apron and sat down across the table. "So neither I nor Grannie is under suspicion for anything?"

"I suspect you of playing loose with the law and the rules."

"But you owe me for catching your murderer."

"Okay, I owe you. What do you want?"

What did I want? A booming pie business. A social life. A better relationship with the Chief of Police. A chance to get to know him again. A chance to let him know me. And that was just for starters. The list goes on.

THE END

GRANNIE'S PRIZE-WINNING FUJI APPLE SOUTHERN PECAN CARAMEL PIE

One all-butter, deep-dish pastry crust.

Filling

   ½ cup sugar

   3 tbsp flour

   1 tsp cinnamon

   pinch of salt

   6 cups Fuji apples, peeled and sliced

Stir together the first four ingredients. Add the apples and mix. Pile apples into unbaked crust.

Crumb Topping

   1 cup brown sugar

   ½ cup flour

   ½ cup rolled oats

   ½ cup unsalted butter

   ½ cup pecans, toasted

Stir together the first four ingredients to form coarse crumbs. Sprinkle topping over apples.

   Heat oven to 375° F. Cover edges of crust with foil. Bake for 25 minutes. Remove foil and bake another 25 minutes.

Remove pie from oven and sprinkle with the toasted pecans. Drizzle with Caramel Sauce.

Caramel Sauce

    1 stick unsalted butter

    1 cup light brown sugar

    ½ tsp salt

    1½ tsp vanilla

    ½ cup evaporated milk

Place butter, brown sugar, and salt in a small saucepan and melt over a medium heat. Turn up heat and bring to a boil, whisking constantly. Remove from heat and stir in vanilla and milk. Serve warm over pie.

HANNA'S ALL-BUTTER PIE CRUST

For a single-crust pie

    1¼ cup flour

    1 stick cold unsalted butter

    pinch of salt

    3 to 4 tbsp ice water

Blend flour, butter, and salt with your fingers until mixture is like coarse crumbs. Drizzle ice water over flour mixture and mix until dough holds together. Put dough on your work suface and form into a disk. Refrigerate for an hour. Roll out to fit a deep-dish pie pan. Dough will keep refrigerated for a day, or freeze for later use.

HANNA'S BLACK-BOTTOM RASPBERRY CREAM PIE

Crust

    30 chocolate wafer cookies

    1 stick unsalted butter

    ¼ cup sugar

Spray a 9-inch glass pie pan with nonstick cooking spray. Crush the cookies and mix in the sugar. Add butter and mix until crumbs form.

Press the crumb mixture over the bottom and sides of the pie pan. Chill the crust for 30 minutes then bake in a 350° F oven for about 10 min. Cool.

Filling

    ½ cup sugar

    ¼ cup cocoa

    2 tbsp cornstarch

    ¼ cup whole milk or nonfat half and half

    2 egg yolks and 1 whole egg

    4 oz. semi-sweet chocolate chips

    2 tbsp unsalted butter

Combine the sugar, cocoa, and cornstarch in a saucepan. Gradually add the milk or half and half, then the egg yolks and the whole egg. Stir over medium heat until pudding thickens and boils, about 8 minutes. Remove from heat and add the chocolate chips and butter. Whisk until smooth.

Spread pudding into cookie-crumb crust. Cover with plastic wrap and refrigerate overnight.

Topping

1 cup whipping cream

1 basket fresh raspberries

Peel plastic off pie. Whip cream until stiff. Spread over pie and garnish with raspberries. Chill pie again for one to four hours.

© CRAIG CULVER

ABOUT THE AUTHOR

CAROL CULVER is the author of over thirty books, including many bestselling Harlequin romance novels. She has a BA in French and studied at the Sorbonne in Paris. This is her debut mystery novel.